A LOVE
OF
Her Own

HEART
of the WEST ✳ 3

A LOVE
OF
Her Own

A NOVEL

MAGGIE BRENDAN

Revell

a division of Baker Publishing Group
Grand Rapids, Michigan

© 2010 by Maggie Brendan

Published by Revell
a division of Baker Publishing Group
P.O. Box 6287, Grand Rapids, MI 49516-6287
www.revellbooks.com

Printed in the United States of America

Library of Congress Cataloging-in-Publication Data
Brendan, Maggie, 1949–
    A love of her own : a novel / Maggie Brendan.
        p.   cm. — (Heart of the West ; bk. 3)
    ISBN 978-0-8007-3351-3 (pbk.)
    1. Montana—Fiction. I. Title.
  PS3602.R4485L68 2010
  813'.6—dc22   2010000661

Scripture is taken from the King James Version of the Bible.

This book is a work of fiction. Names, characters, places, and incidents are the product of the author's imagination or are used fictitiously. Any resemblance to actual events, locales, or persons, living or dead, is coincidental.

Published in association with Tamela Hancock Murray of the Hartline Literary Agency, LLC.

10   11   12   13   14   15   16   7   6   5   4   3   2   1

In memory of my mother, Maggie (Mary Magdalene), and my father, John Samuel O'Neal, who loved a good Western. And in memory of my sisters Gail and Estelle, and my brothers Sam and Orville. I love and miss you all.

> Many waters cannot quench love,
> neither can the floods drown it.
>
> Song of Solomon 8:7

1

The Yampa Valley, Colorado
September 1896

The brisk Colorado wind tugged at April McBride's silky tresses underneath her Stetson hat, tickling the exposed skin at the nape of her neck. She threw her head back in delight, and her laughter spilled across the valley floor, causing her roan's tail to twitch. There wasn't anything April would rather do on a fall day than be out riding with total abandonment. She pushed her mount higher up the slope.

A half hour later she reined her horse in as she reached the crest of the craggy ridge overlooking the Yampa Valley. Her gaze traveled down to the rumbling Blue River below where a familiar figure on horseback had stopped to give his horse a drink. *Luke Weber.* But this time her heart no longer thumped with excitement. Luke paused at the river's edge and rested his arms across the saddle horn. He glanced up to her on the ridgeline above him and lifted his hat in greeting. April returned the greeting with a wave. After a brief moment, Luke gave his horse a nudge and continued on downstream.

Who would have thought that she and Luke would be just friends one day? Certainly not April. It all seemed so long ago now . . .

Her world had come crashing down the day Luke told her there would be no wedding. Her shock had been profound, and April, who was never at a loss for words, was speechless. She'd tried to absorb what he'd said while her heart, frozen in pain, threatened to stop beating altogether. How could he not love her? She had loved him deeply and was ready to begin their life together.

Her ego had suffered terribly, and she wondered what was wrong with *her*. But how could she argue with someone who told her he didn't share the same feelings? She couldn't. If it had been the other way around, she wouldn't have wanted him insisting that she marry him just because he loved her. No . . . it wouldn't have worked. April could see that now, but it had taken a long time to reach that perspective. How many times had her mother told her that she was praying for her and the right man would come along when the timing was right? Too many to suit April.

She'd lived with a shattered heart, refusing to see any of the eligible bachelors in Steamboat Springs who constantly pursued her, and now, after four years, her heart had slowly mended. Luke and Crystal were going to have a baby soon, and she could honestly say she was happy for them. Who wouldn't be when one could see the love in their eyes? Her mother was certain that her mended heart was the work of the Lord. April wasn't so sure about that, but she knew she had finally moved on and was genuinely happy for Luke and Crystal now.

Enough of this reflecting. The day was simply too beautiful to waste ruminating about the past, so she headed the roan back down into the valley, allowing her to take the lead on their way back to the Rocking M Ranch.

Hours later, April stripped off her leather gloves and picked up the mail as she entered the large foyer of her home. With a measure of contentment, she started going through the stack. It was nice to have the house to herself while her parents were away in Ireland for their thirtieth wedding anniversary. She shuffled through the assortment of bills and invitations, releasing a squeal of delight when her eyes latched onto an envelope marked MONTANA in her brother's bold handwriting. It was crumpled and dirty, and the postmark was early August. Where must it have traveled before reaching her? No matter. Seeing a letter from Josh brought a huge smile to her face, and she decided to go sit in the garden, away from the maid who was cleaning, to savor every word privately.

Settling down on the bench near the angel fountain with its soothing flow of water in the background, April picked up her engraved letter opener and slit open the envelope to find a single page from Josh.

Dearest Sis,

Hope all is well with you, and our parents are enjoying their trip to Ireland. Mother wrote me that she was really looking forward to it.

The main reason I write again so soon is to tell you that I am engaged to marry the girl of my dreams! Her name is Juliana Brady, and we are to

*be married September 25. I realize I should have
written sooner, but time slipped away from me
somehow. Now that we've finally set a date, we would
be honored if you would come and represent our
family.*

*Please telegraph me your answer and the time of
your arrival, and I will reserve a room for you at the
Stockton Hotel right away. I can hardly wait for the
wedding and to see you again!*

With much love and affection,
Josh

Tears of joy stung the corners of her eyes. What wonderful
news, but oh, how disappointed her parents were going to be to
miss Josh's wedding. April decided to send one of the servants
into town to telegraph her reply. She should send a telegraph to
her parents as well, even though they would be unable to get back
in time. Maybe Josh had already done that.

A trip to Montana! Maybe that was exactly what she needed
to get excited about her life again. New, fresh faces sounded very
appealing. She rose, stuffed the telegram into her pocket, then
hurried down the brick path to the house, immediately thinking
of what she'd need to pack.

"Tilly!" April called, and the stout maid hurried down the
hallway to reach her.

"Yes, ma'am? What's all the excitement?" She was breathing
heavily when she stopped short in front of her mistress.

"Hurry, I'll be leaving for Montana as soon as I can make the
arrangements," she said, then rushed to the large secretary and

jotted a message down on a piece of letterhead. "Can you fetch Robby to send a telegram?"

"I'll do it right away, and I'll have him get your valise down from the attic too." Tilly turned to go find Robby.

"One bag won't do. I'll need my trunk for certain." April clapped her hands together, then grabbed Tilly's hands and swung her around in a circle. April's straight, silky blonde hair flew about her shoulders until Tilly giggled and they were both out of breath.

"You must be going to see Josh."

"Yes! It's the best news—Josh is getting married!"

"Land sakes, Miss April, you can't go alone. Do you want me to accompany you?"

April stopped and stared at her. "Mmm . . . I think I can do this alone. I'll be on the train and stage the entire way with lots of company. Besides, you're needed here."

"That may be so, but you will need my help."

April clicked her tongue against her teeth. "I'm grown and can handle a trip by myself. Don't forget it's almost the turn of the century. Women are doing many things on their own right now."

"Maybe so, but your parents are not going to like this one bit," Tilly muttered. "No sirree, not one bit."

But April was already taking the stairs two at a time in her riding pants while Tilly stood looking up at her mistress and shaking her head. When April got excited about something, the entire household had better watch out!

"When you're ready, come up to my bedroom. I need to get organized," April called over her shoulder as she reached the landing.

"Yes, Miss April, just as soon as I find Robby to send your

telegram." Tilly scooted her stout frame as fast as she could in the direction of the kitchen.

Billings, Montana, was nothing more than a cow town to April's way of thinking, much like Denver. Lots of dusty streets, rough-hewn buildings, and plenty of bustling activity that she'd observed from her window seat as the train flew past the center of town to the rail depot situated on the eastern outskirts. The smell from the hundreds of sheep corralled near the railroad station overpowered her, and April reached for her handkerchief to cover her nose. Josh had told her in one of his letters that Billings was a major depot to ship the woolies back East. She wondered for the tenth time today why her brother wanted to live in Montana after living most of his life in Colorado. Aching and tired, she was not looking forward to another long ride from Billings to Lewistown. One never knew what kind of characters you might encounter in this part of the country.

Her thoughts were interrupted by the conductor announcing their arrival in Billings in his booming voice.

"Final stop, Billings, Montana!" he called, then continued walking down the aisle.

April couldn't wait to disembark and stretch her legs. She was much more comfortable on horseback and preferred that way to travel. "Excuse me," she said to the gentleman blocking the aisle. He was bent over trying to collect his paperwork in the seat across from her. "This is where I must get off."

"Well, miss, it's the last run of the evening"—he straightened to give her a level stare—"so there's no hurry."

"I beg your pardon." April gazed back at the dark-haired man whose eyes twinkled with mischief in his affable face. He was of medium build with thick, dark hair, neatly combed, and his gray brocade vest stretched snugly across his trim build. He reached down to don his matching jacket, then hoisted a black bag from the train's floor. *A doctor?* she wondered, but she was in no mood for humor. "*Please* don't let me get in your way!" she snapped.

He seemed totally unruffled by her comment. "Can I help you with your bag there?" He indicated the small valise she held in her hand.

"I'm quite capable. Now if you don't mind, could you please let me pass?"

The gentleman bowed, clicked his heels together slightly, then moved aside, gesturing with his hand for her to go before him down the aisle.

"Humph," April muttered under her breath, her skirts swishing in her haste to get out of the train car. She had noticed him ever since he'd boarded the train at Union Station in Denver. There was no ring on his left hand, yet he hadn't even acknowledged her presence throughout the long ride, completely absorbed in whatever he was reading.

April wasn't used to being ignored, especially by a nice-looking gentleman. *Just as well*, she thought, *he's probably engaged anyway.* Or was she losing her looks? The thought gave her a jolt. After all, she *had* aged in four years. At twenty-two now, had she lost her appeal? She wasn't entirely sure that she was looking for more than friendship with any man. She was through trusting a man with her heart.

Stepping down the steep metal stairs with the aid of the

conductor, April turned to thank him, but he had already returned to the boxcar. She looked in exasperation at her bags, which had been deposited at her feet, then saw the words NORTHERN PACIFIC RAILROAD DEPOT painted above the large doorway of the depot.

A young boy of about thirteen ran up to her. "Need some help with your bags, lady?"

April eyed him with distaste. He was nothing but a street urchin, with his pants two sizes too big, held up by suspenders and torn at the knees. A cap sat cocked to one side of his head, covering his longer-than-normal, unruly hair beneath. He looked unbelievably thin.

"Well . . . I . . . guess so. You could carry them up to the ticket station for the next train to Lewistown."

"There ain't one," he said, tilting his head up to see her better.

"Surely there is one leaving in the morning?" April started for the ticket counter.

"No, ma'am. The train won't come again until next week, and the stagecoach left for Lewistown early this mornin'." He wiped his nose on the back of his sleeve.

She looked at him, hardly believing her ears. "I simply must be in Lewistown by Friday for a wedding, and we still have nearly a hundred miles to go. Where is the train conductor? Get him for me." Her voice rose. "How am I supposed to get to Lewistown, pray tell?"

"Same as I will," a voice behind her said.

April turned to see the gentleman from the train. "I beg your pardon?"

"You sure do use that phrase a lot." He flipped the kid a couple of coins, and the boy jumped to catch them, his eyes wide. "I'll get her trunk, but thanks, kid, for your offer."

Now she was really irritated. "Why in the world would you keep count of *how* many times I've said that? I don't even know your name," she said with an icy glare. Her feet were killing her in her tight leather dress shoes. Oh, what she would give to have on her cowboy boots and britches.

He set his luggage down next to hers and stuck out his hand. "Name's Mark Barnum. And you are?"

"April McBride." She eyed him suspiciously and extended her hand into his warm handshake. "So the answer to my question is . . ."

"Stagecoach, but it won't be leaving until the morning."

"In the *morning*! But it's Wednesday, and the wedding is Friday afternoon. That just won't do. I have to have time to rest and clean up."

Mark squinted back at her in the bright sunlight. "I'm afraid that's the only way you'll get there, Miss—it is Miss McBride, isn't it?"

"Of course it is."

"Then I know your brother, Josh."

April drew her shoulders back. "Really? How do you know my brother?"

"I live in Lewistown. It's a small town—hard not to know almost everyone."

"Then you also know that he is *getting married* on Friday? I had planned on being there."

Mark nodded. "With any luck you will. You'll have to spend the night at a hotel and leave bright and early tomorrow."

April rolled her eyes heavenward. She was spitting mad that there was only one stage a day to Lewistown. She didn't come all this way to miss Josh's wedding. She took a deep breath to collect her wits about her. There was simply nothing else to do.

"Could you point me in the direction of the nearest hotel, please, Mr. Barnum? Then I'll be out of *your* way." April placed her small valise under her arm, then gripped the leather strap of her trunk, struggling with all her strength to pull them across the street. Somehow she lost her grip, and her valise slid from her armpit and fell in a heap in the dust. It flew open, spilling its contents, including her unmentionables, right there in plain sight for Mr. Barnum to see. *Lord have mercy! What next?*

"Please, Miss McBride. Let me hire a carriage to take all our bags to the hotel," Mark said. He squatted down in front of April, who felt her face blanch with embarrassment. He picked up one of her dresses off the ground and placed it back in the valise, pretending not to notice the fine silky underwear as April hastily threw them in her case and slammed the lid shut with a vengeance.

They stood up, and April swallowed her pride. "That would be so kind of you. Thank you."

The young boy was hanging back, watching. "I have a wagon, sir. I don't mind helping ya at all. The only other one has already left."

"Wonderful! Lead the way, young man, and take us to the Billings Hotel," Mark replied, lifting his bag and one of April's while letting the young boy haul April's trunk.

April followed the boy toward the cart that he called a wagon. Stopping a few feet back, she almost laughed out loud, but caught herself when she saw Mark's hard look.

"I can't ride in that contraption," she said softly to Mark as she watched the young boy throw her luggage into the cart. "Look at the old horse. She may drop dead before we go a half a block!" April loved horses and hated to see one so old having to work. At home, this horse would have been turned out to pasture long ago.

Mark took her elbow and gently propelled her forward. "Sure you can. It'll only be for a couple of blocks."

April jerked her arm back. "Well, I won't be seen going down the streets in that *thing*," she said through clenched teeth, pointing to the cart.

Mark stopped short with a quizzical frown. "Who cares? No one knows you here, Miss McBride, so what difference does it make?" He looked around. "Besides, I don't see anyone paying us any mind."

April stood with her arms crossed, not moving, surveying the situation. One person couldn't carry all her luggage. The boy was right. Everyone had left the station. She eyed the cart that had room for only two. The boy motioned for them to come forward. She groaned. "Oh, all right. I guess it won't kill me just this one time, but we can't all three fit in that seat."

"Don't worry your pretty blonde head. I'll hop in the back. I don't mind, I've ridden in much worse."

Before he assisted April into the small seat next to the boy, she paused to give the old nag a gentle stroke across her bony back. "Sweet friend, thank you for hauling my bags," April whispered into the horse's ear. The mare responded with a low snort and toss of her mane. The gentleman hopped into the back of the cart.

The boy gave her a sideways glance. "Her name is Ruby, named after my maw." A shadow of sadness flickered in the boy's eyes.

"That's a nice name for your horse, and I'm sure she is honored to have your mother's name." She wanted to say, *I hope she has the energy to pull this wagon*, but she bit her tongue. "My name is April McBride."

The boy touched his fingers to the brim of his cap. "My name is Billy Taylor."

April turned to look back at Mr. Barnum, who had already settled himself on the edge of the wagon with his legs dangling off the back edge, as if he did this sort of thing every day.

"All set?" the boy asked over his shoulder.

"Yes. Drive away, lad, and let's get Miss McBride to the hotel before she perishes."

April twisted back around to the front of her seat as the boy yelled, "Giddyap!" tapping the nag lightly across her rump. At first she didn't move, so he gave her another light tap, then she trotted down the avenue, much to April's surprise.

Billy grinned. "Sometimes she kinda goes to sleep while she's awaitin' my instructions."

April suppressed a giggle behind her hand. "Is that what it is?"

"She knows she's helping me earn a livin'," Billy said in such a serious tone that April looked over at him.

"Billy, you don't look a day over thirteen. You should be in school. Besides, Ruby here should be retired. She's worn out and old. Don't you think this load is too much for her?"

"Heck no! I reckon she ought to retire, but the fact is I need her to help me."

April felt a twinge of pity momentarily for the boy, but it quickly vanished. He was not her problem.

Morgan Kincaid inspected the riggings on each of the six horses harnessed to the Wells Fargo stagecoach for any signs of wear, just as he always did before starting on the next trip to Lewistown. Leon, his partner, was at the back checking over the axle and adding a coat of grease to the bearings in the wheelbase. They'd already swept out the coach from his last crew of passengers when they'd arrived early this morning.

Morgan paused. If development had its way, they'd both be out of a job soon, as the Union Pacific and the Northern Pacific continued to spread out across Montana. People called it progress, but to Morgan's way of thinking, it would be the end of an era that would directly affect him, and he was getting on up in age.

He watched his friend hustle about and thanked God for Leon's friendship. Leon liked to joke, but he was a hard worker and a good companion on the long drives. It was unusual for Morgan to have a white man as his trusted partner, but their friendship was a natural one born out of working together for many years. Morgan had been a shotgun messenger long before he started driving the team, and he was good at it, but with his eyesight not what it used to be, he'd hired Leon.

Morgan had learned to handle the reins of a team when he was in his early twenties. It took great skill to handle six sets of reins wrapped securely around his fingers, then move each of them separately to guide the horses right or left. He'd learned early on how to use the muscles of his hands to adjust the pull of the reins. It allowed the horses some lack of restriction, but not so much that the horses could run free.

He pulled out his pocket watch, and the hands glinted off the silver as he flipped it open. Almost six o'clock. He surveyed the small crowd near the platform of the relay station. An older couple, a young woman with a baby, a man, and a beautiful blonde-haired lady who was clearly agitated made up the list of passengers for this trip. Leon gave him the signal that everything was all set on his end.

Morgan strode over to the group and addressed them in a rich Southern voice. "Good morning, ladies and gentlemen. My name is Morgan Kinkaid, and I'll be your driver. We are ready to start our journey to Lewistown. First I want to inform you of a few rules if you've never ridden our coach before. When the driver asks you to get out and walk, do so without grumbling. I won't request it unless it becomes absolutely necessary. Don't growl at the food at the stations when we stop. Don't smoke or drink on my coach, and don't flop over your neighbor when sleeping." He paused to let that sink in, watching for the reactions on their faces. "Don't lollygag at the washbasin, and don't keep the stage waiting—we may leave without you. Don't think for one second that you are on a picnic; nothing could be further from the truth. Expect annoyances, discomfort, and some hardships, then we'll all get along just fine," he said with authority. "Are there any questions? If not, then let's get started."

Billy came rushing up to him. "Mister Morgan, is there room for one more?" He almost slid into the blonde-haired woman but caught himself on the hitching post.

The stagecoach driver turned around, and the woman drew in a sharp breath. "What are you doing here?" she asked Billy before the driver could answer.

Breathless, Billy explained. "Ruby up and died last night, Miss

April, after I let you off at the hotel. When I got her back to the livery . . . she just dropped." He tried to hold back his tears. "I was just about to feed her oats . . ." He hung his head.

Morgan pulled the lad aside, out of earshot of the others. "Do you have a ticket?" It wasn't the first time he'd seen Billy around the depot. He knew that Billy was an orphan and was always hanging around learning what he could while carting passengers' luggage and earning a bit of cash.

"No, sir, not yet, but I could help with the horses."

"I don't need any help. Why do you want to go to Lewis-town?"

Billy sighed. "Maybe get a better job, and Miss April here was kind to me yesterday, and to Ruby. I thought maybe she needs someone to work for her and look out after her . . . or some-thin.'"

Morgan chuckled. "I rather doubt that. She looks like she can pretty much handle anything."

"Could I squeeze in between you and Leon?"

"Well . . ." Morgan scratched his chin.

"Please, I beg you. I need a fresh start," Billy pleaded.

"All right, Billy, I'll take you as far as Lewistown. You may be fourteen, but you shouldn't be alone on the streets."

Billy murmured his thanks. "Shucks, I've been taking care of myself a long time now. You won't regret it, I promise."

Morgan turned to the rest. "Time's a-wasting and I like to keep on schedule. It's 5:55. Let's get our tails on the road. My partner, Leon, has stored your luggage on top."

They all piled in, April sitting next to the young woman with her baby and Mark on the opposite side with the older couple.

21

The floor of the coach was cramped as well, filled with bags of US mail. April just wanted to sit back and close her eyes. She'd gotten little sleep last night and was up at the crack of daylight in order not to miss this stage.

The stagecoach driver certainly seemed to be in control of things. She'd never been this close to a black person before. He appeared to be quite capable of handling the team, despite the gray in his wiry hair. His face was peppered by a white beard against paper-brown skin that resembled a dried prune. He was tall and muscular, and she noticed that he wore thick leather gloves with cuffs reaching up his forearm. Apparently he'd agreed to let Billy ride, because he'd scampered up to the front seat of the coach.

It wouldn't be too long and she'd be seeing her brother's sweet face. How she missed him. And it was time that Josh settled down. She could hardly wait to meet the woman he'd chosen. April was sure he would have chosen someone equally wonderful. Or at least she hoped so.

With harness rattling and wheels creaking, the coach lurched forward, heading out of town, and was soon rolling at a fast clip. April ignored the passengers around her and closed her eyes, leaning her head against the edge of the window. The rocking motion of the coach was soothing, and soon she nodded off. She dreamed of riding her horse across the floor of the Yampa Valley with the autumn trees shimmering in the distance, nestled below the snow-capped Rocky Mountains. The wind was blowing through her loose hair, and she felt complete freedom and utter happiness.

"Waaaaah!"

The cry of a baby brought April back into the reality of a two-day ride crammed into the stagecoach with complete strangers.

April watched the young woman as she tried to soothe her fussy baby, but nothing would quiet her. The lady's name, she found out, was Beth Reed, and her baby was Anne. The older couple introduced themselves as May and Willard Wingate, going to visit family in Lewistown. Mark Barnum chatted with them and smiled as he watched Beth and her baby. April didn't think she had one thing in common with any of them, and truth be known, she didn't feel like getting to know them. This would be a miserably long ride indeed. She would remind Josh of that very fact when she saw him.

May clapped her hands and held them out toward the baby. "Beth, let me entertain her for a bit, while you rest."

"Oh, I can't let you do that," Beth protested.

"'Course you can. I have six grandchildren myself."

Willard piped up, "Better listen to her. She's good with children."

Beth hesitated. "Are you sure? I've fed her, so she should be able to wait until we make our next stop."

Baby Anne went willingly into May's outstretched arms and cooed while looking into May's grinning face. It wasn't long before the baby was nestled against May's ample bosom, looking around at the passengers with her enormous eyes. Beth relaxed in her seat. April figured that she was worn to a frazzle from wrestling with her baby all morning. Babies looked like a lot of work to her. She'd much rather be outdoors or working the ranch horses or cattle with her father.

"My gout is acting up, and all this jostling around is only going to make it worse," Willard said.

"Humph! You can't be hurting any worse than I am, dear." May glanced at April. "He doesn't know what pain is. My rheumatism gives me constant pain, but you don't see me complaining." She glared at her husband.

"That may be true, but with my heart condition I have to take things slow, you know." Willard winked at April.

"De*aaar*, you think you have a heart condition, but you don't know that for certain because you won't visit the doctor!" May was clearly agitated.

April saw a smile curve Mark's lips as he stifled a laugh, and she glanced at Beth, who looked fast asleep. The baby's eyes were slowly closing as well.

"Perhaps you should get that complaint checked, Mr. Wingate, when you get settled at your daughter's. I'm a doctor." Mark handed him a business card.

April cast a quick look at him. "I expected as much, but you never said anything about that."

"It never came up." Mark directed his attention back to Willard. "Stop in and see me anytime. My office is right on Main Street."

May twisted abruptly in her seat, disturbing the baby, who woke up with a loud whimper. "Then I'll come with him too, so you can relieve me of my terrible headaches."

April saw Willard's face twist into a frown. "By golly, you're going to give me a headache with all your aches and pains!"

April had never heard so many complaints from two people before, and she wished they would stop yakking about it. Maybe she could try to change the subject, but who could be heard above the baby's crying? She couldn't believe that Beth never stirred. All the more reason to just have horses. She could put them in a stall, corral, or pasture and go on about her business. They certainly never complained.

Mark caught her eye. Her disdain must have shown in her face because he smiled at her. "We'll be stopping soon to water the horses and take a fifteen-minute break."

April pursed her lips together to keep from complaining. The break couldn't come soon enough for her. She sat facing the back of the stage and leaned out, gazing at the fast-moving landscape. The stagecoach left a cloud of dust some twenty feet behind them from the twenty-four hooves of the horses as they tore across the trail.

"Those horses can really kick up some dust!" April idly commented to no one in particular. There was a big difference between the Montana and Colorado landscape, but both were equally beautiful. The wind lifted a few strands of her hair from their pins, and April pushed them back into place, but the breeze was a welcome breath of fresh air after the stifling smells of May's heavy perfume mingled with the odor of Anne's soiled diaper.

Wes Owen adjusted his brown Stetson and stared at his reflection in the old cracked dresser mirror. His straight, sandy brown hair fell past his collar. *Should have gotten my hair trimmed,* he thought. But he was trying to be careful with the little money he had, and just because he was going to a wedding, he didn't think it was necessary to spend another fifty cents. It didn't look too bad, as long as he had his hat on. His eyes were clear and bright as he examined the light stubble of growth along his jawline, and he was satisfied that he'd finally shaved off his mustache last week. He thought it made him look younger. He never had been one to shave every day, and he wasn't about to start.

He knew that he wasn't exactly handsome but was rugged-looking from his deep tan and lines that crinkled around his eyes, a result of the sun. It'd have to do—it was the face God had given him. *If* it was God in the first place. He had his doubts, though his friend Josh had tried to convince him otherwise.

Frowning at his reflection, he pulled on his shirt and faded jeans, thinking how flattered he was to be invited to Josh and Juliana's wedding. He ran his fingers over the hand-tooled leather belt that matched his brown boots, loving the feel of the smooth leather and the rich smell of it. He'd spent more than he'd intended to on the boots and belt. He'd ordered it straight from Texas through a friend of his, and he knew that both pieces would last a long time. They'd have to, just like his saddle. Besides breaking horses, he'd always wanted to own a store where men who appreciated fine leather saddles and implements could be outfitted in the very best. But that was merely a dream.

Wes glanced at the clock. He'd have just enough time to check out Lars's wild mare before scooting on over to the wedding. He threw on his deep brown duster to ward off the September cold that had suddenly descended the last few days, and hurried out to get his horse. He saddled Dakota and slipped the bit into the horse's mouth, then quickly mounted and jerked the reins in the direction of Lewistown.

When the stage stopped, Leon instructed the passengers to get out of the coach in order to lighten the load while Morgan struggled with the stagecoach up the steep road. April sighed. At this rate, she would be surprised if she made the wedding at all. Her clothes were covered with dust and grime, and she dearly needed a bath. But at least she was in good company. The rest of the group didn't look any better than she.

Billy walked up to baby Anne and touched her hand. "Hello, little one," he said, and she jabbered something unintelligible and drooled down the front of her dress. Billy looked at April. "I think she likes me."

April smiled at the young lad. "Of course she does. She's like all females—we love attention," she said, casting a knowing look at Beth.

"Some of them do, but not all," Beth said demurely as she shifted the baby to the other hip. There was a slight frown creasing Beth's brow. "I need to change her diaper, but my bag is in the coach."

April stood watching with her hands folded. She knew nothing whatsoever about babies, except that they demanded plenty of attention.

Leon scurried up to the group. "I'm afraid you're all going to have to walk the rest of the way to the crest of that hill. Once we reach the top, we'll board again for a short ride to where we'll stop for lunch. Follow me and stick together."

"Just what I paid for. A chance to walk part of the way to Lewistown!" April sputtered as she lifted the hem of her skirt in aggravation. The ladies followed the men up the uneven road with Billy offering to carry Anne. The baby snuggled in his scrawny arms. *A half-grown man in an adolescent body*, April thought. She couldn't help but notice how Billy seemed to like everyone and was always cheerful despite his bad fortune.

Morgan had reached the top of the hill and was standing in the road, giving the horses a brief respite, when the group finally made it to the crest. "Folks, I'm sorry you had to walk that last stretch, but it was necessary. Our next stop is about twenty-five minutes away, and we'll stop for an hour."

Beth walked up to the coach where Morgan stood. "Please, before we leave, I need to change my baby's diaper. It'll only take a moment." Billy trudged up the last few yards, lugging Anne on his hip.

Morgan looked at the young woman and her baby. There was something pitiful about her that he couldn't put his finger on. He wondered why she was traveling with a baby and who she would be meeting.

"By all means, for the sake of the rest of us . . . *do* let her have a few minutes to clean up the child," April pleaded.

Morgan turned to give April a sharp look. *Probably never had to lift a finger to do anything in her young life.* He nodded at Beth. "I was just about to say yes, Mrs. Reed. We'll still be able to keep our schedule."

Beth reached inside the coach and grabbed her small traveling bag, then took Anne from Billy's arms. "Thank you, Billy. You were a great help carrying the baby up the hill for me. I don't know if I could have made it."

Billy beamed at her. "Aw . . . it was nothin'."

Beth swept past April without looking at her. Willard and May struggled to join the rest, huffing and out of breath. "Whew! That was some hike," Willard said, supporting May by the arm. Her chest heaved in and out until Morgan thought the buttons on her shirtwaist would pop.

"I'm just glad it wasn't a hot July day," May said between gasps of air. "I really shouldn't have to do this, you know, with my health like it is."

"Yours is no worse than mine now, sweetie."

April walked up to the front where the team was being attended by Leon. "Some nice horseflesh, but they are looking tired."

"Yes, ma'am. They are, but we'll be changing them out at the next stop." Leon paused to look at her. "You like horses?"

April laughed. "Yes, I do. Especially riding them. My father has a cattle ranch, so I grew up around them."

Leon scratched his beard. "Excuse me for saying so, but you don't look the part." His eyes traveled over her smart traveling dress and shoes.

"Don't let my looks fool you," she said, reaching out to stroke one of the horse's withers.

Morgan strode to the front of the stagecoach. "Please go ahead and get back in the coach. Mrs. Reed will be back any second, and we'll be ready to leave."

"I hope we won't get behind schedule, Mr. Kincaid, because of her and our having to trudge that long road." April's eyes flashed at him. "I'm supposed to be at my brother's wedding late tomorrow afternoon. I will be sorely upset if I miss it because of this! I had no idea this trip would be so hard. I'm covered in dust and getting bounced around like a US mailbag."

Like the world revolves around her, Morgan thought. He gave her a level stare that spoke volumes and cleared his throat. "I always do my best to stick to the schedule, and I've been late only a few times because of weather. Changing a baby's diaper, and your complaints, won't stop us from making it." He touched the brim of his hat to her, then signaled to Leon to get started as he climbed back to his perch on the coach. He hoped that would stop her griping. She needed to learn a few lessons about life. Too bad she didn't know Miss Margaret. She could teach April a lesson or two.

Morgan knew he hadn't heard the last of Miss McBride by a

long shot. There would be more complaints when she had to eat Abigail's beans and potatoes. He chuckled under his breath, and Leon cast him a quizzical look. "Never mind me, Leon. Something just struck me funny!"

When the stagecoach finally pulled away from the roadhouse after a brief respite, April found herself anxious to get back on the road toward Lewistown. The roadhouse was little more than a primitive log cabin with a kitchen and large open room where they all shared a questionable meal of beans, potatoes, and tough roast beef.

The cook was known as Abigail, a rotund, middle-aged woman with a gregarious nature. She piled their plates high and served them coffee and water.

April had tried her best to eat, but about the only thing she could keep down were Abigail's biscuits. The coffee was bitter and the boiled potatoes had little taste. She shuddered when she thought about where they would be spending the night before driving on to Lewistown. Her body was already sore from being tossed about on the rough road. And if she had to listen to May's and Willard's ailments for another day, she thought she might lose her mind. She cocked her head. Apparently this was the couple's usual way of conversing. Was that how things were when you'd been married a long time? She did not want her marriage—if she ever got married—to be like that.

She'd tried to talk to Beth when they walked outside after lunch before boarding, but she wasn't very friendly and seemed intent on seeing to Anne. April looked at the baby now curled up in her mama's arms. Her eyes were slowly drooping, now that she'd had her bottle and a diaper change. Soon she was fast asleep with the rocking of the stage. April had to admit that Anne was a cute little one, and even Mark had commented to Beth that the baby was indeed a beautiful child.

This time April sat facing forward with the older couple next to her. April closed her eyes, feigning sleep to keep May's constant chatter out of her ear.

By late afternoon, everyone was tired and cranky, and they had only one other brief stop before traveling on again. Even the good-natured doctor showed signs of fatigue. April felt the stage slowly roll to a halt, and she looked out the window as Morgan and Leon walked over and opened the coach doors.

"Folks, this is where we stop for the night. Supper is served at 5:30 sharp. The cost of a room with cots is two dollars. We'll be pulling out at 6 a.m. sharp once again. Enjoy your respite," Morgan announced.

The passengers were eager to find the outbuildings before going inside the roadhouse. April held her nose as she stood waiting her turn.

"Do you think you could hold Anne for me when it's my turn?" Beth asked.

"Uh . . . sure . . . if she'll let me." April had never held a baby and was unsure of what to do.

"Hold your noses, ladies," May squawked as she staggered out of the outhouse. "I'm warning you. I wonder when it was last cleaned."

Beth handed the baby to April, who cooed up at her. It felt funny to be holding something so helpless and small, but she smelled good and wasn't heavy at all. The baby reached up for April's shiny locket with her tiny fingers. April marveled at Anne's delicate features and thick lashes sweeping against flawless skin. With surprise, April found her heart warming to the baby who smiled up at her with her fat baby cheeks, and she didn't hear Beth step out of the outhouse.

"Don't let her break your locket."

April lifted her head from the small bundle, looking at Beth. "Oh, she can't hurt it. She's been a perfect angel." She handed the baby back to her mother.

"Thank you, April." Beth's expression was warm and friendly. "You'll have your own baby someday."

April shook her head. "I'm not so sure about that. At least, not in the near future. I wouldn't know what to do with a baby."

May harrumphed. "If you can handle a horse, you'll do great raising a baby."

But April remained skeptical where babies were concerned.

After a miserable night sharing a crowded room with Beth, Anne, and May, April's back ached from the cots they called beds. The baby had cried for a long time because she was not in familiar surroundings, and May snored most of the night. Add to that a breakfast of hard biscuits and greasy bacon that left an uneasy feeling in April's middle. Lunch was hardly any better, and the bouncing ride hadn't helped her stomach either.

Morgan was waiting for her after another stop. She didn't want to hold up the stage. Far from it.

"If you're ready, we really must leave now, Miss McBride." April thought he seemed annoyed with her. She couldn't help it if her stomach was clamping her insides.

"I believe so. It was not my intent to interfere with your schedule. I can't help it if breakfast disagreed with me. Perhaps if the meat had been fresh, I wouldn't be feeling this way. What I wouldn't do for a decent cup of coffee. I guess that's not likely to happen. The conditions of what was called a room were disgusting for two dollars a night."

She lifted the hem of her skirt to climb into the waiting stage, and Mark reached down to give her a hand up.

"Not to worry," Morgan said with clenched teeth. "We *will* get back on schedule. It's best if you don't grumble about things you have no control over along the stage trail. The stage companies try to provide the best that they can out here in the wilderness. I did warn everyone. Just be glad that we've not had any robberies along the way this trip."

Before he walked to the front, April leaned out the window. "Bandits won't scare me, Mr. Kincaid. Just get us back on schedule so I don't miss my brother's wedding!"

Morgan gave her a hard stare. "You're not the only one who's paid eighteen dollars for this trip. I want to accommodate *all* my passengers." He strode to the front of the stage and hauled himself up to where Leon and Billy were waiting. He picked up the reins, and after a sharp snap of his whip, the team quickly trotted off, leaving the dust behind them.

Soon after lunch it was apparent that there was trouble. April could feel the stage slowing and finally roll to a complete stop. Mark looked at her, his brow furrowed in question.

Willard, who'd been lounging against May's shoulder, sat up

34

straight. "Why are we stopping?" As he said it, the back left side of the stage seem to lean to one side.

"There must be a problem." Mark opened the door and leaped out. Everyone else piled out of the coach. Leon was stooped over at the rear of the stagecoach, and it was obvious at first glance that the rear axle held a broken wheel.

May gasped. "Oh my goodness. Whatever will we do?"

"Can it be repaired?" Mark asked, walking back to where Leon stood scratching his head.

"Afraid not," he answered glumly.

Morgan joined them. "What rotten luck! Leon, you're gonna have to go back to the last station and see if they have another wheel to replace this one. If not, they'll have to send us a replacement coach if one is available."

"Let me go. I can ride hard and fast," Billy pleaded.

"But that'll take hours!" April shook her head in frustration.

Morgan's jaw flinched. "It can't be helped." He turned to Billy. "Leon will need to go."

"Aw, shucks!" Billy frowned, and Morgan clapped him on the back. "Thanks anyway, Billy. I might need your help here."

Morgan and Leon unhitched one of the horses. Leon hoisted a saddlebag from the front seat, mounted the big horse, and gave it a swift jab with his heels, heading back to the station they'd left just an hour before.

"Now what do we do?" April demanded. She looked pointedly at Morgan. The other passengers shuffled forward.

"We wait. Pure and simple. Looks like you'll be a couple hours late to the wedding, Miss McBride. Maybe in time to send the couple off on their honeymoon," Morgan replied.

"Let's go sit down on one of the rocks just under the trees there. It's a beautiful valley," Beth said, apparently trying to get April calm.

"No, thank you, Beth," April said with a slight shake of her head.

Willard held his arm out to May. "Come on, love. It'll be nice to get some fresh air. We've no hurry. The grandkids will keep." May slipped her hand through his arm, looking up at him as if he were the sweetest man alive.

Mark moved toward April. "Care to take a walk? Looks like we have time to explore."

April stood thinking about the predicament and quickly formulated an idea. "No, Dr. Barnum. I have to get to Lewistown."

"So do we all, and we will."

April saw by the look on his face that he knew she was considering what she could do. She walked toward Morgan, who was taking a closer look at the wheel at the rear of the stagecoach.

Morgan looked up and said, "I'm gonna need the bags unloaded that are strapped on top of the coach. Mark, you think you and Billy could give me a hand with that?"

"Sure thing," Mark answered. Billy hurried over and started climbing on top of the coach.

April shielded her eyes from the sun to look up at Billy. "Could you throw mine down first?"

Morgan threw her a questioning look, but she pretended she didn't notice. "I'm going to change clothes."

"Whatever for?" Beth asked, swinging Anne back and forth in her arms.

"If Mr. Kincaid will let me, I want to borrow one of the horses and ride on into Lewistown."

April heard Beth gasp.

"What? Are you crazy? You'll wait just like the others," Morgan sputtered.

"Mr. Kincaid, I'm a good horsewoman, and you'll have a fresh mount when Leon gets back. Besides, he may have to wait for another coach. In the meantime, I could take one of your horses and might be able to get to Lewistown before the wedding at five."

"What makes you think I'll let you do that, Miss McBride?" Morgan pursed his lips into a fine line. "You can wait right here like the rest."

April dropped her shoulders, momentarily deflated. "Because I'm begging you. I'll take care of your horse and you won't be responsible—"

Mark interrupted. "I say if she can stay on one of those huge beasts, then let her give it a try. It'd be a shame to miss her only brother's wedding." Mark glanced at Morgan.

"I have a feelin' that I'm gonna regret this . . . but since I know Josh personally, I'll agree, Miss McBride, but my horse better not come back lame, and you better not fall off. I'm still responsible for my passengers." He walked toward the team and started the process of unharnessing another horse. "I don't know what you'll do for a saddle, but that's your problem."

"I can ride bareback for a few hours, if you have a blanket."

Morgan grunted. "I have one under the driver's seat that we use for sudden cold spells. I'll grab it." He climbed up to the seat and came back with a woolen blanket and handed it to April.

"Perfect," April said, taking the blanket. Morgan watched her, his eyes narrowing in thought.

"Billy, would you drag my trunk over to those bushes there?" April turned to Mark. "And thanks for the vote of confidence."

Mark stood with his hands in his pockets, rocking back on his heels. "I feel pretty sure you can handle just about anything you set your mind to."

April felt her face burn. "I'm not sure about that, but I'm determined to make it to Lewistown."

"If I don't make it to Josh's wedding, please give him my apologies, and I'll catch up with him and Juliana later," Mark said.

April hurried over to where Billy had dragged her trunk and opened the lid with her key. Mark and Beth went to find a grassy area to play with the baby while they waited for Leon to return.

After digging underneath her dresses and petticoats, she pulled out a pair of men's jeans, a light blue flannel shirt, and a pair of boots. She'd keep her split skirt that she normally wore for later. No point in getting it filthy. Making certain that she wasn't going to be seen behind the chokeberry bush, April scrambled out of her traveling skirt and jacket, yanked on the jeans, then quickly buttoned the shirt, stuffing the tails into her waistband. She put a few necessary items in her tapestry valise, along with the soft yellow dress that she would wear to Josh's wedding. The rest of her things, including their gifts, she would retrieve when the stage arrived in town. She pulled her long hair into a knot, shoved it underneath her felt cowboy hat, and donned her black duster.

Billy's eyes opened wide at April when she stepped from behind the bush. "Wow, Miss April. I hardly recognized you!"

"Good! I'll be safer on the trail that way. Which horse did you decide to let me borrow?" she asked, fixing her gaze on Morgan.

"This here's Gus. He'll get you there in a hurry and is easy to control. When you check into your hotel, just have the livery take him over to the stage station until we arrive." Morgan led a huge sorrel over to April, then gave her directions to Lewistown.

"I'll take good care of him. I promise." April patted Gus's broad face and he snorted.

Morgan raised his eyes heavenward. "Lord, I hope I don't regret this," he prayed underneath his breath.

"Did you say something?" She turned to Morgan.

"I was just telling Billy to get your trunk."

Billy piped up. "I'll take care of it myself, Miss April. Hope I'll see you in Lewistown later." He gazed at her sheepishly.

"Thanks, Billy. I'm sure we'll run into each other." April dismissed him with a wave of her hand and turned to Morgan. "Mr. Kincaid, if you could just give me a hand up, I'll be on my way."

Morgan laced his fingers together, and she placed a booted foot inside it, throwing her other leg across Gus's broad back. Morgan handed her bag up to her. "Thanks, Mr. Kincaid. I owe you one." April looked down at Morgan, probably knowing he wasn't too happy about his decision.

"You've got that right, Miss McBride. Do be careful. You ought to make it to Lewistown in just under two hours." Morgan stepped back to let her pass. He watched her gallop down the trail, kicking up a cloud of dust, looking like a man from the back with a long coat and hat. He admired how she held her seat in spite of not having a saddle. He watched as she and Gus became one fluid motion until he could no longer see her on the dusty road.

As much as he hated to let her take off on Gus, Morgan was glad to be rid of April and her constant grumbling and complaining.

If it wasn't the food, it was the stops they had to make and where they stayed. She complained about the other passengers too. He was sure that she was used to having her every need met whenever she snapped her fingers. He hoped she didn't return home by his stage. He had just about all he could take of her and her attitude.

Morgan turned to Mark. "I pity the man who tangles with those beautiful blue eyes."

Mark chuckled. "Shoot, she'll have him roped and lassoed quicker than a wildfire spreads."

Wes thought he'd be able to get a handle on Lars's mare in the corral at the edge of town and still have time to make it to the wedding. He hadn't seen a horse that he couldn't break. It was something he was proud of. But this mare might become the first.

He stepped back, letting the rope that he'd looped around the mare's neck go slack. She was a beauty for a fact. Jet black, about sixteen hands high. Her sides heaving, she stopped pawing the ground before her in anger and stared him down with her huge, gleaming black eyes.

"Hey, girl, nobody's gonna hurt you none," Wes whispered, keeping his distance for a bit. He had to earn her trust. He tentatively took a step toward her, and then another with his palm faceup. The mare rose up on her back legs, pawing the air with her front hooves and tossing her head, which sent her mane flying.

Wes yanked down hard on the rope, and the mare screamed. He dug his heels into the ground, trying to hold the rope taut while speaking quietly to her.

"Hey, you there! Stop that!"

Wes turned to see a young lad canter toward him on the back

41

of a big sorrel, sending rocks and dirt flying as he reined his horse in. The rider stopped some distance away, but Wes could tell that he must have been on the trail for a while. He couldn't help but notice that he used no saddle, only a blanket. Still holding the rope, Wes pushed his hat back to get a better look at who was yelling at him. The young man leaned over his horse's neck to stare at him. His jeans and duster showed dirt from a long ride, and his floppy felt hat shaded most of his face.

"If you are trying to break that horse, those tactics won't work!" Wes heard a squeaky-pitched voice laden with anger say.

"Boy, I've been doing this most of my life, and I don't believe I asked for your advice!" he yelled back. *Snot-nosed kid sure has a lot of nerve. Must not be from around these parts, or he'd know better.*

"Leave that mare be. I'll take her off your hands." The rider pulled out a wad of bills from his hip pocket and threw them in the dirt, and the mare snorted her displeasure. "That ought to be more than enough to cover the cost. I'm in a bit of a hurry, but I'll be back to collect her in the morning."

"She's not for sale. She belongs to Lars, the smithy, for your information." Wes drew his lips into a tight line.

The young man's horse danced back and forth in agitation. "He'll sell her just to get her off his hands. Right now, I have a wedding that I must attend." The rider yanked the reins in the direction of town and cantered off.

Wes picked up the money. *Whew! This high-strung mare is probably not worth this amount for all her aggravation.* Wes wondered who that person could have been. No matter, he was going to the wedding too, and he'd just hand the money right back to him.

Wes let the rope drop and left the corral. The mare immediately ran to the far side. She would get used to walking about with the rope, and then maybe he'd try to put a bridle on her. But now he needed to wash his hands and hightail it to Josh's wedding. Maybe he'd see Natalie there. She had been friendly to him at the art sale and at church, when he'd let Josh talk him into going. Would she remember him?

April could hear the bells tolling the five o'clock hour from the white clapboard church at the end of Main Street. She realized that she was already late and decided that if she went on to the hotel now to change, she would miss the entire wedding. She could slip in the back of the church unseen and then hurry to change for the reception. Her mother would be mortified if she knew that she'd taken off from the stagecoach alone with a borrowed horse, but she didn't want to endure two days on a stage just to miss her beloved brother's wedding. Too bad their parents wouldn't be here.

It took only moments to find Beaver Creek Church on the edge of town. Looking around the churchyard, April saw that it was filled with horses and buggies. She tied Gus to a hitching post, tiptoed up the steps, and eased open the church door. Good, no squeaking. She breathed a sigh of relief. Closing the door behind her, she turned to see the church pews filled with people and decorated with white bows and orange chrysanthemums. The wedding party was already assembled at the altar.

She took one tiny step over to the nearest pew, and the floor groaned in protest. She held her breath, but in the quiet sanctuary, the guests turned around to see who the latecomer was. She quickly sat down, her hat still on to help hide her face, but not before Josh's eyes locked with hers and a huge grin spread across his handsome face. April placed a finger to her mouth, indicating for him to be quiet, so he turned to face his bride. She wouldn't be able to skip out early now that he'd spotted her.

She tried to ignore the stares around her, but she was acutely aware of her grimy appearance and knew her cowboy garb was not appropriate for a wedding. With her hair pushed under her cowboy hat, perhaps they would think she was a man.

April squirmed in the pew, a bit warm with her duster on, but she dared not remove it and cause any more distractions. After the ceremony, she'd hurry out before she would have to speak to anyone else.

She focused on the reverend as he spoke the wedding vows to the couple. Josh's bride, whom she now knew as Juliana, was tall with dark hair, and from her profile April could tell she was attractive. Josh wore a navy blue suit and matching string tie with a chrysanthemum in his lapel, and black leather boots. Juliana was dressed in a white gown with delicate lace inserts at the bodice and sleeves. Around her head she wore a crown of mock orange blossoms and a trailing veil of frothy tulle. They made a handsome couple. Her brother was looking at Juliana with complete adoration, as she smiled up at him with trembling lips. April adored her brother and prayed that Juliana would be a good wife for him.

The vows were repeated and rings exchanged, and the groom lifted the lacy veil and kissed his bride, lingering a moment on her lips. The smiling couple faced the congregation before walking the length of the aisle. Everyone stood up clapping and cheering. As they neared April, Josh stopped and leaned over for a kiss from his sister as she congratulated him. April noticed the questioning look Juliana gave him.

In a quiet voice so as not to be overheard, Josh said, "Juliana, meet my sister April. Apparently she just rode up. Literally!"

April shot her brother an impish look, then smiled at his new wife. "Nice to meet you. I'll see you at the reception in the fellowship hall once I've changed."

"Lovely to meet you as well," Juliana murmured shyly.

"Don't take long, sis," Josh said, guiding his bride back into the aisle to go outside.

April was right behind them and ran to mount Gus. She gave him a swift kick in the ribs while holding her hat with one hand, her coattail flying in the wind.

Josh laughed when Juliana stared after April. "I warned you that she was someone to be reckoned with. I suppose there is a good reason for her showing up that way," he said, patting his bride's hand in the crook of his arm.

"Yes, you did, and I can't wait to get to know her better." Juliana smiled up at him.

Josh stared down at his lovely wife. "And you will soon, my beautiful bride, and you and I will get to know each other better too . . . alone," he whispered in her ear, ignoring the guests who began spilling down the church steps.

Juliana blushed prettily and hauled him toward the side door to the fellowship hall.

April stopped Gus directly in front of the Stockton Hotel and hurriedly slid off his broad back. It would feel so good to clean off the trail dust and change her clothes. She marched up to the front desk, yanking off her hat. No one was about, so she slammed her palm down on the bell sitting on the counter. Where was everyone? She didn't have all day. An older man shuffled from the back room to the front desk in no apparent hurry, picked up his spectacles, and looked at her quizzically.

"May I help you, er . . . miss?"

"You may. I'm April McBride. Josh McBride made a reservation for a room for me." She laid her hat on the counter and tried to pat her flyaway hair back into place. The hotel seemed to be beautifully furnished, the hardwood floors gleamed with high gloss, and potted ferns graced either side of the front desk.

The older gentleman glanced down at his book and slowly followed each line with his bony finger. The time seemed to stretch into long minutes. He shook his gray head. "I'm sorry, but I see nothing on the books for your reservation."

"What? There must be some mistake."

"Afraid not, ma'am." He shoved the sliding spectacles back up on the bridge of his nose. "It seems that your message was not received by us, or it would be here." His face was serious.

April put her palms on the counter and leaned over as he turned the registrar's book toward her. With irritation, she could see that he was right. "I see. Well . . . go ahead and make a reservation for me to stay about two weeks."

"I'm afraid we have no vacant rooms tonight, but if you'll check back tomorrow, we'll probably have a room for you."

"But I need one now!" April raised her voice and tapped the toe of her boot impatiently. "What'll I do? I need to change clothes for my brother's wedding reception that's going on right now!" She felt like crying. Every problem seemed to be joined by another one.

The clerk's eyes raked over her appearance with a grimace.

"It's a long story."

He shrugged and pointed to his right. "There's a necessary room over there where you can change clothes. When the reception's over, you could check down the street at Miss Margaret's boardinghouse. She may be able to accommodate you."

"Boardinghouse?" April waved a hand at the clerk when he started to speak. She didn't have time to quibble. She picked up her valise and headed to the water closet.

"Miss McBride? You left your hat."

April paused, grabbed her hat, and stalked off. How in the world had they not received her telegram? She was sure that Robby had sent it.

She shook out her wrinkled yellow dress and matching cape as best she could and placed it over the back of a chair. Pulling off the dirty pants and shirt, she packed them at the bottom of her bag. She was grateful she had water to wash her face and arms. Her hair would just have to hang straight down since there wasn't time or a hot iron to curl it now. She brushed the silky length of blonde hair that hung past her shoulders, then pulled her dress on. Staring at her reflection, she thought, *Not too bad considering I'm tired and haven't had one good night's sleep in a week.*

Throwing her matching woolen cape around her shoulders, April stepped out into the foyer. She saw the clerk's eyebrows shoot upward.

"My, that was a quick change, and one for the better, I might add!" He stared at her over the top of his spectacles.

"Thanks. Do you think that you could hold my bag until this evening when I come back to collect it?"

"No trouble at all," he said, taking it from her outstretched arm. "I'll store it right here behind the front desk for you."

"Thank you . . . I'm afraid I don't know your name."

"I'm Ed Rankin. Are you Josh's sister?"

"Yes, I am. Do you know Josh?"

"Not personally, but I've heard good things about him through Marion Stockton."

"Oh? She must be a friend of his."

"I believe so. Her father owns this hotel."

"How very interesting," she said, trying to edge toward the door to leave. She didn't want him to keep jawing about the townsfolk. When she reached the door, she turned. "Do you think you can have someone take the horse that I rode to the stage depot?" She laid a silver dollar on the counter for his trouble.

"Sure thing, Miss McBride. We'll see to it."

"I'd be grateful. I must hurry, but I'll be back. Thanks for your help."

April hurried out into the late afternoon's lengthening shadows to take the short walk down the boardwalk to the church. Lewistown was a quaint, small town with a few people and wagons moving about as the close of day was near. Not nearly as big as Steamboat Springs, but still she looked forward to peeking around the following week. She was not in any hurry to make the long, grinding trip home.

When April arrived at the church, the hall was full of guests

48

enjoying punch and the sounds of a string quartet. Several couples were waltzing, and candlelight cast a romantic glow about the decorated room befitting a wedding party. Several said hello as she swept past them, and she nodded a hello, not stopping until she found the happy couple sipping punch amid a small group of friends.

Josh saw her coming and walked up to draw her toward them. "I'm so happy you could make it, April. Why in the world were you dressed in men's clothes?"

"My dear brother, I doubt that Juliana wants to hear my she-nanigans on her wedding day!" April said.

"On the contrary, I want to know." Juliana smiled at her new sister-in-law. "How about a glass of punch?"

"I'd like some. I'm so thirsty after that trip." April got a closer look at her new sister-in-law and was surprised to see that she looked very young. Josh wasn't old, but Juliana was definitely still wet behind the ears. She was not beautiful but was attractive with brilliant blue eyes that seem to stare right into April's thoughts. April followed the couple over to the punch bowl.

"April, I'd like you to meet some of our friends." Juliana smiled. Two women serving the punch and cake paused when they approached the table.

"Back for more punch?" One of the women reached for her cup.

"Thanks, but no. We want to introduce Josh's sister April to everyone." Juliana turned to April, who paused next to Josh. "April, this is Natalie and Louise, who are sisters and my best friends." Juliana beamed at them. "They helped me plan everything for the wedding."

April nodded and said hello. The sisters looked as different as day and night. The talkative one was pretty, the other one quiet and retiring.

"Josh told us he had a sister, but we didn't know you were coming all the way up from Colorado. It's so nice to meet you." Natalie handed April a cup of punch.

"Thank you, Natalie. I never thought I'd get here," April said. "The stagecoach broke down."

Louise looked at her thoughtfully. "Were you the one who came in the black duster right before the ceremony?"

Josh laughed. "You bet it was her. She was not about to miss her brother's wedding," he said with a twinkle in his eyes.

"You are so right." April looked down at her dress. "That's the reason for all the wrinkles in my dress."

"It looks okay, really. Don't worry about that," Juliana said. "So how *did* you get here?"

"Let's just say I borrowed a horse from the stage after pleading with the driver."

"Sounds like something you'd do, sis." Josh downed his punch and put his arm around Juliana's waist. "Want to dance, Jewel?"

At that moment a tiny gray-haired lady leaning on a walking cane walked up to congratulate the couple, and Juliana introduced her. "This is Miss Margaret, Natalie and Louise's mother. Also a dear friend."

"My, but you seem to consider everyone a good friend." April's lips curled into a tight smile.

Miss Margaret held out her hand. "I'm Mrs. Spencer, but everyone calls me Miss Margaret. I run the boardinghouse in town."

April barely touched the old lady's hand. "Hello, Miss Margaret. In fact, I heard your name earlier from Ed at the Stockton Hotel. Seems as though they didn't have a reservation for me and their rooms are booked. He told me to inquire at your boardinghouse."

"Ed's right. I do have a room. How long will you be staying?" Miss Margaret was gazing at her with gray, watery eyes as though sizing her up. Somehow April felt uncomfortable under her intent look. *Why is she looking at me in that strange way? Old people are a mystery to me.*

"She can stay until we get back from our honeymoon," Josh commented, squeezing Juliana. "Then she can come to the ranch."

"Oh no, Josh, I'm not getting in the middle of newlyweds while they're adjusting to living together." April turned to Miss Margaret. "It may be as long as a few weeks. I really don't know yet."

"No problem, April," Natalie answered for her mother. "We've got room for you." Miss Margaret nodded in agreement.

"Well . . ." April hesitated.

"It's settled. You can come stay with us. We can have your luggage brought over," Miss Margaret insisted.

"My luggage hasn't arrived yet. You see, the wagon wheel broke and I rode in on Gus, one of the coach horses." April watched as Miss Margaret's eyes narrowed.

"You did? How very unusual, my dear."

Josh chuckled. "Not if you know my sister. Sis, Jewel and I are going to dance. Get to know everyone as if you were home." Josh led Juliana to the dance floor, leaving April floundering for something to say to the group she barely knew. So they all stood watching as Josh and Juliana, whom he affectionately called Jewel, moved around the floor to the beat of the music. Complete happiness was evident on Josh's face, and by the way Juliana's eyes gazed into his, April could tell the feeling was mutual.

April wanted a love just like that.

She glanced across the floor to the doorway and saw the man who had been wrangling with the horse when she'd ridden into town earlier. He was tall and lanky and still wearing his hat. He wore no suit coat but had on a leather vest the color of butternut squash and wore tight jeans. He walked with fluid assurance, crossing the floor with a purpose, his spurs jingling. He headed toward the reverend, who stood talking with a stout man wearing a badge. April assumed he was the town sheriff. If she got an opportunity, she would make sure the wrangler had taken care of the mare for her. She had given him most of her cash.

There was something almost overconfident about the man and the way he swaggered in that she couldn't put her finger on as she watched him out of the corner of her eye. Cocky. That was the kind of man she took an immediate dislike to. He was probably rough in his treatment of horses in order to break them down. She could not tolerate the mistreatment of animals, especially horses.

The dance ended, and Josh and Juliana walked off the dance floor, laughing. April saw the horse wrangler walk over to them. *Josh's friend? Not Josh's type.* She turned her head toward them just as the lanky man looked right at her, and Josh gestured toward her. *Oh no, they're walking over to me.* April dropped her eyes, pretended she hadn't seen them, and tried to encourage Miss Margaret to tell her about the boardinghouse. She hoped Josh would not play matchmaker. *Heaven forbid it!* She mentally shook herself and straightened to stand as tall as she could, shoulders back and ready for a battle she knew was coming.

4

Wes followed the sound of music to the fellowship hall where a good number of people were already in the throes of celebrating the nuptials of his good friend Josh. He had been to church a few times in the past but was uncomfortable in this setting. Never in a million years would he have thought he'd go in the first place, but Josh had been pretty persuasive. Wes's father would roll over in his grave if he knew Wes was here, or, for that matter, reading the Good Book.

He spotted Josh and Juliana accepting congratulations and hugs from friends. As he made his way over to them, he felt a bit envious. While he didn't know either of them very well, through a strange set of circumstances, they had become friends in the last few months.

Josh grinned as Wes walked up and stretched out his hand to congratulate him. "I'm not much on weddings and funerals, but yours was very nice. But then, how could it not be with that beautiful bride of yours?"

Juliana smiled shyly and looked at her husband, hugging Josh's arm. "We thought it turned out nice too."

"Thanks for coming to share in our happiness, Wes." Josh gripped his hand. "One day it's going to be your turn."

"Oh, I doubt that. I'm not the marrying kind."

"Don't you mean no one could put up with you?" Josh teased.

"You may be exactly right. Horses are my main focus, and I haven't found a gal yet who wanted to share in horse training for her future." He shrugged.

"You never know, Wes. When one falls in love, stranger things can happen," Juliana said.

"Anyway, I'm looking for a young man who rode up this afternoon when I was training Lars's mare. Never seen him before, but I think he must have been one of your guests who came in late."

"You must mean my sister April." Josh pointed across the room, indicating a woman in a yellow dress.

Wes looked to where he pointed. His jaw dropped. An attractive, slender blonde stood chatting with Miss Margaret and Louise. "No, Josh. It was a young man in a long duster and floppy hat." There was no way that this was the same person he saw in dirty jeans and a duster, shouting at him earlier!

Josh shook his head. "I'm trying to tell you—it was April, my sister. Come on, I'll introduce you to her. Excuse us a moment, Jewel."

"You go ahead. I want to speak with Helen and Cynthia."

Josh brushed her fingertips with a kiss. "I won't be long."

Wes swallowed hard and suddenly found himself being introduced to Josh's sister. April was exquisitely beautiful, and she held herself in a regal way and looked in complete control of her emotions. She was tall and slender. He liked that. The sunlight streamed through the window and enveloped her profile with its softness, casting glints on her silky blonde hair that lay against the yellow silk gown.

"Sis, I want you to meet my friend Wes Owen." Josh touched April on the arm.

April half turned, revealing her creamy white shoulders and slender neck, then slowly lifted her eyes to meet Wes's. For a moment he felt like he had been kicked in the chest just by the depth of them. She had clear blue eyes with large irises that gave him a cool look, unnerving him somehow.

He heard himself mumble a greeting, but instantly he felt awkward and out of place. She was a well-bred lady. He could tell, not that it made any difference to him. Was she really the same woman he'd seen dressed in pants earlier? He hadn't exactly cottoned to her interjecting herself into his horse wrangling. He thought it very odd that she dressed the way she did, riding up on her horse without a saddle. She was definitely out of the ordinary—and out of his realm.

"Hello." April lifted her hand to touch his in a brief handshake, then quickly dropped her hand to her side. She glanced at Josh. "I believe we already met this afternoon."

"That's a fact, Miss April," he stuttered, feeling like his tongue was as thick as the hide on his horse's back. He hurriedly regained his composure. "I'd like to give you this." Wes handed her the small drawstring bag of cash. "As I said before, the horse is *not* for sale."

"You can't be serious. That's a great deal of money there. I'm sure more than that wild horse is worth."

They had forgotten that Josh and Margaret were still there and continued on.

"I'm as serious as the blush on your cheeks. The horse belongs to the blacksmith."

April harrumphed. "If you knew anything at all about horses, you wouldn't have been so harsh with the mare."

Wes felt his face go red, and the collar of his shirt suddenly made his neck itch. He turned to Josh, who didn't seem to know quite what to make of their exchange. Wes needed to be careful. This was his sister. "Josh"—he nodded to him—"I think your sister doesn't know that I make my living training horses for some of the best ranchers around."

"He sure does, April, and he's known in these parts as one of the best."

"Exactly as I thought—your reputation precedes you." April hitched an eyebrow upward.

"Wes, I believe you've met your match. I need to tell you, April has a way with horses—I'm not sure what my father would do without her. But I'll let you get to know each other. I'm going to find my bride. I've been away from her too long already!" He clapped Wes on the shoulder, nodded to Miss Margaret, and hurried away.

The two stood sizing each other up. Finally Wes spoke. "Maybe we should start over. If you're in the market for a horse, I have several at my place that you can come look over."

"I would hardly do that. I'm just here for a couple of weeks. I can borrow one of Josh's horses."

"Uh . . . don't think so. He only has one, and Juliana would not part with her horse for anyone."

"Surely Josh has more than one horse?"

"I'm telling you straight. He's a sheepherder now, not a cattle-man." Wes let that sink in for a moment.

"Sheep . . . those disgusting little creatures. How he got into that I'll never understand."

"You can make a good living out of sheepherding," Wes said.

"Well, it's not being a cattleman, now is it?"

"Ma'am, around here they both count." Wes had lived in Mon-tana all his life and knew that in the beginning of sheepherding, there had been a lot of animosity between ranchers and sheep-herders. But eventually the ranchers had to admit there was a lot of money in sheepherding, and Montana had quickly risen as one of the main centers of sheepherding in the country.

Miss Margaret cleared her throat. Again they'd forgotten she was still there, all eyes and ears. "Wes, perhaps you could bring April over to the boardinghouse after the reception. She can have Juliana's old room," she said with a smile.

April tossed her hair off her shoulders. "No need for that. I can find my way, and I don't have my luggage yet."

Wes felt relief. He didn't want to have anything to do with someone as high-strung and egotistical as she. He stood with one hand resting on his hip and tilted his head, pretending to watch the dancers, but out of the corner of his eye he observed April turn down several invitations to dance. He certainly wasn't about to ask her. In fact, he was just about to go look for Natalie when she walked up to Margaret.

"Mother, are you holding up okay?" Natalie asked, touching her mother's sleeve.

Miss Margaret peered at her daughter through the tops of her wire spectacles and laughed. "Not to worry, dear. I'm feeling just fine. I can always rest, but I can't always be around gaiety such as this."

Natalie turned to April with a friendly look. "I've heard so much about you."

April gave her a curious look. "You have? All good, I hope."

"Yes, of course. I hope we can become better acquainted."

"There will be plenty of time for us to do that before my brother returns from his honeymoon."

Miss Margaret shifted her gaze from April to Natalie. "April will be staying with us in Juliana's old room. Won't that be nice?"

"Oh . . . I'm glad that Louise and I spent this morning cleaning. Juliana had her things moved to Josh's house before the wedding—"

"Thank you, but I won't be with you long," April said. "I'll be moving to the Stockton Hotel as early as tomorrow. I'm more suited to a staff."

"I see," Natalie said, and shot her mother a quizzical look.

From the look on her face, Margaret didn't let on that it mattered to her one way or the other. Wes didn't know the old lady very well, but it was apparent to him, from the few times he'd gone to church, that she adored Juliana.

Wes, sensing the awkwardness of the conversation, approached Natalie for a dance. Sweeping his hat off, he took a deep breath. "Miss Natalie, would you care to have a whirl on the dance floor?" He tossed his hat back and forth from one hand to the other. Josh had reminded him to take his hat off on certain occasions, which was something he usually didn't do except when he bathed or went to bed.

"Why . . . uh . . . sure. I'd like that," she said with surprise, then turned to the others. "Will you excuse us?" She slipped her arm in the crook of Wes's elbow.

The tune was a waltz, and Wes stumbled his way through it, trying to move with the music, but he felt like he had grown two left feet since he took to the dance floor. He felt about as comfortable as a fly in a bowl of milk . . . drowning.

"Ouch!" Natalie yelped. "That was my foot, or what's left of it!"

Wes pulled away but still held her hands in his sweaty palms. "I'm so sorry. Did I hurt you?" He wanted to sink into the floor and hoped April wasn't watching with her dignified nose in the air. Somehow he knew she thought him uncouth. He wasn't exactly sure how he knew, other than the way she looked at him, and now he could probably say Natalie thought that as well.

Natalie squeezed his hand. "My goodness! Don't take it so hard, Wes. I'm not the best dancer in the world either." Her brown eyes flashed up at him.

Wes laughed. "Maybe we should just go have some cake and punch instead. That way I can't land on your feet."

Natalie slowed her steps. "Fine with me. Why don't you lead the way."

As he directed her toward the refreshments, he thought to himself that this was going even better than he thought. He had a pretty lady on his arm, and having become acquainted with Josh and the reverend, he didn't feel too out of place. Now if he could just learn the waltz. . . .

A half hour later, the music stopped, and Louise clapped her hands together to get everyone's attention. She looked over the crowd. "Friends and family, it's time to say good-bye to the happy couple. Be sure and pick up small packets of rice by the vestibule door, and then wait outside until we see them come out."

People started moving to the front of the church, talking with excitement about the bride and groom, then formed a line on either side of the church steps. As they waited, the sun sank to the edge of the horizon, its waning light casting shadows through the trees scattered about the churchyard. The wind blew lightly, giving April a chill.

She noticed a young girl in a wheelchair along with a woman, probably the girl's mother, standing at the top of the stairs waiting for someone to help bring the girl down. To her surprise, Wes, spurs jingling, strode over and lifted the girl out of the chair into his arms, then carried her down the stairs. He waited as the reverend carried the wheelchair and deposited it on the ground, and the girl gave him a quick kiss on his cheek. His face mirrored surprise, leaving April to speculate that he must not know her very well. She wondered why the little girl was crippled and felt a momentary pang of sadness for her. The girl's mother, a retiring redhead, fussed over her and straightened her dress after Wes sat her in the chair.

"Did you pick up your rice?" Miss Margaret asked, coming to stand next to her.

"Yes, ma'am. I wonder what's taking them so long." April began to untie the ribbon wrapped around the net material. "It's been a very long day. I think I could go to sleep in a heartbeat."

"You poor thing. You can do just that when we get you to my place. You can sleep late, and no one will disturb you in the morning."

April sighed. "Sounds heavenly. The stagecoach ride was a rough one, and I'm not anxious to repeat it soon."

"I'm sure Morgan did the best he could to accommodate his passengers. He's a very considerate man and well respected in Lewistown."

"You know the coach driver?" One of April's eyebrows shot up.

"You seem surprised."

"Well, yes, I am. I've never really been around black people much, and I'm not sure what I think."

Margaret shook her head. "Well then, you have much to learn."

"I beg your pardon? I don't believe I need to be educated about whom to be friends with." Who did this old lady think she was?

"Excuse me, April. I didn't mean to imply that anyone could pick your friends. It's just that sometimes you may be surprised by who your friends are."

Loud cheering rose from the crowd when Josh and Juliana appeared at the top step. They skipped down the stairs, holding their hands up to ward off the rice that pelted their heads but laughing the entire time. April laughed with everyone else, and Josh gave her a brief hug before assisting Juliana into the waiting carriage decorated with flowers, ribbons, and a sign saying JUST MARRIED on the back. Waving furiously to the crowd, the couple was soon rumbling down the drive to begin their honeymoon.

5

"Here's your room, April," Natalie said, taking her key out of the lock and swinging the door wide. She allowed April to enter first, as if waiting for her reaction to the toile furnishings.

"Mmm . . ." was all April said through pursed lips.

"Is there something wrong with the room?"

April tossed her handbag on the bed, looking around. She waved her hand. "It'll do, Natalie. It's just a little too frilly for my taste. I prefer simpler decor."

Natalie placed April's satchel next to the dressing table, then reached over to close the open window that she'd left cracked an inch for fresh air. "If you'd like, I can move you to another room across the hallway." Natalie forced a smile.

"That won't be necessary. I'll move to the Stockton Hotel to-morrow, I'm sure."

April sank down in the plush toile boudoir chair and bent to remove her shoes. "How anyone wears these miserable tight heels all day over a pair of broken-in riding boots is beyond me."

Natalie smiled at her. "I guess I'm just used to them. I take it that you wear boots most of the time?"

April wiggled her toes. "I certainly do. Boots and my split skirt, though I prefer men's Levi's for riding. You should give it a try." April rubbed her feet. "Tell you what—when the rest of my bags arrive, I'll let you try a pair. I can't live without them." She yawned, stretching her arms overhead.

"I'll let you get settled. If there's anything you need, just let me know." Natalie turned to leave.

"Thank you." April fished in her purse for some coins and held them out to Natalie.

"Oh, no thanks. I can't take that. We aren't running a hotel, and we have no servants. I carried your bag up, knowing you're tired from the drive, but our boarders are on their own except for meals taken in the dining room." Natalie reached for the doorknob then paused. "That includes making your own bed. If you choose to eat breakfast here, it's served at seven, or there's a couple of cafés within walking distance."

Louise tapped on the open door as she stepped into the room. "Before I retire, I thought I'd see if Natalie got you all settled in your room." Louise looked down at April still rubbing her feet. April could tell the elder sister considered herself in charge of the boardinghouse.

"Quite fine, for the time being. I'll be at the hotel tomorrow."

Louise exchanged a look with her sister. "Very well then. It looks like you could use a warm footbath. Would you like me to send up some warm water? I know that dancing can be hard on the feet."

April waved her hand. "No, it's more the shoes than the dancing. I only danced once or twice."

"If you're sure . . ." Louise sounded relieved.

April walked the sisters to the door. "Thanks, Louise, but I just want to crawl into bed. It's been a long day."

Natalie handed her the key. "Then we'll just say good night."

After they left, April quickly shed her clothes, leaving them right where they dropped, and slipped into her nightgown. She was so tired that she couldn't see straight. Crawling between the crisp linen sheets, she breathed a sigh of relief, grateful for the first real bed in two weeks. She wondered how in the world cowboys slept on a bedroll for days on end.

Her mind wandered back to the cowboy she'd met wrangling with the mare earlier. He didn't seem like the kind of person Josh would have as a friend. Too rough around the edges. Maybe Josh had changed since moving to Montana. He seemed very happy with his pretty bride. She couldn't wait until they returned from their honeymoon to learn more about how they'd met, and she'd ask about Wes too. It was a pity that her parents weren't here to see the joyous occasion.

Her eyelids became heavy, and in a matter of minutes she was fast asleep.

It seemed only moments had passed when loud knocking on her door roused her. April pulled herself to a sitting position and blinked. It couldn't be morning already, but the knocking sounded again.

Irritated, she yanked the covers back, pulling on her robe.

"What . . . who is it?" She stood near the door and listened.

"Dear, it's Miss Margaret. Are you up?" April heard the older lady say.

Exasperated, April opened the door. "I am now!"

The tiny lady stood leaning on her cane with a patronizing look in her gray eyes that made April feel uncomfortable. "It's a bit early for a social visit, Miss Margaret. I've barely had any sleep." A whiff of liniment that April found distasteful hung in the air.

"Really? But it's eleven o'clock now. The sun will warp your ribs if you lay about too long."

April tossed her hair to one side and smoothed it with her hand. "That's hardly your concern, now is it?"

Miss Margaret straightened her spine, fingering the lace on her collar. "You're right, it's none of my business. But I did want to tell you that the stagecoach got in late last night, and your bags were left at the depot to be picked up. You may need assistance in getting them."

April could tell from Miss Margaret's chilly tone that she felt rebuffed. "Sorry. I guess I'm still a bit on the weary side. How did you know they arrived?"

"I saw Leon at Power Mercantile, the general store, this morning. You remember him, don't you?"

"Yes, I do. I'll see about getting them sent over today. Now, if you don't mind . . ."

Miss Margaret backed away and turned to leave, but then paused and tapped her finger to her face in thought. "Oh, there was a young lad there with him, looking for work. Said he knew you . . . I think he said his name was Billy?"

April laughed. "Yes, the sweet kid who rode on the stage with Leon."

Miss Margaret said quietly, "I think he's an orphan, but he seems like such a nice young man." She clucked her tongue. "And him without a mother or father. He said he'd be happy to deliver your bags wherever you wanted them."

"That would be perfect! How do I contact him?"

Miss Margaret gave her a motherly smile. "I'm not exactly sure, April. Like I said, he was at the general store this morning, but I don't know if they hired him. I told him to check with the Stockton Hotel too."

"Thank you, Miss Margaret. I'll locate him today."

Miss Margaret nodded with a smile, and April shut the door, leaning against it. Her eyes caught the clock on the secretary. Miss Margaret was right—she had slept most of the morning away. She'd get changed and find Billy. It'd be nice to have some fresh clothes, but for now she'd have to wear the wrinkled yellow dress that she'd worn to the wedding.

Suddenly her stomach reminded her that she hadn't eaten since the stagecoach stopped for lunch the day before. Hmm . . . she'd have to do something about that as well. She wasn't used to having to *find* her own breakfast. Tilly saw to that. What had Natalie said about a café just down the block?

But first things first. She'd freshen up, then get something to eat and see about getting her belongings sent to the boardinghouse for the time being.

Margaret finished her lunch with her daughters, then retired to the parlor as was her afternoon habit. She wiped her spectacles with the edge of her knitted shawl and picked up her Bible and little brown journal. She flipped the journal open to where she listed all her prayer requests, and with great pleasure she placed a check mark and date next to Juliana's and Josh's names. Her prayers had been answered where they were concerned.

Today she decided to make two more entries. She scrawled Billy's name just under Jane Hood's name. She'd prayed for Cynthia Hood to find a husband once she'd heard about Jane's accident.

Now why couldn't that child walk? Dr. Barnum had said there was nothing physically wrong with her. Which left only one thing—it was a problem in the mind. The child was angry about her father's death in the mining accident. It was similar to what Juliana had gone through, except for the horrible way Juliana had found her father after many years of separation. But she had come through it all a better and stronger person. Now Margaret had two young people to pray for.

One more name was added to her list, right under her two daughters. April McBride. *That one is going to need some special prayers or my name is not Margaret! Spoiled little rich girl.* So unlike her brother Josh. One would never have known that he was from a wealthy family in Colorado. He was so gracious and kind. Just perfect for Juliana.

Well, one thing I know for sure, she won't get her way around here. All the more reason she'd pray for April as long as she was in Montana. Margaret laid her journal aside and picked up her Bible. She started reading from Proverbs and then saw April bounce down the front porch and walk down the street in her yellow party gown with a determined look about her. Margaret couldn't help but chuckle.

April loved how the lush mountain peaks jutted up from behind Lewistown, creating a pleasing backdrop to her visitor's eye. Not as high as the peaks that she was used to in Colorado, but still impressive. The fresh outdoor air filled her lungs and the sun shone brightly. She was glad for her cape, if for nothing else than to cover her rumpled dress. *Guess I could've asked Natalie for an iron.* That would have been the sensible thing to do, but she was in a hurry to get something to eat and then see about her clothes.

She spied a faded sign swinging just ahead of her, boasting Maggie's Café, and she picked up her steps a little. A delicious whiff of fried chicken assaulted her nostrils, making her mouth water, and her stomach growled so violently that she placed her hand over her waist. Chicken would be just the thing. Reaching for the doorknob, she was suddenly overshadowed by a burly man in a red flannel shirt and suspenders. She noticed an odious smell of perspiration as he leaned over to get the door for her. She paused at first, but he indicated with a sweep of his hand that she should go first, so she nodded slightly and stepped through the doorway.

The lunch hour was a busy one this day, and she scanned the room for a seat, hurrying to get away from the burly man behind her. She located a vacant small table nearest the window, but as she reached it, she saw a gentleman's hat lying in the chair. It was obviously taken, so she turned away, but as she did she felt a tap on her shoulder. *Please don't let it be the man in the flannel shirt . . .* Even as hungry as she was, she knew his smell would surely keep her from taking the first bite of food.

When she turned around, she recognized the doctor from the stagecoach. Except now he looked quite spiffy in his gray suit with matching vest and bat-wing tie. Without his hat, she noticed his chestnut hair was parted slightly to the left and combed straight down, which April thought very fashionable for the times.

"April, how good to see you! There's room at my table." He motioned to the table where he reached down to lift his hat. "Please, allow me," he said, pulling the chair out for her.

"Oh, then this was your hat? Well, if you're sure . . ." She looked up at his eyes that crinkled at the corners when he smiled.

"I'm sure. Take a seat."

April did his bidding, and he pushed her chair in, then took his seat as he laid his hat in the windowsill. She picked up her napkin and started to speak just as he opened his mouth to say something, and they laughed.

"Excuse me, April. You go first." He smiled and leaned back in his chair.

April let her cape drop to the back of her chair. "I was just going to say that I was starving. I haven't eaten since I don't know when."

Mark returned a dimpled smile. "Oh, I thought you were at the wedding last night."

"I was, but to tell you the truth, all I saw was cake and punch, when what I needed was a meal. I'm not much on sweets," she said, unfolding her napkin. Drat! She hadn't much money on her.

"Ha! That's what I like, a gal with an appetite!" His laughter reverberated about the room. "And not too shy to admit it!" Mark motioned to the waiter, a skinny young man with thick brown locks falling across his face. "Pete," he said, taking the menu from the lad's hand, "we need to feed this lady right now. Give us two minutes and we'll order."

Pete pushed the lock of hair out of his eyes and bobbed his curly head. "Right away, sir. I'll be right back with two waters and take your order." He sped back to the kitchen.

April laughed softly. "You must eat here often, if you know the waiter by name."

"It's usually where I have lunch before seeing patients in the afternoon." His eyes were soft and warm as he stared back at her. "Take a look at the menu, April. I highly recommend the roast beef sandwich."

"I'm tired of beef. I think I'll take the chicken and dumplings!"

"Does that mean you eat a lot of beef?" Mark asked as he opened up his napkin.

April did likewise, smoothing the napkin over her dress. "I guess so. On a cattle ranch, it's the most common staple served."

"Josh told me that your dad raises quite a number of cattle. Do you help out, or do you just enjoy being a cattle baron's daughter? From what I've seen of you in the last few days, I'd say it was the former." He chuckled.

"And you would be correct, sir. I can't imagine being indoors all the time, tending house and children. I don't mind getting dirty, and I enjoy being with horses. I pretty much grew up on horseback. My daddy used to tease that Mama had me while on the back of a horse!"

Mark laughed and remarked, "Then I would say that's why you had the skills to take off on your own out there in unfamiliar territory after the stage broke down."

April watched as the waiter returned and filled their glasses with water. "I had to be here for Josh's wedding." She turned to the waiter. "I'll have the chicken and dumplings, and make certain they are hot!"

"We wouldn't serve them any other way," Pete said, eyeing her warily.

"Well . . . just make sure you're as good as your word." Her solemn tone held no hint of good humor, especially when she caught him looking at her wrinkled dress.

"I'll have the roast beef sandwich, Pete," Mark said, handing him the menus. "It's the best."

"Right you are, sir." Pete winked and shoved his pencil behind his ear, then slipped away.

"So, tell me about the wedding. Was Josh nervous?" April saw Mark's eyes sweep over her crumpled dress. "And do you normally wear your evening gowns to breakfast?"

April laughed heartily. "Actually, no. I'm not comfortable in this type of dress for very long." She paused and reached up to scratch where the edge of lace met her collarbone. "I'm normally in jeans or a split skirt. It's all that I brought with me when I left the stagecoach." She caught his raised eyebrows. *Let him think what he likes.* She didn't have much choice. Her riding gear was filthy. "As soon as I eat, I'll go collect my bags from the depot."

"Mmm . . . I see." He leveled a look at her. "But you didn't answer my question—how was my friend? Nervous?"

April hooted. "If he was nervous, he didn't show it."

"He married a very nice lady." Mark glanced away momentarily.

Did she detect a bit of regret in Mark's voice? "I guess so. I haven't had a chance to get to know her, really, but it's apparent he's smitten with her. She seems very young."

"She's not *that* young. Innocence always makes someone look younger. She's had a hard life for one so young and recently lost her mother. But I think she's a determined young lady."

71

"Maybe you can tell me what you know about her. Is she from Montana?"

"I believe she's been here awhile, but that's all I know." Mark's eyes narrowed in thought. "So, April, tell me a little about your father's ranch."

April had no problem talking about her home or her father's success. She told him about the cattle her father raised, her participation on the ranch, and how she'd learned everything firsthand by trailing her father around. Mark seemed to enjoy listening to her talk.

The waiter appeared and placed their lunch on the table and slipped away. April picked up her spoon and dug into the bowl of dumplings. Before long, she turned sideways in her chair, motioning for the waiter. When he sauntered over, her lips drew into a tight line and she said, "I thought I told you to make certain the dish was hot!" She shoved the bowl toward him. "Take this back to the kitchen and heat it up. You must have allowed it to be dipped up awhile before bringing it to me."

With a slight bow, Pete lifted the bowl and felt it. "But it is warm, madam."

April nearly rose from her seat but instead crouched forward. "Are you arguing with me, young man? There is no steam coming from this bowl of dumplings!" Out of the corner of her eye, she saw Mark pause with his sandwich nearly to his mouth, shifting uncomfortably in his seat.

Pete backed away with the bowl, stuttering, "I'll see that it's reheated." He started toward the kitchen, shaking his head.

"You bet you will." April turned and waved her hand at Mark. "Don't wait on me. Please go ahead and eat. I don't know whatever happened to good help!" Her mouth watered at the size of his thick roast beef sandwich, and her stomach growled loudly. She hoped Mark hadn't heard its noise.

"I can wait. I'm sure he's really busy. There's quite a lunch crowd today," he said rather sharply. He looked around and waved to the table across the room, and April turned to see the lady with the crippled girl she remembered from the wedding. The lady beamed back at him.

"Who is that?" April asked just as Pete returned with her bowl of dumplings. This time there was steam rising that could be seen with the naked eye as he plunked it down in front of her. April ignored the fact that he stood waiting to see if it was to her satisfaction, and she continued to eat as if he wasn't there.

Mark nodded his thanks, so Pete went on to another waiting table to replenish their drinks.

"That's Cynthia Hood and her daughter Jane. Jane was hit by a speeding carriage this winter and hasn't regained the use of her legs. But as her doctor, I'm not sure why. I can find no medical reason whatsoever. I'm beginning to think this is all psychological." He chewed his sandwich with a thoughtful look.

Even though she had sat across from Mark on the stagecoach, she was struck afresh with his dark good looks and easy way of talking. He had nice hands and fingers that picked up his food with certain gentleness. Almost as if it were someone's heart he was tending to. She dragged her eyes away.

"Mmm . . . interesting. But what would cause that?" April was now enjoying her bowl of dumplings and felt like licking her lips.

"I'm sure I have no idea. I just started to get to know Cynthia a little after the accident. She's a widow now."

Ah, so the wealthy doctor must have his eye on the little blushing widow. Why else would he be gazing at her and her crippled child when I'm sitting directly across from him?

"Jane is a very beautiful young girl," April commented, looking again at the young woman with large hazel eyes and blonde hair. "Perhaps she needs something to take her mind off her situation." April patted her lips with her napkin.

"Do you have an idea?"

April's eyes narrowed thoughtfully. "Hmm, I just may," she said, polishing off the last bite of her lunch.

"I'll be glad to introduce you to Cynthia and Jane after lunch."

April scooted her chair back. "Maybe another time. I've got to go now." She pretended to look in her handbag for money, stalling for time.

Mark stood. "You're leaving? I'll take care of the lunch," he said as she rose and picked up her cape.

She closed her handbag. "Oh, thank you, Dr. Barnum. I hope I'll see you around town." She pressed the sleeve of his arm with her hand and gave him her sweetest smile.

He tilted his head toward her. "I'm sure you will. If there's anything I can do for you before Josh returns, please let me know."

"I certainly will. Thanks."

Stepping out into the brilliant sunshine, April squinted, wishing she had worn a cowboy hat. Then she thought how ridiculous it would have looked with her fancy yellow dress. *I could get some attention fast that way.* She laughed to herself.

She made her way toward the depot, her tummy full, feeling satisfied that she'd just had lunch with a well-to-do doctor. April intended to make certain that he would want to see more of her while she was here. She'd keep an eye on Cynthia just in case Mark had more than just a friendship with her. She couldn't let that happen as long as she was in Montana, or she wouldn't have a ready escort. It couldn't hurt to be seen around town with a prominent member of Lewistown either. No reason not to have some fun away from home while in this boring mining town.

6

Morgan jumped down from the stagecoach seat and directed Leon to get the horses unharnessed while he headed inside the depot office. He was glad that he had the rest of the week free before the next scheduled departure on Thursday. He'd been going for two weeks now with no respite. He intended to make the most of his time off. Although he loved his job because he met interesting people along the stage run stops, it was time to rest up in his own bed tucked away above the depot, perhaps visit a few friends, and maybe catch a church service. His soul needed it.

The stiffness in his hips reminded him that he was getting older, and sooner or later he'd be forced to cut back on the long hours of driving the stagecoach anyway. His rheumatism would see to that. He made a mental note to ask Miss Margaret if she used any tonic for her aches and pains. Maybe he'd see her at church or run into her around town. Could be soon that he'd just work behind the scenes and run the stage operations. Not a bad idea at all.

He couldn't help but notice out of the corner of his eye that a trunk was sitting off in the edge of the clearing underneath the towering ponderosa pines. He paused, placing his hands on his hips. Now what in tarnation was it doing over there? Did one of his passengers forget to pick up their luggage last night?

He strode through the door and walked up to the ticket counter where Will was counting the day's receipts. Will paused and glanced up, looking through the grilled window.

"Well, howdy, Morgan!"

Morgan nodded. "Whose luggage is piled out there under the trees?"

"A lady by the name of April McBride. Don't know why she hadn't come for it, but we had a skunk problem out back yesterdee, and her trunk may have picked up some of the odor, so I drug it off a ways, until she can come and have it hauled off."

"Ah . . . yes, April." Morgan took a deep breath. "She's not gonna be too happy about this."

"We had to smoke the place to get rid of the smell in the yard. You should've been here yesterday. It stunk something awful outside."

"I'm glad that I wasn't, Will. 'Course, I can't say that it smells all that great now," Morgan teased. Walking over to the stove, he lifted the coffeepot lid with a dubious sniff at the day-old coffee. "I'm gonna make us some fresh coffee. You interested?"

Will closed the cash drawer. "Nope! Soon as I'm finished here, I'm heading to the bank with this deposit. I don't like having that much cash on hand. You want to check it, Boss?"

Morgan shook his head. "I trust you, Will. You know that."

Will left, and Morgan filled the pot with coffee and placed it on the potbellied stove. Leon trudged in and plopped down into the rickety wooden chair by the front door, removing his hat. "I could shore use a cup of that coffee, pardner," he said, wiping his brow with his handkerchief. He yanked his boots off, wiggled his toes, and exhaled. "Ahh . . ."

"Doggone it, Leon!" Morgan walked over and poked him in the shoulder. "Put your boots back on, or the office will need fumigatin' again."

"There ya go again, telling me my feet stink," Leon sputtered. "I can't smell a thing."

"That's just my point! You can't smell it!"

Leon laughed heartily. "Okay, okay. I get the point. After that coffee, I'm goin' in search of a good hot bath." He snapped his boots back on as fast as he'd pulled them off.

"Makes perfect sense to me—" Morgan stopped short at the sound of footsteps on the porch. "Oh no . . . here comes trouble, Leon," he whispered right before April swung the door wide open. Her honey-gold cheeks were stained red with irritation.

Even with the annoyed look on her face, Morgan thought she looked pretty, but like a spoiled, unpleasant child. It was hard to overlook the sunlight that touched April's hair, and it appeared as fine as the spun silk of an angel's wings, but not quite—he knew better. And he knew that she wasn't a child. She looked a little the worse for wear in what appeared to be a party dress. *A little too early for that*, he surmised. Out of the corner of his eye, he saw Leon gape.

"Mr. Kincaid! Where in the world is my trunk?" She sashayed in like she owned the entire worn-out depot. "I was told that it was left on the porch here until I could have it transported."

Leon jumped to his feet, his hat in his hand, nearly toppling the wooden chair. Morgan threw his eyes heavenward. *Lord, I need me a huge dose of Your patience right now.* He meandered toward her.

"Miss McBride. Nice to see you again," Morgan said, ignoring the question for the time being, which only irritated her more. "How about a cup of coffee? Just brewed up a fresh pot myself."

April blinked at him and tapped her toe again on the floorboard. "I'm not here to have tête-à-tête. I came to get my trunk."

Leon shifted on one hip as he watched Morgan take his time stirring sugar in his tin cup. Morgan took a sip before looking April squarely in her narrowing eyes.

"Will dragged it to the edge of the woods. He said there was a skunk around and he was afraid your trunk might have been affected."

"What?" April expelled a breath of exasperation. "How can that be? Was mine the only one? Sounds pretty suspicious to me." She tossed her head angrily.

Morgan briefly closed his eyes then snapped them open. "Yours was the only trunk that wasn't picked up when I left the depot late last night. With all due respect, ma'am, I don't think anyone knew where you wuz staying." Morgan shook his head. "No one is to blame."

April stalked out the door, then said over her shoulder, "Well then, someone should have at the very least gone to enough trouble to find me! How ridiculous!" She grabbed her dress in her hands and tripped down the porch steps with Leon pounding down the steps behind her.

"Miss McBride, don't get all het up. I woulda brung it to you myself personally, if I'd known where to haul it to."

April hurried on, but just as she reached the last step, she heard the rip of material as a rusty nail poking out from the handrail snagged her dress, tearing it halfway down and exposing her naked calf. Stopping in her tracks, she turned sideways and looked down at her exposed leg. She had foregone her stockings this morning, waiting until she'd retrieved a fresh pair from her belongings.

"Creeping spiders and slivering snakes!" April yanked the rest of her dress free. "I don't need this aggravation today!" Behind her, she heard a chuckle from Morgan and an "Aw, shucks" from Leon.

She looked back over her shoulder to see Morgan and Leon staring at her leg. "Well, what are you staring at? Never seen a woman's leg before?" Morgan's stupid grin was getting under her skin.

"Leon"—Morgan shot him a look—"put your tongue back in your mouth and go help the lady out. Take her trunk wherever she wants."

With all the dignity that April could muster, she tripped toward the clearing but then stopped and turned around. "Oh, Mr. Kincaid . . . I guess I should express my thanks for the use of your horse." She watched as he stood on the porch saying nothing. His lips were pulled into a tight scowl as he cleared his throat. "No trouble—glad I could help you out, Miss McBride."

April straightened her shoulders, lifting her hand to shield her eyes from the bright afternoon sun. "Yes, well . . . thanks to you I made it to the wedding, but just barely."

"I'm sure that made your brother happy," Morgan said dryly, then he scooted back inside the depot.

Leon waved his arm. "Come on, Miss McBride. Let's go see about that trunk."

"Mr. Kincaid is a man of few words, isn't he?"

Leon chortled. "Yep. Morgan is not one to waste his time repeating words."

April was curious that Leon wanted to help and thought him an odd sort. The kind of man who respected his friend but at the same time liked having someone else in charge.

As April neared the clustered pines with the largest tree trunks she'd ever seen, a peculiar smell caused her to catch her breath, threatening to dislodge her lunch. "Oh no. Is that my trunk I smell?" She stopped two feet away, covering her nose with her hand.

"Reckon it is. That's too bad, but I think Will said the skunk just barely caught the edge of the porch and your trunk, so it might not be too stinky inside." Leon held out his palm as if it were the most natural thing in the world for him to do. "Your key, ma'am."

April took a couple of steps closer, handing him the key. Leon walked to the trunk. "It could be worse. Just be glad that Will smoked the entire area, or you wouldn't be standing this close." With a serious glance at her, he bent over, inserted the key, and flipped the lid back, exposing not only her outerwear but also lacy cotton underwear.

Leon's eyes slid discreetly away from the trunk's contents. "Aw . . . not too bad. You lucked out, but you need something else to put your clothes in. Then we can burn the trunk." He stood back up to face her.

"What do you mean, burn my trunk?" April exclaimed.

Leon scratched the scruffy stubble on his jaw. "You heard me right."

"But I have nothing to put my clothes in! Those are all the possessions I brought with me. Now what do I do?" April looked around in desperation.

"Excuse me, Miss April," a voice said behind them. April and

Leon wheeled around simultaneously to see young Billy walking over to them. "I can help you with that."

"Now how do you figure that, young man?" Leon squinted at the kid.

"I have a burlap sack here that she can put all her things in. I just told Mr. Kincaid that I'd carry them over to the creek to be washed for you."

"Washed? I think that's a hopeless thing to do, Billy. Thanks all the same. I'm afraid my clothes are ruined!" April tossed her head in the direction of the depot. "The stagecoach manager is at fault. They should have put my belongings inside the depot for safekeeping overnight!"

"Now see here, you can't go blaming our operations for what happened," Leon said sharply.

April lifted her torn skirt, walking toward the depot. "Who's in charge of the stagecoach, Leon? I need to talk to him."

"You just did," Leon replied, indicating the depot's office with a nod of his head.

April stopped short and looked from Leon to Billy. "*Mr. Kincaid?* How can that be—why, he never said a word."

"Why should he? He owns the franchise for Overland Stage here in Lewistown."

Billy added, "That's right, Miss April. I just talked to him about working here. And he's gonna let me lend a hand at the depot. He told me that my first assignment was to get your belongings to you."

April laughed. "Is that so?"

Leon turned to the boy. "Let's put everything in that sack, but before you go a'washin' your clothes in the creek, Miss McBride, you need to soak them in a tub of tomatoes. It'll get most of the smell out, and you'll be all set."

April rolled her eyes, finally comprehending what he was telling her to do. She hadn't washed an article of clothing in her life and didn't want to start now. "All right. I'll put them in the sack myself, but where are we going to find a tub filled with tomatoes and a creek, pray tell?"

Billy handed her the sack, grinning from ear to ear. "I'm glad you asked that question."

April took the sack and marched back to her trunk, then looked helplessly at Billy.

"I'm gonna leave you two to take care of that. I'm off in search of a bath and a nap. Billy, welcome aboard, as we say on the stage." Leon smiled and winked, then extended his hand to Billy's smaller one in a firm handshake.

April saw Billy's eyes shine like the rhinestones on her favorite concha belt while he stood watching Leon mosey off. *Poor little guy, bet he's never had a real father.* Behind her, she could hear Morgan singing in a rich baritone voice, "'Tis so sweet to trust in Jesus . . ."

Wes pulled back on Dakota's reins, listening. Off to his right, he thought he heard the sound of a woman's laughter. *Couldn't be. Not way out here.* Still, since he was in no hurry today to return home after spending the night in town, a rare luxury he allowed himself, he urged his horse down the grassy slope in the direction of the creek where the laughter came from. He knew of no ranch close by. *Probably just travelers stopping to water their mounts.*

As he drew closer, a young boy and a woman, both fully clothed, were splashing each other in the creek with great frivolity. What appeared to be laundry was strewn across the bushes to dry. *Wait a minute . . .* That yellow dress, now sodden and clinging to the shapely woman who was wet up to her waist, looked very familiar. Wes pushed his hat back and folded his arms across the saddle horn, quietly watching the two of them totally unaware of an outsider's presence. His eyes narrowed to be sure, but he realized that the woman was Josh's sister April. It was the same Miss High and Mighty who'd tried to tell him how to tame Lars's wild mare.

They looked to be having a good time, and for a moment Wes

wished that he was a part of the fun. He had never had that kind of fun, even as far back as he remembered when he was a little boy. His father would have skinned him alive if he'd slipped away to play in the creek. There were always chores he had to do, and though his father could've helped out with some of the work, he chose not to. He'd said he was better at giving orders.

Wes shook his head. No point in going back over that again now.

Suddenly, April stopped splashing water on the young lad and stared up the hill at him. The kid turned around, and Wes touched his finger to the tip of his hat. Hmm . . . maybe the lad was her son. She didn't seem old enough, though. He tapped Dakota lightly with the reins, and he tossed his mane and picked his way down the path to the creek bed. Wes slowly slid off the horse's back.

"Y'all havin' a party of sorts? Or is today just laundry day?" He watched as April's face flushed all the way to the widow's peak at her forehead, making her even more attractive.

She motioned to the lad. "Billy, we need to get going." She started sloshing through the water toward the edge of the creek, her clothes plastered to her slender form.

Wes tried not to stare and held out his hand to assist her back onto dry ground. He firmly pulled her up the slippery grass and over the rocks covered with algae. The boy she called Billy hurried up behind her. Without much ado, April released Wes's hand and crossed her arms over her chest. Droplets of water dripped from her hair onto her shoulders and slid into the secret place between the swell of her breasts. Tearing his eyes away, Wes looked at the boy, who couldn't have been much more than thirteen or fourteen. "Miss April, is this your son?"

April laughed. "Hardly. I'm not *that* old. Billy, meet Wes Owen."

Billy pumped Wes's outstretched hand. "I've heard about you."

"You have? Well now . . . what have you heard?" Wes grinned at the boy.

Billy wrung out his shirttail as he spoke. "Just that you're about the best horse trainer in these parts! According to Mr. Kincaid."

Wes saw April roll her eyes upward. *Now, why'd she do that? She knows nothing about me. Nothing!* "I don't recall seeing you around Lewistown."

"I came on the stagecoach late last night, and that's how I met Miss April. I was looking for a job, and Mr. Kincaid who runs the stage line said he'd give me a chance helping out doing odd jobs for him."

Billy's eyes were bright and held a pure zest for living. Wes knew he himself had never been that happy as a kid. Billy seemed all right. "Good for you, Billy. I've known Morgan Kincaid for a long time. He'll treat you fairly."

Billy looked down at his bare toes as a brief shadow of sadness crossed his face. "I hope so. I'd like to hang around here. I really need the job."

April started picking up clothes from the bushes, turning to Billy. "If you're finished jawing with Mr. Owen, I'd appreciate it if you could get me back to the boardinghouse."

Wes stared at the pile of laundry. "I never knew anyone who needed to wash clothes as soon as they got to town," he commented wryly.

"Never mind that, Mr. Owen." April's eyes snapped as she pulled the clothes off the nearby bushes, throwing them into a washtub. "You should get on back to whatever you were doing before you stopped by." He watched as she stopped and propped her backside against a rock, then slid her shoes back on. Briefly he caught a glimpse of her legs and noticed for the first time that her dress was torn. She was definitely a strange one to contend with. At the same time, he envied the carefree manner about her.

"You sure you don't need some help with all that?" Wes walked over, intending on helping Billy load the washtub back onto the wagon. The horse was tethered to a chokecherry bush nearby.

"Thanks, Mr. Owen, but I can handle it. I'm used to hard work," Billy said.

Wes helped him lift the heavy metal tub into the wagon anyway. "It's no bother, kid. You look like you have a strong set of arms on you."

"I do? Gosh, maybe I do," he said, holding up his bicep for inspection.

Wes reached out and felt it. "Yep, strong as steel, boy." Wes gave his muscle a brief squeeze. He knew what it was like to be Billy's age—it didn't seem all that long ago when he'd tried to prove himself. Wes shut out those memories for now and smiled at the kid.

April tossed her damp hair back over her shoulders and walked toward Dakota. She stood admiring him, speaking in a hushed voice, then glanced back at Wes. "Mr. Owen—"

"Please, Miss April, just call me Wes. No need for ceremony in these parts."

"Er . . . Wes." She stumbled over his name. "Is this horse you're riding for sale? He's a mighty fine specimen of horseflesh." She patted Dakota's muscular neck as Dakota nuzzled her hand in search of a treat.

Wes removed his hat and slapped the dust off against his thigh before placing it back on his head, then laughed heartily. "Not on your life, ma'am. But if it's a horse you're looking for, you can ride over to my farm and look-see for yourself."

"But I'd like this one. He's a beauty." She ran her hand slowly across his haunches, then checked out his legs. Her lips curved into a tantalizing tilt. She was trying to speak like a serious horse buyer, but she looked like a homeless, rumpled stray. Wes almost laughed outright at the picture she made.

"Well, you can just keep on a-wantin'. Dakota will *never* be for sale. If you change your mind, you can come look over the mares and geldings I have for sale." He leveled a dark look directly into her blue eyes. "Everyone knows where you can find me." Slightly irritated, Wes grabbed the reins and pulled his long legs into the saddle.

April gave him a taunting look. "There's not a horse that can't be bought." She staggered back just before Wes kicked his heels into Dakota's side, forcing him up the ridge. Wes turned and waved good-bye to Billy.

Shadows of the town's outline, created by the late afternoon sunlight, were imprinted in the dusty streets of Lewistown by the time April and Billy stopped the wagon in front of the Stockton Hotel. April scrambled down, ignoring the pointed stares of two ladies conversing on the porch. "Billy, you can bring my things on in."

She swept through the entryway and marched straight up to the front desk. Not seeing the desk clerk, she slammed her hand down on the bell, causing it to jangle loudly throughout the grand parlor.

Ed walked out from behind the walnut paneling and gave her a cheery smile. "I see you're back, Miss McBride."

"I am indeed, and I have my things right outside. I'd like my room to face the street if possible." She pulled the ledger to her and picked up the pen, ready to sign in.

Ed cleared his throat and coughed slightly. "I'm sorry, there are no vacancies at the moment, I'm afraid."

She slanted an eyebrow upward. "You must be kidding." She set the pen down, feeling foolish. She really didn't want to go back to the boardinghouse and the watchful eyes of Miss Margaret and her daughters. She was hoping for more privacy.

Ed's faced turned a mottled pink. "Please, Miss McBride, I wouldn't joke about a thing like this, but I'm sure if you check back next week, there should be vacancies. September is a busy time for the hotel. You know, people wanting to get away from the big city of Billings to enjoy the mountains and the fall color."

"Is there a problem, here, Ed?" A tall woman with auburn hair piled high on her head walked over to them and propped an arm against the counter.

"Er . . . no, ma'am," Ed answered nervously. It was obvious that he was trying to be as polite as possible to her.

The woman turned, and her hazel eyes swept over April's appearance. "Haven't I seen you somewhere? Oh yes, now I remember. You were at the wedding yesterday." Ed scurried back to what he was doing, leaving the matter in the woman's capable hands.

"Yes, I was." April extended her hand. "I'm April McBride, Josh's sister, but I don't believe we've met." April could tell by the woman's forward style that she could be someone to contend with.

"Nice to meet you," the woman replied. She quickly shook April's hand, then took a step back, an odd look registering on her freckled face. "I'm Marion Stockton. My father owns the hotel. I am sorry, but I'm afraid that Ed is right. We are booked."

The odd look was not lost on April. "I see. Well then . . . I'm sorry to have troubled you. I guess it's meant for me to stay at Miss Margaret's boardinghouse until my brother returns."

Marion arched an eyebrow. "You *could* do worse. Miss Margaret is a very sweet old soul." Her gaze flew to the wide double doors just as Billy carried a washtub into the foyer.

April had her doubts about that but turned to Billy as he approached. "I'm sorry, Billy, but you'll have to carry my things back to the wagon."

"How come?" he asked with an inquisitive look on his face.

Marion answered for her. "The hotel is booked solid for now. From the looks of it, you need a trunk for your clothes, Miss McBride. What happened to your luggage?"

April felt suddenly weary and dragged a loose hair across her forehead, tucking it behind one ear. "You're right, Miss Stockton. I do need a trunk. But for now, this will have to suffice." She chewed on her bottom lip, knowing full well that she didn't have a lot of money left at the moment, and she almost laughed hysterically. The daughter of a wealthy cattle baron with little money, wearing a crumpled party dress, dragging around a tub filled with damp and wrinkled clothing, and living at a boardinghouse. How ludicrous she must look. No wonder Wes gave her a strange look. "Billy, just take me to Miss Margaret."

"Whatever you say, Miss April." He lifted the tub with a groan while Marion opened the door for him and watched as he disappeared down the stairs.

Marion turned to April. "I'm truly sorry for the inconvenience. And please, call me Marion—Miss Stockton sounds *sooo* old."

Guessing the fact that she was unmarried was a thorn in her flesh, April said nothing but nodded her head. "Agreed, if you will call me April." She started to leave. "I need to go get changed. Nice to have met you, Marion."

"I'm sure we'll run into each other around town. If there's anything at all you need or if I can help in any way, let me know. Your brother Josh is a very special man."

Was April imagining it, or did her eyes mist up? She made a mental note about that. "I'm sure I'll be fine, Marion. I'm a very resourceful person. Good day." She lifted her skirts, then hurried outside and climbed back into the wagon with Billy. April couldn't help but notice the disgusted looks cast her way from the same two ladies on the porch twittering behind gloved hands.

Marion watched from the door with a curious look, but April paid her no mind as Billy led his horse and wagon away with a flick of the reins.

Margaret helped Louise set the table for supper and listened to Natalie happily humming a tune over the din of the rattling of pots coming from the kitchen. Tonight she and Natalie had a big pot of chicken and dumplings simmering, and she hoped that her daughter kept her mind on the task of dinner; otherwise the dumplings would stick to the bottom of the pan. Margaret was pleased that she had a couple of new boarders—a somewhat retiring young woman with a small baby, and an older couple. It was always better to have more at the table to ensure engaging conversation—and it was good for business.

"Mother, I'm going to go check on dessert. Back in a few moments." Louise pushed open the swinging door to the kitchen and disappeared.

Margaret watched her daughter hurry into the kitchen and marveled at how conscientious she was. Everything she did must be perfect, whether it was her sewing, helping at church, or helping to run the boardinghouse. Natalie and Louise were entirely opposite in their manner and attitude. Margaret wished she could get Louise to relax and enjoy living more than worrying about every little detail. She knew that Louise could come across as overbearing, but her daughter only desired to please others, to the point of not caring for herself. *I wonder how I can get her to soften her approach and get her to dress a little less matronly, so some nice man could penetrate that austere exterior of hers . . .*

The front door rattled open and the bell overhead chimed, so Margaret laid down the handful of forks and made her way to the entryway as fast as she was able with the aid of her cane. It was April, looking a little the worse for wear, along with the lad Billy. April's hair was a mess, and her dress was torn and dirty.

"April! Are you all right?" Margaret touched the sleeve of April's dress.

April giggled. "Oh, hi, Miss Margaret. Excuse my appearance. I had a little washing to attend to today." She turned to Billy. "Just set that tub at the door of my room, number 6, at the top of the stairs on the left."

"Yes, ma'am." Billy hoisted the tub to his shoulder and started up the stairs.

April turned back to Margaret. "What time is supper? I'll need to get changed."

"Indeed you will. We'll eat at 5:30 sharp. We have several new boarders joining us tonight and I don't want to keep them waiting, so you'd better hurry on up if you intend to eat with us." Margaret saw April's brows knit together in a frown on her pretty face.

"Hmm . . . I guess I may as well. It'd be fun to meet some new people in town, and I have no one else to have dinner with tonight."

"Yes, I can see that, but I'm sure that will change soon, my dear, when the word gets out that there is a pretty *and* available young lady in town."

April stared back at her as though she thoroughly agreed with Margaret's assessment. "You're probably right. It'll be a week before my brother returns."

Billy came back downstairs, taking the steps two at time. He nodded to Margaret and turned to April. "If you decide that you want to go over to Wes's and pick out a horse, I'd like to go with you. I know a little about horses myself. Just let me know. I'm going on back to the stage depot now." He stuck his hands in his pockets.

April fished around in her coat pocket, and Margaret saw her distress. Margaret reached into her dress pocket, handed Billy a quarter, and winked at April, who looked relieved.

Margaret wondered if Billy had found a job and a place to sleep, so she decided to just ask him. "Billy, where are you staying?"

He smiled. "Miss Margaret, thanks for asking. Mr. Kincaid is letting me bunk at his place and gave me a job too." His voice cracked a little with a high pitch, then returned to normal, but he didn't seem embarrassed by it.

"Ah, that's wonderful. He will treat you fairly while you're in his employ, and you'll learn a lot from him." Billy was bursting with youthful eagerness, and Margaret was eager to find out more about him but refrained from plying him with too many questions.

"Yes, ma'am! I think he will. I'd love to learn how to drive that team of horses, but he won't let me . . . at least not yet." Billy shifted from one foot to the other. "Well, Miss April, if you won't be needin' anything else . . ."

April crooked her arm through his and walked him to the door.

"Thanks for all your help this afternoon, Billy. I don't know what I would have done if you hadn't stepped in to assist me."

Margaret watched Billy's face light up as he gazed up at April.

"Shucks, anything you need, Miss April, just let me know. I'd better get back over to the depot now and see what else needs to be done before dark." He turned, flashing a smile at Margaret. "This is a job that I intend to keep. Good-bye, ladies." Billy turned to go and winked at Margaret.

"Good-bye, and stop back by anytime, Billy," she answered, leaning forward on her cane. "Anyone who's new in our town is entitled to a free supper at the boardinghouse."

"Is that a fact, Miss Margaret?" Billy paused. Margaret's eyes flicked over his thin frame. *Yes, he could surely use a good home-cooked meal and a haircut!*

"Of course, my dear boy." Margaret touched his arm briefly, peering over her spectacles into his warm brown eyes. She noticed fine peach fuzz along his upper lip and jawline. *Soon to be a man,* she thought. "Supper's always at 5:30."

"I promise to take you up on that real soon. It sure smells good!" He pulled open the oak door with its lace-curtained window and skipped on down the sidewalk, whistling a tune as April stood on the porch and waved good-bye.

What a sweet attitude he has, Margaret thought. He reminded her of Albert growing up—a hard worker and full of energy.

"Miss Margaret, I'll need an iron to press my dress for dinner. Where might I find one?" April asked. She knew better than to ask if there was someone else who could do the ironing for her, since Natalie had already informed her that they were merely a boardinghouse and not a hotel with extra services. She would have to figure some things out on her own. But there was no need to let them know that.

"You'll find one in the closet at the end of the hallway on the second floor, right down the hall from your room." Miss Margaret turned to go back to the dining room. "See you at supper, April. I must go finish setting the table."

April watched the older lady as she tapped her cane against the hardwood floor toward the other side of the house. She must have arthritis like her own grandmother had in her old age. She had to admire that it didn't appear to slow Miss Margaret down at all. From what she could tell, Miss Margaret was definitely a strong, feisty old lady.

April took out her key and unlocked her door, then dragged her tub of clothes into her room. After several frustrating attempts, she was able to strike a match on the hearthstone and start a decent fire in the fireplace. After retrieving the iron, she set it on the grate to heat while she stripped off her ruined dress down to her chemise. Then she started working on her tangled hair. She stared at her reflection in the mirror. What a sight she was! She'd never looked worse. She quickly lifted her mass of hair, and after giving it a swift brushing, she pulled it up into a chignon with the use of her tortoise hair combs. She poured cold water from the pitcher into the bowl on the sink table and splashed her face. The fire radiated nicely, and her skin felt warm.

The iron should be hot now. It looked simple enough. She'd observed her maid ironing before, but she had never *really* paid much attention to how she actually did it. It couldn't be that hard, could it?

She draped the striped percale dress over the ironing board and touched the fabric with the hot iron, running it up and down along the skirt material, but she wasn't sure what to do about the folds gathered at the waist. Every time she pressed one fold out, it seemed that she only made matters worse and wrinkled the other folds gathered closely together, causing long creases down the front. How was she going to keep from having so many creases with all those pleats? She had no idea, so she paused to contemplate the problem. Suddenly she smelled scorching fabric and quickly removed the iron to reveal its outline transferred nice and brown onto the blue material.

April muttered an oath. "It's like trying to saw sawdust—next to impossible!" She decided that it wasn't too noticeable since it was in the back fullness of the dress. She had never liked women's work and didn't suppose she would start now. *Oh well, I won't be meeting royalty.*

She glanced at the clock and realized she had only minutes to spare. She flicked the hot iron over the worst of the wrinkles and slipped the dress over her head, being careful not to muss her hair. It would have to do. It was too much folderol for her to care one way or the other. She splashed a tiny bit of rose water on her neck and wrists, then stepped back to admire her slender figure with an appraising smile.

Delicious smells led her to the dining room, where the sound of chattering voices greeted her. She was looking forward to meeting the new boarders. But after entering the dining room, April tried to hide her disappointment when she saw who the boarders were.

Seated left of Louise were Willard and May Wingate, the boorish older couple who had traveled with her on the stage. The shy Beth sat next to Miss Margaret.

Willard stood as she approached the table. "What a nice surprise, Miss McBride!" he said, hooking his thumbs into his worsted vest. Its buttons threatened to fly off in all directions at any given moment from the taut pressure on the fabric.

"Hello, Mr. and Mrs. Wingate. So we meet again." April took the seat next to Natalie in a chair that Willard pulled out for her. "I thought you would be staying with your family."

May jumped right in. "Oh heavens, no! They have a full house. It's much easier to stay here and have a room all to ourselves, isn't it?" She squeezed the top of her husband's hand firmly and smiled sheepishly at him.

"Yes, dear . . . unless you make my heart work overtime." He winked at May, and her round face turned pink.

"Since you've met the Wingates, you probably know Beth Reed," Miss Margaret said as she lifted her napkin.

Beth lifted her chin and, with a timorous look at April, said, "Good to see you again, April."

"And you, Beth. Where is little Anne?" April asked.

"Sleeping well in my room. Thanks for asking."

Natalie said, "Since we all have met, why don't we say grace and then we can converse as we eat?"

"Excellent idea!" Willard said. "I confess I'm nearly starving."

"Then you'll love Natalie's chicken and dumplings," Louise said. "She makes the best!"

April frowned inwardly. Having had that meal for lunch, she didn't find it appealing. What she really wanted was a steak or roast with potatoes and gravy.

Miss Margaret said grace, and Louise served the steaming dumplings from a huge tureen in the center of the table while everyone passed their bowls to her. Louise passed warm rolls around the table. Ahh, hot bread . . . now that was April's weakness. She could make a meal out of bread and strawberry jam. Surprisingly, the dumplings were light and fluffy and definitely better than what she had eaten at the café.

Conversation flowed about the mining and the town's activities, and April was enjoying the warmth of Miss Margaret's home. Louise asked her if she would tell them a little about herself.

April thought a moment before answering. "My father—and Josh's father—raises the best cattle in Colorado. I guess you could say I'm a bit of a tomboy. I prefer riding horses and the outdoor range to being inside doing ordinary woman's work."

"What's wrong with being a woman and doing household chores?" May said, a tinge of pink staining her cheeks.

"I didn't say there was anything wrong with it. It just doesn't hold *my* interest," April answered. Natalie and Louise stared down the table, silent.

"Well, I never—" May sputtered.

Willard cleared his throat. "Doesn't matter, dear, when she finds the right man, I'm sure she'll settle down and become a wonderful housewife."

"Oh, Mr. Wingate, I hardly think that will happen." April hurried to assure him of how she felt. "Training horses and running cattle are more to my liking. I don't need a husband to do that."

"But surely you want a husband and family." Louise's wide eyes showed surprise at April's admission.

"I wouldn't say never, but I can't see myself sitting home darning socks and washing clothes." Suddenly April thought of earlier this afternoon as she and Billy had doused her clothes in the creek. She almost laughed out loud but hid her smile behind her napkin.

Willard grunted his displeasure at her remarks. "It'll happen to you, just like it does to every female I know who wants to take care of her man and make him happy and give him children. A woman's place is in the home."

"That's what I say too," May said.

April shook her head. "No, I don't agree that every woman wants to become a slave to a man's desires and stay home tied down with children, wiping noses and changing diapers—sorry, Beth. Why, some women even go to college and become doctors or nurses or work in offices. There are other things in life than a man's ego!"

"My! You just canned him like a cleaned peach, April." Miss Margaret chuckled. "Perhaps we need to be clear that God wants each of us to aspire to our dreams and the abilities He has given each of us in order to have a good future. For some, that means family and children, and we are not to point fingers when someone else's ideas don't line up with what *we* think one should be doing." She looked over at Beth, who was staring down into her plate with a face of stone.

April was acutely aware that she shouldn't have made the remark about children, despite her brief apology. "Again, Beth, I'm sorry. I didn't mean for it to come out sounding that way about children. I'm sure you are very happy being at home with your baby."

"You have no idea what it's like." Beth's face showed little expression as she pushed her chair back. "If you don't mind, everyone, I need to go check on Anne," she murmured, then turned to Natalie.

"Thank you for the delicious dumplings." She quickly left the dining room.

After dinner, Natalie rose from the table. "Anyone interested in Louise's cherry pie?"

"Sounds like a delicious way to top off the meal," Willard said.

"Then why don't we retire to the parlor. We can have our dessert in there and relax a bit." Margaret stood and the others did likewise.

"Mother, Natalie and I will bring the tray in a few minutes," Louise said.

"What fine daughters you have, Miss Margaret." Willard took his wife's arm and followed Margaret into the parlor.

Margaret's heart warmed at his words. "Indeed I do. I couldn't ask for any better than my two girls."

As they entered the parlor, she couldn't help but notice the scorched spot in the shape of a flatiron on the back of April's dress. *Dear me . . . first the tub of laundry and her torn dress, now this. Whatever has April been up to? Not to mention that peculiar smell mixed with rose water that clings to her.* It was very apparent to Margaret that April was indeed a free spirit. April caught her staring, but Margaret only gave her an amused smile.

9

Miss Margaret stepped out onto the front porch, thanking God for His beautiful cloudless blue sky this September morning. Sighing deeply, she embraced the day and thanked Him for living to see another one, though she longed for her husband. On days like this, when her stiff knees didn't want to carry her, joining him would be a blessed relief. She knew in her heart that God had a reason for her to still be alive. Two daughters who needed her, for one thing.

She'd been a spinster and had long given up on love when she'd met and married George. He had swept her off her feet, and right away they'd started a family. Maybe that was why she had such sympathy for Louise. Being the eldest daughter, she seemed to be destined to spinsterhood. *Well, not if I have anything to do with it!* It was Margaret's dream to have her daughters settled before the Lord took her home—as if she had any choice in the matter.

She turned to go back indoors and hoped the girls were up now and dressing for church. She wasn't too sure about the rest of the boarders. She'd invited everyone at dinner last night and watched as April raised an eyebrow.

That April was quite different from the boarders she was used to dealing with. Maybe the hotel would have a vacancy and April would move back over there where she could be waited on properly, as she seemed to think was her due. Then again, Margaret was interested enough in April's shenanigans to want to keep her around, if for nothing else but pure entertainment. Besides, she needed Margaret's prayers.

Natalie and Louise met her in the foyer, all set to go to services. "Mother, April asked if we would wait for her. She's changed her mind and decided to join us," Natalie said with a doubtful look at Louise.

"Wonderful! As long as she doesn't take too long. Nothing's worse than walking into church after the preacher has started his sermon."

"I told her not to take too long, but I don't think hurrying is in her nature." Louise twisted her lips together.

Natalie touched her mother's arm. "Mother, I think you should say something to her about the condition of her clothes. Perhaps we should have her see about having them sent out to the laundry down the street."

"There's a peculiar smell that seems to linger too," Louise said with a disapproving tone. She stood with her arms crossed. "I don't want to be late today since I'm playing the piano—"

Margaret interrupted. "I know what you mean, Natalie." She smiled up at her daughters. "I'm not too sure she would appreciate us being nosy. And Louise, we have plenty of time to get to the church before the service starts." Putting a finger to her lips, she shushed them. "Here she comes. Now be kind."

April joined them in another poorly pressed morning dress of pale green, its white collar curling up at one edge. "I'm sorry if I've kept you ladies waiting. I guess I sleep better than I thought in the toile bedroom." She laughed.

Natalie pressed her gloved hand to her mouth to stifle a giggle as her eyes swept over April's appearance.

"We must hurry now," Louise said tersely. "Had I known we would have to wait for you, I'd have hitched the team to the wagon, but since we're walking, we really must go or I'm going to be late!"

April rolled her eyes and gave Natalie a conspiratorial glance. "Isn't it just a short walk to the church?" she asked, but Louise simply ignored her question.

"Don't worry, April. Louise is not happy if she isn't ahead of schedule, no matter what it is."

"Humph! You're not the one playing the music at church." Louise proceeded to fling open the front door after giving her sister a sharp look.

"Girls, please! This is the Lord's day. You *will rejoice* and be glad in it." Margaret heard another "humph" escape Louise's pursed lips. Her voice softened. "Natalie, fetch my Bible for me." Motioning with a wave of her cane for them to follow Louise, Margaret stepped through the door.

It was only three short blocks to the church whose steeple was sparkling white against the cloudless blue sky. The adjacent cemetery was enclosed with a wrought-iron fence, and its tombstones were aged gray from the passing of time and harsh winter weather. Tall spruce trees, bent permanently from past Chinook winds, leaned against the fence. Several people were standing about in quiet conversation near the church entrance when Margaret and the girls arrived. Louise scooted on past them with a nod and hurried inside.

"Well, I declare! If it isn't Morgan Kincaid in the flesh!" Margaret hobbled up to her friend standing at the top of the church's broad steps.

The tall man turned, and a generous smile split his face as he reached out his large hand to Margaret's small one. "Miss Margaret. Good to see you again." Turning to Natalie and Louise, he said, "Hello, ladies."

"Hello, Mr. Kincaid. Nice to see you taking some time off," Natalie said.

"My sentiments as well," Margaret agreed.

Morgan smiled back at them, then turned to April and asked, "How's it working out for you living at the boardinghouse, Miss McBride?"

April crossed her arms. "It's okay for now, since the hotel was full. After Josh returns, I plan on staying with him and Juliana at some point before I return to Colorado."

"Really?" Morgan's eyes squinted from the morning sun. "He has Andy and Nellie living with him. It might get a little crowded."

"I daresay I have no idea who you are talking about." April shrugged.

"I thought you met them at the wedding," Margaret said.

"Did I?" April was looking around the church grounds as though she wasn't interested in the couple staying at her brother's ranch.

Morgan chuckled. "Well, if you didn't, you will soon. Andy

works for your brother herding sheep. Nellie is his wife. You'll like them. They're a sweet couple."

"Is that so? I guess I'll find out for myself soon enough."

"Oh, I'm sure they're inside the church already. I'll introduce you afterward," Natalie said.

The church bell pealed the hour, and they all went inside. Louise was playing the piano while everyone scrambled for a seat, and the preacher took his place at the podium to greet the congregation. The singing commenced, and after several hymns Reverend Carlson gave a message about putting others before your own needs, bringing an "Amen" or two from the crowd.

Later, Morgan stood outside under the huge cottonwood tree talking with Margaret. "It's good to be in church today. When I'm on the road, I really miss Reverend Carlson's sermons," he said.

"I know what you mean, Morgan. How have you been? Are you taking a little break from the stage routes this week?"

"Just a little. We'll be back on the road Thursday on the route to Billings." He peered down at her, his face serious. "I'm having some rheumatism in my hips and wondered what you take when you feel like your joints just won't move."

Margaret patted her upper lip with her lace handkerchief. "So that's what's ailing you? Probably too many years sitting on that stagecoach perch." Margaret considered Morgan a true friend, having met him years ago on her first stage ride to Billings. She'd immediately appreciated his good humor and the way he treated most everyone with respect, even ones who didn't deserve it.

"Well, are you gonna tell me or just keep it to yourself?" he teased.

"I'm sorry, my mind was wandering—it's been doing that a bit more with every passing day. I use salicylic acid. It's an alkaline treatment I got from Dr. Barnum. He said to take it when my rheumatism is acting up. It's a bicarbonate of soda or something like that. I'm trying to remember exactly what it was that he told me . . . Anyway, you take it every three or four hours. I add a little lemon juice for taste, but don't take it on an empty stomach."

"Then I'll drop in to see the doctor about getting some. The older I get, the stiffer my hips and fingers are," Morgan said, rubbing his hands together. "Is that April gal giving you any trouble?"

Margaret just laughed. "No, not really—she's just different. Not at all like Josh," she said, gazing over at April talking with Wes and Natalie. As she watched the three young people, it suddenly struck her that Natalie was looking up at Wes like he'd hung the moon. Now why hadn't she seen that look on her face before?

"Is something wrong, Miss Margaret?" Morgan asked, following her eyes to see what had captured her attention.

Margaret wrinkled her forehead. "That all depends on whether my daughter has set her eye on Wes, especially after the way April's face softened when she looked at him."

"April—are you sure?" Morgan's bushy eyebrows raised in question.

She adjusted her glasses. "I know my eyes aren't as good as they used to be, but I think I know what I saw in their faces. I never would've dreamed it."

Morgan lifted his hat off the hitching post, placing it back on his salt-and-pepper head of tight curls. "Natalie might have a little competition in that area. But I'd say Wes is not April's type of man. Besides, she's only staying until Josh returns."

Margaret laughed. "You have April pegged about right.

Underneath all that air of authority hides a spoiled little girl who's always had her way, but she's secretly hoping for someone to take her in hand. She may not know it now, but she will sooner or later. Mark my words, Morgan."

"Spoken with wisdom, Miss Margaret." Morgan bowed slightly.

Margaret started toward Louise, who had now joined the group of young people with Billy at her side, but then she turned back to Morgan. "Why don't you and Billy join us for lunch today?"

Morgan shuffled his boots in the dust. "Well, I'm not sure—"

Tapping her cane in the dirt, Margaret interrupted. "No need to be sure. I'm the one asking, so I'll take that as a yes."

"Then we'd love to have lunch with you."

"You can invite your sidekick too." Margaret watched as Morgan's face softened. "Is he here?"

"You mean Leon? I don't even know where he is this morning. I'm not sure if I want to know . . ."

"Then just come on over whenever you're ready—all we have to do is heat up the roast. It won't take long to do. See you in a little bit." Margaret walked over to let the girls know she was ready to start back home.

Nellie and Andy had joined the young people, and Margaret's heart warmed as she watched the affection between them. "April, did Natalie introduce you to Nellie and Andy?" she asked, joining them.

April turned from the cluster. "Yes, Miss Margaret, she did," she answered. "I've learned that Josh and Andy get along like brothers." Margaret thought there was a slight edge to her voice. Could it be that April was jealous?

Andy patted Nellie's hand in the crook of his arm. "Josh is about the best employer and friend I could ever hope to have, and we miss him. Don't we, Nellie?"

Nellie answered in a thick English accent. "To be sure, Andy. Josh and Juliana have made us feel right at home."

"Yes, I guess he did," April said coolly, her eyes narrowing.

"Oh, but me and Andy can make up a pallet in the upstairs bedroom, if you'd like to come home with us. It'll be no problem at all. Or better yet, we could give you our bedroom and we'll sleep on the pallet, right, dear?" She looked at Andy.

"Of course we can. I'm sorry, guess I wasn't thinking. Josh hasn't had time to furnish the rest of the house yet. I reckon that Juliana will be busy with all that when they return."

April straightened her shoulders. "No, no. Don't do that on my account. I'm comfortable at the boardinghouse for now."

Wes, who stood quietly by, made a move to leave. "Excuse me, I've gotta head on back. Miss April, I'll be at the ranch this afternoon if you decide you want to ride over and check out my horses." He touched his fingertips to his hat and winked at Natalie, who blushed and looked away.

"I can loan you my horse until you return to Colorado, April," Nellie offered.

"Thanks, but I wouldn't want to put you out." Turning to Wes, she said, "I'll come over after lunch then."

Wes's eyes locked on April's. "Okay," he answered. "I'll be waiting."

Margaret watched the exchange with interest. She knew Nellie, but she hadn't been around Andy much. He seemed to be a right likable chap. April's comments didn't appear to bother him much, which was good. She doubted that much of anything bothered Andy for very long. He was simply good-natured.

Margaret noted that Natalie and April both watched as Wes mounted his horse and rode off, leaving a trail of dust behind him. Natalie's look was wistful, but Margaret couldn't tell what April was thinking.

10

April could hardly wait to slip out after lunch at the boarding-house, leaving Miss Margaret and her guests in the parlor to relax or play checkers or just nap. But napping was not on April's mind. It was a glorious September afternoon, and she was going to enjoy it. She changed her clothes to her riding jeans and slipped on her boots for a ride out to Wes's ranch. She loved the smell of her leather belt and the feel of the embossed leaves on her matching cowboy boots. April had paid a pretty penny for the set. She'd also ordered the smallest pair of men's Levi's from the Montgomery catalog when she was only fourteen. She remembered how her mother had gasped when April first donned her riding outfit. It had taken some convincing for her to allow April out of the house. No one at home seemed to mind anymore, and now her curves filled out the jeans in all the right places.

I'll bet Wes has a nice ranch with good horseflesh, especially if he's the expert everyone says he is. It'd be good to have her own horse to ride while she passed the time in Montana. She was looking forward to exploring what the countryside had to offer.

She passed the parlor and heard Willard and May talking about their family to Miss Margaret. She was glad she didn't have to stay and listen to their constant banter and lovesick talk.

April walked in the direction of the depot. Billy had told her he'd have a horse saddled for her that Mr. Kincaid said she could borrow for the trip. Billy planned on going with her, but she would tell him that today she'd rather take a ride on her own. He was a good young man, and she wondered how hard it must have been for him growing up the way he did. April couldn't imagine life like that. She'd always had everything she needed in life given to her. In fact, she'd never wanted for anything.

April's conscience pricked her, and she felt a momentary twinge of sadness for people like Billy, or the crippled girl Jane, whose sad eyes haunted her. And she wondered too about Beth and her baby, Anne. But thinking there was not much she could do for so many less fortunate, she shifted her mind to more pleasant things, like having a horse to ride.

Rounding the corner to the depot, April saw Billy on the porch waiting for her. He hopped up and ran to greet her but stood back a ways. His eyes swept over her outerwear, but he simply said, "Ready to go? The boss isn't back from Miss Margaret's yet, but I came on back here and saddled up a horse for you and one for me—if you want me along."

Such eagerness in his face was too hard for April to refuse. "All right then. I'm ready to go if you are."

"I'm more than ready. It sure beats sitting around with old folks talking about rheumatism and such."

Billy hurried over to the corral adjacent to the depot building and led two horses out. He handed April one set of reins. "You've already ridden Gus, so I know you can handle him. I'll take Star. Do you know the way to Wes's place?"

"No, I thought you knew." She grinned at him from under the brim of her hat.

Billy laughed good-naturedly. "I do. I asked Mr. Kincaid this morning." He led the way past the corral and to the road. "We'll just follow this wagon road until it ends and then veer off through the meadow for another couple of miles. His place is not too far after that."

They cantered along in silence, each enjoying the carefree afternoon ride. April observed that Billy knew how to handle a horse well and seemed very confident.

"Billy, how do you like your job?" He appeared happier than the day he'd picked her up in his cart at the stage depot in Billings.

"I like working with Morgan. I don't even have to call him Mr. Kincaid. He's different from anyone else I've worked for and treats me just like a son."

"Is he married?" April asked. She'd never seen any women other than passengers around the depot, and certainly not dark-skinned ladies.

"I think he is, but I'm not sure where his wife is. It's not polite to ask him since I just work for him. But I'll bet you could." Billy reached down and patted Star's neck affectionately.

"I'm glad you're working for him. Maybe someday you can drive the stage—who knows?"

"Now that would be just dandy! I'd like that. Maybe if he'll let me learn how, he could take some time off."

April smiled at Billy. "You know what I think, Billy? I think you're a pretty bright young man. I'm truly sorry for whatever happened to your parents."

Billy looked straight ahead at the dirt road. "Aw, I'll make it—been taking care of myself since I was ten years old. My parents died young. A horse threw my father and he broke his neck. My mama took sick not long after. It seemed like she just couldn't bear losing my father. She passed away a year later."

April felt a pang in her heart as she listened to him talk. "Couldn't a relative have taken you in?"

"Only relatives I have live back in Nebraska. I didn't have no way to get back there and didn't really want to. I just found odd jobs here and there and slept in the stables for one of the men I worked for. But I did okay, till Ruby up and died on me. That's why I figured I'd just leave for a new town when I met you and Dr. Barnum that day." He sighed. "So far, it's worked out. I have a job and a place to sleep."

April was quiet for a minute, suddenly realizing she had no idea what it was like to go to bed hungry or not know where you would lay your head at night. It was a reminder to give the Christian charity the preacher had talked about this morning. "Billy, I'm sorry. You're so young to have to support yourself. Maybe I could take you back with me to Colorado when I go. I know my dad would hire you."

"That's so nice of you, but don't feel sorry for me, Miss April. I kinda like it here, don't you?"

"It's all right, I guess, but there's no place more beautiful than Colorado."

Billy tipped his head, looked her square in the eye, and said, "My mama always said that God created beauty everywhere. Besides, a place can't love you back no matter how pretty, only people can do that."

"Hmm . . . I've never thought of it that way before. You may be right, though I can't imagine living anywhere but Colorado."

Billy pulled back on the reins, slowing his horse. April stopped and turned around. "Something wrong?"

Billy slid down off his horse before answering. "Star's limping all of a sudden. I need to check out her foot."

April dismounted and stood holding her reins as Billy lifted Star's front hoof. "Hmm, she's got a pretty bad cut—must've picked up a sharp rock or something. Tell you what, I'm going back to take care of her. No need for me to be riding her like this."

April examined the hoof. "Yes, I can see you're right. I can find my own way over to Wes's ranch."

Billy turned Star in the direction of town to walk her back. "When you come to the end of this road, go through the meadow a ways to a path on the right. Take that trail to his place. A sign that says 'The Rusty Spur' hangs over the gate. You sure you don't mind going alone?"

"I'll be fine. I'm used to roaming the countryside alone." April grasped the saddle horn and pulled herself back into the saddle. With a clicking sound to Gus, she trotted across the tall grass. Brilliant blue asters dotted the meadow, and against nearby rocks, evening primroses still bloomed freely.

She loved being alone on the back of a horse, the wind in her hair and the power of the horse underneath. Not that she minded having Billy along, but this was real freedom. Soon she came to the trail, which was barely more than a path, so she slowed Gus to a walk. It was thickly covered with hanging tree limbs and underbrush, and she picked her way carefully, pushing aside the hanging branches to avoid being stung in the face. Wes must not have too many visitors . . . Maybe she should've waited for Billy to be able to come with her after all.

It was much cooler under the thick canopy of spruce and pines mingled with the pungent smell of the forest. April loved the mountain air fragrance and at home would sometimes cut boughs from a spruce tree to give the house a fresh aroma.

Finally, the path sloped downward and opened up into a lush valley. The ranch couldn't be too far away now, and the sunlight warmed her up once again. Gus nickered as though he too appreciated the sun's warmth.

April suddenly remembered that she hardly had enough money to pay for her lodging this week, much less a horse. Her father had always taken care of everything for her, and she never had to worry about details like having cash. It just never occurred to her until now that she'd need more money than she brought. She'd have to wire the bank in Steamboat Springs.

Now how in the world am I going to buy a horse? I wonder if Wes rents them out. She laughed out loud, startling Gus, and his ears twitched.

Up ahead the trail widened into a wagon road that led to the Rusty Spur. As she approached, she was not prepared for what she saw. In her mind she expected a well-appointed horse farm. But what she saw was a worn-out homestead.

As she rode under the Rusty Spur sign, which was indeed rusty, she sighed. The perimeter of Wes's property looked neglected from what she could tell. It was overgrown with brush and high grass, but the corrals looked to be in decent repair. A few shingles were loose, their edges curling on the roof of the house, which badly needed painting. In the yard was a haphazardly stacked woodpile, and leaning against the side of the house were several cans of paint, probably waiting for someone to open the lids. A rusty plow was nearly covered in the tall grass. Not what she expected. Not at all.

It was very quiet, and April was beginning to wonder if Wes was even home. She wondered if he lived alone. Sliding off the horse, she looped the reins around the hitching post, made her way up the unsteady steps to the front door, and rapped hard. No answer. *To think I rode all the way out here for nothing!*

As minutes passed, she walked to the end of the porch and looked out at the empty corral. April tapped the toe of her boot and crossed her arms. Where could he be? She turned to leave, and as she did, Wes rounded the side of the house on horseback, leading three mares and a filly. He seemed unaware that April was there. So she watched as he leaned down, opened the corral gate, and led the horses inside. Not until he'd latched the gate and trotted back to the barn did he turn and wave his hand in greeting to her. April walked over to where he stood and unsaddled his horse.

"Howdy." Wes nodded as his eyes appraised her. Why was he looking at her like that?

"I didn't think you were here, and I was about to turn around and go back to town," she snapped. "I told you I was coming to look at your horses."

April watched as Wes removed the saddle and bridle, in no apparent hurry, and carried them to the tack room. "I remembered," he said as he walked back out. He gave Dakota some oats, then wiped his hands on his blue bandana. He wore no gloves, and she noticed his long fingers, then looked up at his hazel eyes, which held a glint of mischief in them when he slanted a glance at her. She looked away, pretending to be more interested in his horses.

"Well, I'm here now and want to see the horses, if it's not too much trouble," she said.

Wes paused, resting his hands on his hips. "I heard you the first time, Miss April." He pushed his hat farther back on his head. "Follow me over to the corral." Wes kept a good distance between them.

This was not going the way she thought it would. He was acting unfriendly, and she couldn't figure out why. He seemed lacking good manners. Well, she'd just pick out a horse, get out of his way, and go riding before she returned to the boardinghouse.

Wes walked to the corral with April following. He didn't want to look at her too closely again for fear that he'd stare too long. The clear blue in her eyes, framed in long, thick lashes barely darker than her blonde hair, was like the Montana sky. He was all too aware of the curves hidden under her jeans. Few women wore jeans, although many ladies were riding straddle-legged across the saddle nowadays. But April sure looked good as she stood there next to the railing, thumbs hooked into her belt. She wasn't like any woman he'd met before. Kind of bossy—in fact, she acted much like a man in some ways, and he didn't know how to react.

He watched her climb the tall wood railing of the corral fence and hold her hand out to the horses, who came clopping up close, sniffing her fingers. She reached into her hip pocket and gave them each a sugar cube. "Beautiful horses, Wes. I think I like the chestnut filly."

"You want to have a ride and see how she handles? I haven't named her yet since I intended to sell her." Even from where he stood, Wes caught a peculiar odor that clung to April. The same odor he'd smelled at church. He reached up to help her down, and she took his outstretched hand. She gazed right into his eyes, and he swallowed hard, dropping her hand.

He lifted a bridle hanging on the fence post and flipped the latch on the gate to fetch the sorrel for her. "I have to warn you, she has a mind of her own—kinda like you." He winked, slipping the bit into the filly's mouth.

April took the reins from him. "Then we shall get along famously, won't we, girl?" She patted the copper-red coat of the horse, admiring her.

"Want me to saddle her for you?"

"No need—if you would just give me a hand up . . ." The filly backed up a little and tossed her head when April approached her. "Hi there, my beauty," she said quietly, allowing the filly to get used to her up close. "Wanna go riding?" The horse swished her tail and gazed at her with huge eyes. April took a few steps closer. "I thought you might want to break outta this corral." April's voice was as thick and warm as honey when she spoke, and Wes liked the sound of it. *Oh, to be that horse.*

Wes approached her and bent slightly, cupping his hand, and she placed her foot in it and swung her other leg over the horse's back. Mercy! There was that peculiar smell again. He stepped back. "Take her out to the back pasture and run her a little."

April nodded and cantered out of the yard, heading beyond the house to the pasture. She gave the horse a light tap on her sides, allowing the horse free rein. Her hat fell back, but the string kept it from flying off. Wes sucked in his breath. He wasn't ac-customed to seeing a female ride with such abandon, but she could definitely hold her seat without a saddle. It was a sight to behold, woman and sorrel moving as one in fluid motion. He had no doubt that she would pick the chestnut. They were so alike, but he wasn't sure that he understood her need to have a horse unless she stayed in Montana. Guess it was none of his business as long as she was buying.

He watched her slow the filly down and make another lap, guiding the horse from right to left with slight pressure of her legs. Wes knew she was checking out whether the filly followed directions and was testing Wes's skill as a trainer at the same time. He hoped she'd be satisfied, but he wasn't sure after the way she'd yelled at him the first time he laid eyes on her.

April had a broad smile on her face when she returned, and Wes took that as a good sign. "So what did you think?"

She laughed in a delightful way. "Oh, she's something all right, wantin' her own way. But that makes it all the more fun!" April leaned down to stroke the horse's neck. "She is so beautiful. I'll take her. How much are you asking?"

"I'll take two hundred dollars for her." Wes watched as the smile slid off April's face.

"Uh . . . I don't have that much with me. Do you ever rent one out—say, for a week or two?" She chewed her bottom lip with a doubtful look.

"I haven't, and I'm not about to start now," he answered. "Only a buzzard feeds on his friends. How much do you have?"

Her eyes blinked in thought as she tried to come up with an answer. "That's just it. I'm a little low on cash at the moment, but

I can wire the bank in Colorado first thing tomorrow morning." She flipped a leg over the horse's back and dismounted, her eyes searching his for a suggestion.

"Tell you what. You have something to barter—say, like that nice leather belt you're wearing and those matching cowboy boots."

She drew in a sharp breath of surprise and flashed him a look that said he'd lost his mind. "I should say not! It cost me a lot to have these made especially for me, and it took months. Can't you trust me until I receive a wire to the Lewistown bank?" Her eyes pleaded, and at first he thought she would cry. Wes could tell right then that she was a true lover of horses to want one so badly that she couldn't even wait another day to have her own. *Spoiled little darling.*

He took a step toward her. "I'm afraid not."

April's face darkened. "What would you do with them anyway? Neither the belt nor boots will fit *you*."

Wes swaggered closer. "I have just the gal in mind who might take a likin' to 'em!"

She hesitated.

He waited.

She blinked.

Their eyes locked.

She spoke first. "Oh, blast you! You know I like the chestnut." April loosened the belt, removed it, and threw it at him, but he caught it before it hit him in the face. He chuckled, then pointed to her boots.

"I hope your gal knows how to appreciate good leather when she gets this." She hopped on one foot as she clumsily struggled to pull a boot off. Wes reached out to hold her steady, but she quickly pushed his hand aside. "Don't touch me, you smelly horse trainer!"

His eyes snapped. Wes lost his temper and the composure he'd tried hard to learn from all Josh's advice about how to treat women. He grabbed her wrist and said, "*Smelly*? So that's what you think?" Her eyes widened, but then she compressed her lips in a defiant smirk. "I'll tell you who stinks, madam. You do!"

April exploded. "Of all the nerve . . . How dare you say that!" She tried to turn away from him, but he held her fast by her wrist.

"Just be glad you have the fancy belt and boots off," he barked as he dragged her by the arm toward the horses' water trough. When she realized what he was intending to do, she struggled to free his grip, but Wes knew he was stronger.

April, with just socks on her feet, dug them as hard as she could in the dirt and fell on her backside. Wes dropped her belt in the dust, and with his hand free now, he clasped both of her wrists, pulled her up, and heaved her over his shoulder. She pounded his back with her fists, squirming and writhing for all she was worth.

"Put me down, you skinny brute! You'd better do what I say!"

"I'm sorry, April," he said as he strode to the water trough, "but since no one would tell you, it's left up to me. You are close to smelling like a skunk, and we're gonna take care of that here and now!" With that, he plopped her lengthwise into the trough and pushed her down while she flailed about in indignation, sucking in water and air. She tried to climb out but lost her footing and fell backward again. Wes picked up a bar of soap next to the water pump and tossed it to her. It landed with a plop on her chest. "If I were you, I'd lather up."

"Oh—" she muttered through clenched teeth. She threw the bar back at him, but he ducked and it missed its target. The look on her face was worse than the one on his bandy rooster, and Wes roared with laughter. He moved aside quickly as she lunged, avoiding the swing of her small fist. He calmly leaned against the fence post, watching as she picked up her hat, which had fallen into the dust during the fracas. Though her hair was dripping with water, she slapped the hat back on her head. "You're going to regret this," she sputtered, clenching both fists to her sides.

Wes regarded her, and his eyes traveled to the wet chambray shirt clinging to her bosom, which heaved in and out with her fast breathing. He tore his eyes away and said, "April, I'm sorry. You can go inside and take off those wet things and I'll loan you some clothes."

"I'll be fine just like I am. I don't need your help in any way." She stared down at her feet in wet socks now muddied from the water and dirt. Her features softened and her anger melted momentarily, and she started to giggle like a woman who'd been cooped up in a cabin for the winter. Wes joined in with a hoot, and they both laughed at the ridiculousness of it all.

Finally, April straightened and asked in a shaky voice, "Did I really stink? Billy and I washed my clothes, and Leon smoked the area around the depot before I got there."

"Sooo, I was right. It was a skunk. You may have gotten rid of the worst odor, but not all of it. I think you got used to the smell. You didn't smell *terrible*, just not good. Didn't you notice the way people kept their distance with you?" Wes grinned. "If I were you, I'd bury those clothes and buy new ones."

"Wipe that silly grin off your face if you're being serious with me." April spun around to where she left Gus and untied the reins. "Can you get a rope around Sassy's neck so I can lead her back with me?"

"Sassy? Is that what you're gonna call her? I reckon it suits her well enough, just like you. Wait here and I'll get a rope."

He returned from the barn and slipped the rope over Sassy's neck. "Sure you want to do this?"

"We struck a bargain, didn't we? Better tell that girlfriend the present came with a price."

Wes quirked an eyebrow at her. Amusement touched his face, and he almost laughed. She must think the gift was for his girl-friend. Let her think whatever she wanted. "At least you smell a little better now, thanks to me. Sure you don't want to take a *real* bath? I can leave you alone in the house." He shifted on his boot heels.

April climbed up onto Gus's broad back. "Not hardly. What would people think?"

"No more'n what they'll think if they knew you came all the way out here alone and going back looking like you do. But suit yourself." He saw her hesitate, thinking about what he'd just pointed out.

"Is that how you treat your lady friends so you can lure them into your home? Well, Mr. Wes Owen, I'm not one of your girls. Please step aside."

"Have it your way, Miss April." His jaw clamped. "I wouldn't want to lay claim to being the one to tell you how to live your life."

"You'll never have to worry about that, I assure you." April cut him a hard look as she scrambled into the saddle, holding Sassy's rope. She tore out of the dirt yard, maneuvering just right to leave Wes choking on a big cloud of dust.

He just stood there. What a temper she had! What had he done that was so wrong? Somebody had to tell her about the odor, didn't they? Otherwise he'd never be able to get close to her, even if she'd let him. Aw, heck, he could just hear Josh say, "Don't you have a lick of sense when it comes to women?" Wes decided it was easier to live without 'em. They were just too hard to unscramble.

11

Lengthening afternoon shadows fell across the dusty trail by the time April neared the wagon road that would lead her back to town. After galloping away from the Rusty Spur, she rode back around to the meadow, then stopped the horses to allow them a cool drink in a small rushing creek. She sat there staring across the stream watching a bald eagle fly to his nest high up in the towering ponderosa pine trees. All was peaceful and quiet—in total contradiction to how she was feeling inside.

What was happening to her? In just a short time after being on the stage ride, then meeting Billy, Wes, Mr. Kincaid, and Miss Margaret and her daughters, she was beginning to feel inadequate somehow. Before, she could have cared less what other people did, how they made their money, or what struggles they faced. But now, after being here only a few days, she noticed her outlook included a more serious consideration of some of her new friends. Maybe because they cared about her? Oh, April had been cared for—her father had given in to her every whim, but did he really want to know her and what she was thinking? April chewed her bottom lip. If she was honest with herself, the answer would be no. She was more like a pet or a trophy to introduce to his friends, just like her mother was.

These intruding thoughts scared her. She'd never considered them before now. It was shameful to admit, but it was true. Now April found herself wanting to do something for Billy and Jane. But what? She realized that she'd never devoted one minute to helping out someone else.

Suddenly, April wondered what people thought about *her*. That had never seemed important to her until now.

From her afternoon experience with Wes, it was obvious to her he owned very little other than a few good horses, a run-down house, and a few measly acres—along with a very hard head! He acted as though he owned half of Montana. His place was disgusting to her. If he was the only one occupying the place, wouldn't he keep it up? Mend a fence, cut the grass, repair the rickety steps, or replace the shingles?

She'd never understand someone like him, and didn't want to. So why did she find him attractive? He wasn't her type at all. He had a scruffy jawline, which told her shaving was hit-or-miss with him. But he sure wore fine, supple boots and a nicely rolled Stetson. He was leaner and more wiry-looking than she cared for. April was normally attracted to men who could wrestle a bear or erect a barn in one day flat, and for a brief moment she thought of Luke back in Colorado. But this time her heart didn't hurt.

She couldn't put her finger on exactly what it was about Wes, but something was there, all right. From what he'd said, he already had a lady he had a fondness for, and on top of that, April had noticed how he and Natalie flirted at church.

It seemed that her good sense had flown right out the stagecoach door during the arduous ride. April blamed it on the clear mountain air or Montana's big sky.

With annoyance, she tugged on the reins, guided Gus out of the creek while still holding the rope tethered to Sassy, then started back to Lewistown. How ridiculous that she was even contemplating a man like Wes when she was going back to Colorado after Josh and Juliana returned.

"April, you got yourself a horse!" Billy shouted when April came riding into the depot clearing.

April was grateful no one else was around to see her beltless and bootless and her hair a tangled, wet mess.

He reached up to grab Gus's reins as she stepped down. "My, she is a beauty." He frowned, looking at her dirty socks caked with dried mud. "What in tarnation happened to you? Where are your boots? Did you forget them?"

"Never mind that, Billy. Please tell Mr. Kincaid I appreciate the use of his horse," April said, climbing onto Sassy's back. She looked down at Billy. "Her name is Sassy. You can ride her just about anytime I'm not riding her, but right now, I need to get on back to the boardinghouse. It's getting dark." April's voice softened. "Do you think you could give Gus a rubdown? I'm going to owe you for helping me out. I do appreciate it."

Billy stepped back. "Sure thing, Miss April. And I'd love a chance to be able to ride your horse."

"I appreciate that. We'll talk more later on." She made a clicking sound against her teeth and set off down the street toward Miss Margaret's.

After getting Sassy settled in Miss Margaret's barn with fresh water and oats, April led her into a stall and swung the gate shut. *I'll have to ask about boarding her and the cost of food*, she thought as she hurried toward the house. Her feet were beginning to get cold now that they had come in contact with the ground. In the mountains, no matter the seasons, the temperature always dropped near dusk. Her own stomach rumbled a bit, reminding her it was nearly supper time, and she knew how Miss Margaret was about punctuality. It's was almost five o'clock. She decided to try to slip up the stairs without being seen before supper. She could just imagine Louise's scoffing.

The back door opened quietly enough, and April started tiptoeing down the long hallway past the kitchen toward the foyer. So far, no one was around. Good. With only her socks on, no one would hear her . . . or so she thought.

"April," Miss Margaret called. "What are you doing in dirty socks, leaving a trail of footprints down my clean hallway?"

April spun around to see Miss Margaret in the doorway of the kitchen, wiping her hands on the white apron covering her housedress. April could hear Natalie and Louise chattering in the kitchen along with a bang of the oven door and the rattling of pans.

"I was hoping no one would see me like this. This is the second time I've come back looking like a drowned rat. I must look a mess." April removed her hat and hitched up her jeans drooping at the waist.

Miss Margaret gave her a quizzical look. "Well, I must say it's disconcerting to see you like this twice in a row. If I didn't know better, I'd say you had a penchant for swimming in the creek with your clothes on." Her mouth twitched sideways, suppressing a laugh.

April was glad Miss Margaret didn't scold her. "It's not what you think."

"Perhaps you'd like to tell me about it later? Don't look so sad, April. I tend to look at the inside of people, not the outside. That never reveals one's true character."

April didn't know what to say to her comment. "Excuse me. I'll run upstairs and get cleaned up." But suddenly she realized she didn't have anything to change into that didn't have a smell clinging to it.

Miss Margaret stopped her with a hand on her arm. "Not until you take off those muddy socks. No need to leave another trail on my rugs on the stairs." She wrinkled her nose as April held on to the stair railing for support and stripped off her socks. Miss Margaret reached out and took them with the tips of her thumb and forefinger, holding them away from her body. "April, I fear there's no need to try to wash them. Do you agree?"

April smiled. "You're right, of course. I guess tomorrow I'll have to do a little shopping."

"Mother," Natalie called from the kitchen.

"I'll be right there," Miss Margaret called back. "See you at supper, April. We just have light sandwiches and refreshments in the parlor on Sunday nights, unless you have other plans."

April paused on the stairs. "Hardly, but later I would like to talk to you about something."

Miss Margaret tilted her head to look up at April with a

questioning look. "I'll be looking forward to it." She turned back to the kitchen, and as she did, May and Willard burst through the front door, laughing and chattering away. Not wanting to get waylaid by them, April hurried up the stairs to clean up.

Preferring not to be alone after April left, Wes saddled up Dakota and decided to pay a little visit to Jane. Josh had asked him to look in on her until they returned since Juliana had sort of taken an interest in Jane and her mother, Cynthia. It was not yet dark, so he had time for a short visit.

On his ride he kept remembering the tips Josh had given him on how to act and talk around females, if he ever intended to court someone. Wes hadn't held out much hope and hadn't been trying . . . until April came along. At the wedding, he was hardly able to tear his eyes away from her. She looked so lovely in the pale yellow dress with her big luminous eyes. Well, the outward appearance was nothing like what the inside was, apparently. She was in a different class than he was.

He supposed it had been a dumb thing to dump her in the water trough, but at the time, it seemed the best way to handle the smell quickly before she had a chance to argue with him. He chuckled, thinking about how fetching she'd looked as she angrily floundered around in the water. Well, he figured he could give up the idea of courting her after that. She'd never forgive him. If Josh were here, he might be able to help Wes figure out what he should do. But for now he'd put April out of his mind.

Before he knew it, he was at the home of Cynthia Hood. He looped Dakota's reins around the white picket fence and grabbed the sack from across the saddle horn. Cynthia had a green thumb from what he could tell. Her small yard was immaculate. Fall chrysanthemums of yellow and orange decorated the stone pathway, and potted plants that he guessed were ferns framed either side of the front door. Wes didn't have much knowledge about plants, and he sure didn't know how to put together the look he saw, but he knew he liked it. Maybe that's what his place needed.

He rapped on the thick door and could hear Cynthia's heels on the floor just beyond the door as she approached and swung it open. "Well, Wes. What a surprise." Cynthia stood looking at him, waiting for the reason for his visit.

"I hope it's not too late to drop by for a few minutes." He felt awkward holding the bag in his hands.

Cynthia paused, then swung her arm inside. "Where are my manners? Please come in." She moved aside to let him enter. "Jane and I were in the parlor reading and taking it easy this afternoon. You know, I work at the boardinghouse on weekdays." Cynthia walked toward the parlor with Wes behind her.

"Josh and Juliana asked if I would just drop in from time to time, to check on Jane or see if you needed anything." Wes remembered to remove his hat, but only because Josh had insisted he do that when he entered someone's home.

"I'll take your hat and hang it right here on the coatrack."

Jane sat in her wheelchair with a cat curled in her lap and a book in her hands. She looked up as Wes walked into the homey room. "Wes, I'm so glad you came to see us! What have you got in that bag?"

"I'll tell you about that in a little while, after we talk," he said, taking a seat in the stuffed chair near Jane.

"Would you like to share some tea or coffee with us? We were just about to have a light snack."

"No thank you, Cynthia." He placed the bag next to him.

"Then I'll go make Jane and myself something and be back directly." Cynthia proceeded to the kitchen, leaving the two of them to talk.

"So, little miss. How do you think you're doing? Have you tried to stand or walk?" Wes watched Jane's reaction to his question. Her young face registered surprise, but Wes didn't know how to be anything but direct and to the point. He wanted to get to the real reason he was there.

"Why . . . you know I can't walk!" Jane shoved the sleeping cat off her lap, and he leaped with surprise and ran out of the room. "I can barely stand with assistance."

"I wasn't sure, Jane. But I have an idea. Are you interested?"

"Maybe," Jane answered with a weak smile. "What's your idea?"

"You know I raise horses. I thought that it might be fun to take you riding sometime—let you get some outdoor exercise. Might be good for your legs," Wes said. "What do you think?" Jane's face was too pale, he thought. The fresh outdoors would be good for her.

"I . . . I'm not really sure. I might fall off. Besides, I have no proper riding clothes."

Wes opened the sack. "I have something to get you started." He pulled out the soft leather belt and the matching brown boots. "You can wear these boots, and I guess your mother could go over to the general store and buy you a small pair of Levi's."

"You mean I'd have to sit astride the horse?" Jane seemed curious about the whole thing now.

"That's the idea. I think it would help you use your leg muscles and stimulate circulation."

"Hmm. I don't know . . ." Jane looked at him, but he couldn't tell what she was thinking. Was it fear?

"Don't know about what?" Cynthia said. She carried a tray laden with a silver teapot and cookies, placing them on a nearby table flanked by chairs.

"Wes has invited me to go riding!" Jane answered, taking a cookie off the tray.

"Is that so?" Cynthia poured the tea into their cups, added sugar, then handed one to Jane.

"It'll get her outside, and the action of riding may be beneficial," Wes said as he watched Cynthia sip her tea with a brooding eye on her daughter.

"I see. What an unusual idea. Would you enjoy that, Jane?"

Jane shrugged. "I guess so. It might be fun. I'll go if you think it's okay." She held up the boots and belt. "He brought these for me to use. I'd need to ride like the men do."

Cynthia reached down to finger the belt. "Very nice. What a clever idea."

"If you could get her a pair of jeans and bring her over one day, say, the middle of the week, we could give it a try." Wes stood up to leave.

"I guess there's no harm in trying, and Mark told me that you have the best-trained horses around." Cynthia set her cup down. "I'll have to make arrangements for her to be taken by wagon to your place, since I work all week at the boardinghouse."

"Don't you worry about that, ma'am. Just leave that to me and I'll see to it." Wes reached for his hat and walked toward the door.

"I might be able to get Billy over at the stage depot to give me a hand."

Jane squirmed in her wheelchair. "Do you have to go? We could play checkers or something."

Wes almost said no, but the pleading in her voice made him change his mind. "Okay, but just a couple of games. I don't want to keep you ladies up late," he said with a wink, making Jane laugh.

"We'd be glad for the company, wouldn't we, Jane?" Cynthia beamed at her daughter.

"Oh yes. Mother, can you pull out the checkerboard?"

"In that case, I'll take a cup of that coffee," Wes said, hanging his hat back up.

Soon the three of them were having a wonderful afternoon. Wes noticed more than once how the little girl seemed to manipulate her mother into jumping at her every request. But then Wes remembered she *was* crippled. When Wes got up to leave, the doorbell sounded, and he said good-bye to Jane while Cynthia greeted Mark Barnum.

She turned to Wes. "You know Dr. Barnum, don't you, Wes?"

Mark nodded, and Wes reached his hand out to shake the doctor's. "Yes, we've met a time or two."

Mark looked from Wes to Cynthia. "I hope I'm not interrupting your evening."

Cynthia clasped her hands tightly, looking uncomfortable.

"Not at all, Doc. I was just leaving. I came by to check on Jane as a favor to Josh."

"I see. That's wonderful. Jane needs friends," he said, smiling.

"Wes thinks horseback riding may encourage Jane to regain the use of her legs," Cynthia remarked.

"Is that so? Well . . ." Mark clapped Wes on the back. "It certainly can't hurt. Good thinking, Wes."

"Mother!" Jane yelled.

"Excuse me." Cynthia left the two men talking and hurried back into the parlor.

Mark walked with Wes to the front door and looked at him intently.

"Is there something on your mind, Doc?"

Mark cleared his throat before speaking. "I don't mean to interfere or be nosy, but are you planning on courting Cynthia?"

So that's why he'd stiffened when he saw Wes there. Wes's face broke into a wide smile. "The answer is no. It's as I said—I really came to talk to Jane about going riding at my ranch."

Relief flooded Mark's face. "Wonderful. I mean, that's good. Please don't take offense. I've been trying to get to know Cynthia better since her daughter's accident."

Wes reached for the doorknob. "No offense taken. But you may have your hands full where her daughter's concerned."

Mark rubbed his chin thoughtfully. "I know exactly what you mean, Wes. It's something we'll have to work on."

"Be seeing you around, Doc." Wes stepped out into the dark night and paused, listening to the night sound of the sighing wind through the trees. He dreaded going home to a cold house once again and longed for companionship. A vision of April crossed his mind. *Give it up, man! You two are from different worlds.* About the only thing they had in common was a fierce love of horses.

The more he thought about it, the more agitated he became. He needed a drink. He hadn't been to the saloon since that night he'd been reading Scripture and wrestling with the Lord, and he'd finally accepted His Word about who He was. If it hadn't been for Josh, he never would've even picked up the Good Book. But just for tonight, maybe he'd drop over to the saloon and have a quick drink before hitting the trail. One little drink couldn't hurt, could it?

12

When April reached her room, she could hardly wait to remove the heavy, wet jeans. She had to nearly peel them off, which only made her madder than a rider being thrown from a horse. She threw them into the corner and started to unbutton the chambray shirt when she spied something draped across her bed, which mysteriously had been made while she was out. *What in the world . . . ?* Someone had left a simple calico dress in a soft shade of rose trimmed in delicate velvet piping, and a fresh set of undergarments were laid out next to the dress. She almost squealed in delight. She had something fresh to wear! She didn't know whether to be insulted or flattered. But Wes was right. Her clothes held an odor despite the bath in the tub of tomatoes and a rinse in the creek. The dress was an older style but looked almost new.

As she lifted the dress and held it up to herself, a piece of paper fluttered to the floor. In bold handwriting the note said:

> *I'm sorry for what I know I'm about to do, but you'll understand by the time you read this.*
>
> *With regards,*
> *Wes*

April was so shocked that she thought she was going to swoon. How did he manage to do this? He couldn't have slipped in here before she got back. Or could he? She *had* spent awhile at the creek just thinking . . .

Dare she wear the dress? Would everyone know? How did he get in?

Well, she'd worry about all that later or she'd miss the light supper in the parlor. She decided she would wear the dress, so she hurriedly took off her shirt and undergarments and got dressed. It was just a tad big in the bosom but fit her in the waist and lengthwise. It really was a pretty everyday dress, the kind her mother would wear.

April rubbed her hair dry with a towel and pinned it up. She walked over to the cheval mirror, did a quarter turn before the mirror, and was satisfied with her appearance. She'd have to talk with Wes about sending her gifts. It just wouldn't do. But maybe no one knew but her and Wes. Her face burned at the thought of him buying undergarments. She put a hand to her midriff to calm her stomach, then inhaled deeply and started for the parlor.

"Oh, hello there, April," Natalie said when April walked into the parlor. "You look lovely and fresh as a primrose in the meadow."

"Hello, everyone," April said, tilting her head to May and Willard, who sat in the settee across from Miss Margaret. Louise was bent over a small table slicing lemon cake. Beth was sitting on the floor with baby Anne, who played with a stack of blocks, cooing in pure enjoyment. This was the quietest the child had been since April had been around her.

"We're glad you could join us this evening." Louise straightened, holding the knife in one hand with her other hand cupped beneath to keep the crumbs from falling to the floor. "We do things informal on Sundays. We only cook one meal on the Sabbath."

"Yes, so I heard. Can I help you serve the cake and sandwiches?" April surprised herself in asking, but the question suddenly rolled off her tongue.

Louise's face showed surprise as well. "Thank you. Natalie is so engrossed in the book she has her head stuck in." Louise glanced at her sister with a frown, who poked her tongue out at Louise, then smiled impishly. Louise just shook her head. "You can start with the egg sandwiches, April." She indicated the plate next to the cake. "If you could just put one on each of the plates stacked there and hand them out, that would be a help."

April moved toward the platter and began picking up the sandwiches, trying to be mindful of the egg filling that oozed out when she lifted each one. She was tempted to lick her fingers but refrained.

"How was your afternoon?" Miss Margaret asked, taking the offered plate from April.

She hesitated, wondering how she should answer without telling about the scene with Wes. Finally, she said, "Good. I just went for a ride with Billy in the countryside."

"That's nice. It was a good day for that," Louise remarked and continued cutting the cake.

"You look lovely in that shade of rose, April." May smiled up at her in her engaging way.

Miss Margaret agreed. "It becomes you." April noticed Miss Margaret's soft, wrinkly face held just a hint of a tease, and her gray eyes danced.

"Well, thank you, Mrs. Wingate. It's very comfortable, which is a lot for me to say about a dress."

"Please just call me May, and I'm sure Willard would be just as happy if you'd call him by his first name, right, dear?"

"By all means. Mr. Wingate sounds old and stuffy!" His breathing labored as though he had just run a foot race. April watched him take another bite, leaning over a well-formed belly that seemed to perch on his lap.

May tilted her head at him and teased, "Which is exactly what you are!"

Willard wiped his perspiring brow with his handkerchief and winked at his wife. "Watch out, woman, or I'll have to haul you upstairs and take you upon my knee! Now pass me a nice thick slice of Miss Margaret's lemon cake."

There he goes again with his innuendoes, April thought. *Do married people really talk to each other like that?* Her parents certainly didn't.

"How about you, Beth? Care for an egg salad sandwich?" Natalie left her novel to assist April.

Beth rose from the floor and took the plate. "Don't mind if I do. It looks delicious and so does the cake, Natalie."

Natalie rolled her eyes toward Louise. "I can't take credit for the cake. Louise made it."

Miss Margaret laid her needlework aside and picked up her sandwich. "Louise has become sort of an expert when it comes to cake baking." She beamed at her daughter. "In fact, she made Josh and Juliana's wedding cake."

April watched as Louise's face burned pink. "Really? Then I'm very impressed. I'm afraid I don't cook and I have no creative talent."

"I'll bet you there is something you're good at and just haven't developed," May said, turning to Willard, who suddenly had become very still and quiet. "Don't you agree—Willard, are you all right?" May suddenly shoved her plate aside and leaned over him. She grabbed his hand and slapped it. His face had gone from its normal pink to a pale gray hue, and he seemed short of breath, unable to say a word and looking fixedly at his wife.

Beth rushed to Willard's side, leaned down, and unbuttoned the collar that was restricting his throat. She turned to April. "Quick, grab my handbag on the coatrack under my cape. Hurry!"

May was frantic. "What can I do? What's wrong with him?" The others crowded around.

"Give me some space." Beth motioned to Natalie. "Help me lay him down, please." Quickly the two of them gently laid Willard back, and Beth placed a pillow under his head while May removed his shoes. April was back with the handbag, and Beth quickly reached inside for a bottle of liquid. She twisted the cap off and held it under his nose. After a few seconds, he blinked and looked around, appearing very disoriented.

"Willard, can you hear me?" Beth was certainly in command of the situation, and she seemed at ease and was a calming presence. Willard mumbled something inaudible and tried to sit up, but he was too weak. "You just rest easy there, Willard. Everything's going to be all right."

He closed his eyes and leaned back onto the pillow as though grateful he didn't have to get up. May's eyes were filled with tears, and she wrung her hands in panic. Beth took her elbow and walked her to the doorway, motioning for the other ladies to follow. "It's best we don't move him, May. We need to send for the doctor. I'm afraid he may have had a heart attack."

"I'll go after the doctor," April offered.

Natalie took her arm. "I'll go with you."

"Please just be quick about it," May cried.

Miss Margaret put her arm around May's shoulders. "Come sit down, May. There's nothing you can do until we see what the doctor says." She guided May to the chair nearest the settee. May reluctantly sat down, gazing teary-eyed at her husband. She held his limp hand in one of hers and clutched a hanky to her mouth.

April and Natalie rushed out of the house and down the sidewalk in the direction of Mark's home and office. Though it was dark now, gas lamps lit their way through the quiet Sunday night. Most people were already in for the evening or dining at the hotel or one of the local cafés.

"I hope Willard will be okay," Natalie said, trying to keep up with April's long strides. "May adores him and they're a devoted couple."

"Me too. I wonder how Beth knew what to do." April could see that Natalie was having trouble keeping up with her, although April had no clue where Mark's place was.

"Mark's office is beyond the sheriff's sign and just past the saloon there," Natalie said, as though she'd read April's mind. She picked up her pace to match April's.

Tinkling music could be heard from the saloon as they drew closer, and April saw a familiar lanky cowboy heading toward its door. Was that Wes? She hoped her eyes were deceiving her. As they neared, he paused with his hand draped across the swinging doors and looked right at her.

"Good evening, Wes," Natalie said, slowing her steps just a bit.

Wes tipped his hat, looking at Natalie and then April. "You ladies seem to be in a hurry to put a fire out." His hazel eyes lingered a moment longer on April than was decent. She fought the queasiness that rose when she realized he was visiting a saloon. Just the thing she figured Wes would do. Why did the fact bother her? It wasn't any of her business what he did. But she halfheartedly wished he wasn't going in there.

"We can't stand here and chitchat." April gave him a frosty stare, and a scowl flittered across his face. "We are going to fetch the doctor for Mr. Wingate." She started to walk past him but he grabbed her arm. April looked down at him as though his hand was a snake. "Please let go."

Releasing her arm, he said, "I'm sorry . . . I was just trying to find out if I could be of any help."

"Not this time, Wes," Natalie said, and they hurried on, leaving Wes looking after them.

Wes hit the saloon doors hard, his fist knocking them aside as he made his way into the saloon and strode straight up to the bar like he'd done long ago. Or at least it seemed that way. A few patrons looked around, the noise startling them from their card game or gabbing as they shared a drink. He put his hat on the counter and ordered a whiskey when Mel, the bartender, walked up. He wanted to get his mind off April in the rose dress, which was totally out of style for her but in near-perfect condition. He should know. He had taken it from his mother's cedar chest. April looked delicate, fresh, and sweet as a mountain morning. Goodness! He wanted to pull her to his chest and breathe in the scent of her silky blonde hair. Yes, he reckoned a drink would help remove that image.

While he waited for Mel to fetch the drink, he turned and leaned against the bar's counter, looking around for any familiar faces, but he didn't see anyone he knew. Several ladies wearing low-necked satin dresses, their faces painted heavily, perched on the laps of several men, laughing and drinking as someone doled out a deck of cards. The piano player, cigar hanging out of his lips, pounded on the keys enthusiastically. Some men staggered toward the dance hall girls as they danced. Out of the corner of his eye, Wes watched a couple pair off and wander upstairs.

Suddenly he felt out of touch. This is how it must look to the person who wasn't drinking—not a pretty sight. He felt uncomfortable in his own skin and decided he'd had enough. He'd seen that look of disgust in April's eyes too. This wasn't for him anymore, and he couldn't step back into this life again. Not now, the good Lord willing.

Mel plopped the drink in front of him as Wes picked up his hat and turned to go.

"Aren't you gonna have your drink, Wes?" Mel placed both hands on the counter and leaned over, staring at him.

"I changed my mind, Mel," Wes said, flipping two coins onto the counter. "Be seeing you around."

April was grateful for the soft feather bed as she sank down into it and pulled up the toile comforter. It had been a long day. The moonlight danced against the walls, creating shadows from the voile sheers that moved gently with the breeze. She'd left the window open slightly to cool off her upstairs room. Soon she wouldn't be able to do that if the cold weather appeared before she left for Colorado.

Since leaving home, she had made some nice friends that made staying until Josh returned bearable. The weather was almost perfect, so she couldn't complain about that either. And now she had a fabulous horse to ride. But she was beginning to miss her own bed and surroundings. She decided that once Josh and Juliana returned, she'd stay only a few more days.

The incident with Willard had been scary, but it had turned out better than April thought it would. Mark told them that Beth had been right. Willard had suffered a mild heart attack and would need to stay in bed for a few weeks. Since he was unable to climb the stairs, Miss Margaret made up a bed in a smaller downstairs bedroom to move the Wingates into. Everyone pitched in to help. May, still somewhat frazzled, thanked everyone for their help and Beth for her quick action. They discovered from the questions Mark asked of Beth that she used to work for her father as his nurse before her baby was born. April was surprised that they hadn't discovered this bit of information on the long stagecoach ride. But then, she had never even tried to reach out to Beth.

April had enjoyed the rest of the evening with Miss Margaret and her daughters. She had to smile when she saw how the two sisters liked to tease each other unmercifully.

April stayed behind to talk to Miss Margaret. She was nervous about telling her what had happened at Wes's and having to admit that he was right about her clothes.

Miss Margaret put her at ease and gently told her, "No one wanted to say anything to you to keep from hurting your feelings."

"I don't understand," April said. "I would have wanted to know. As it was, Wes figured that he owed it to me to not only tell me but also throw me into the water trough with a bar of soap!"

Miss Margaret laughed and said, "So that's why you had no belt or boots on. I wondered."

"Well, I bartered the boots and belt for the horse," April said. "He said he was going to give them to his lady friend. I'd rather he not tell me that part."

Miss Margaret raised an eyebrow. "Does that matter to you?"

"Of course not! I hardly know him—and what I do know is he is not what my father would approve of at all."

"Your father's approval obviously means a lot to you—but does his approval mean more than how you may feel about someone? Remember, it's not what a man possesses that shows you his heart."

April sensed that Miss Margaret had taken Wes's side. "Well, I've seen his place and he doesn't seem concerned about taking care of it. Only his horses."

"Wes cares about many things . . . but some men have to be shown what a woman likes. Could be he feels he's never had anyone to care about him or about what he thought one way or another. Maybe he had little direction in his life. Your brother had some influence on him just in the last couple of months, and Wes is trying so hard."

April knew that he and Josh were friends but was still doubtful.

Miss Margaret continued. "How do you think he was able to get that dress for you?"

"How did you know about the dress, and how does that have

147

anything to do with what he's like?" April asked, wanting to know more of the older lady's wisdom. Her own mother had never talked with her like this.

"It has a lot to do with his character, April. When I saw him at church, he pulled me aside and asked me if I had talked to you about the peculiar smell on your clothes. When I said no, he said he had an idea that might solve it and would need my help. So I helped Wes by sneaking the dress in your room before you got back from the ranch today. It was his way of trying to help you without further embarrassment. I noticed that you seem to like the dress you're wearing, even though it's probably not the kind of dress you'd own."

"You're certainly right about that. It's more like something my mother wears. Funny thing is, the fabric is very soft and the simplicity of it suits me," she said. Then she confided in Miss Margaret that she'd seen Wes going into the saloon earlier and how it bothered her.

Miss Margaret said softly, "April, don't judge a book by its cover. Look beyond what you see on the outside. Why don't you think about what really matters to you?" Miss Margaret then leaned over and gave April a quick hug, much to April's surprise, then bade her good night and left her wondering about the tall, lanky cowboy.

So here she lay in bed, ruminating about a man she thought was trying to humiliate her, and Miss Margaret told her just the opposite was true. Why get mixed up over someone with as tough an exterior as Wes when her time here was short? Her parents would not approve at all! That she knew for certain. But Miss Margaret had gone right past that by asking what really mattered to *her*. What indeed? No one had ever cared enough to ask, and until now, April had never considered it either.

Now she was wide awake. Restless, she got out of bed and dug around in her valise for her Bible. She hadn't spent a lot of time reading the Bible lately, and for a long time now she'd felt like God was far away from her. Tonight she wanted to look to Him for direction and comfort.

She kept thinking about what Miss Margaret said. *What really matters to me?* April wasn't sure she even knew or had a purpose. She turned to Romans and started reading. After a while she landed on chapter 12, and when she got to verse 3, something about it spoke to her.

> For I say, through the grace given unto me, to every man that is among you, not to think of himself more highly than he ought to think; but to think soberly, according as God hath dealt to every man the measure of faith.

April thought about that for a minute. Did that mean the only way she could really begin to understand herself was by learning who God is and what He could do in her life? She had to admit to herself she was not in the habit of putting anyone above herself on a regular basis. A lesson she realized now that she'd learned from her father. Though she loved him, April didn't want to mirror his aloof attitude toward others. Could she change that habit?

No, but I can, a gentle voice reminded her.

April's heart thumped as she bowed her head. *Where do I start, Lord? I've not taken time for You in a long while. Will You forgive me?* She paused, thinking. *I'm a bit out of practice . . . and I guess that's why I haven't been very sensitive to others and say things without thinking how it might make them feel. You know I love my father, but there are things I see in him that I don't want to become. Help me to see others through Your eyes, Lord, and not mine. Change my heart and help me be a better person. Amen.*

April lifted her head as tears wet her cheeks. She felt peace flood her heart and mind and knew she'd have no problem sleeping now.

13

Autumn was just beginning to expose itself with a few dashes of color sprinkled across the mountainside as Indian summer settled over Lewistown. April peeked out her curtained window overlooking Main Street. This afternoon would be a lovely day to go riding. She was feeling energetic and would see if Natalie or Louise would care to go riding with her, but first there were several things she must attend to today. She needed to send a telegraph to her father's bank to transfer cash to the Lewistown bank. Then she'd set about buying a couple of dresses to replace the ones that were ruined. Today, however, April would wear the calico dress again.

She hurried down to breakfast. As usual she seemed to be the last one to come downstairs, and everyone looked up as she burst in. "Good morning!" She took a plate off the sideboard and scooped up some scrambled eggs.

Everyone said hello between bites. "There's fresh coffee or hot tea, April. Would you care for a cup?" Louise asked.

"Coffee would be just the thing. Isn't it a beautiful morning?" April said, taking a seat next to Louise. "Where are May and Willard? Has Beth already had breakfast?"

"You're certainly in a wonderful mood!" Natalie commented, pausing midair with her teacup to her lips.

Miss Margaret dabbed her lips with her napkin. "May took Willard a tray, so she is eating with him in his room. Beth ate earlier and took Anne back upstairs."

"Is there something I can do to help May? I know she was extremely worried." April buttered her bread, then spread a generous helping of huckleberry jam on it. She couldn't help but notice that everyone was silent and looking at her in a curious way.

"What?" April asked, looking around the table.

Louise set her fork down. "It just that we're a little surprised that you'd want to—" She paused, then added quickly, "seeing that you won't be here long."

"Well, that was the old me. The new me wants to see how I can be more useful while I pass the time here until Josh and Juliana return. I may decide to stay longer until my parents return from Ireland."

Miss Margaret cleared her throat. "In any case, I think you should talk to May and ask her directly." She beamed at April. "That's very thoughtful of you to ask."

April swallowed her coffee and said, "I was impressed with Beth's knowledge of what happened to Willard. I couldn't help but wonder if she's looking for a job as a nurse."

"She keeps to herself a lot, so I'm not sure," Miss Margaret said, "but if she is, then Mark might be interested in having a nurse by his side. And a pretty one too, I might add."

Out of the corner of her eye, April saw Louise squirm in her chair and push her scrambled eggs around with her fork. *So, that's who Louise has set her cap for. Poor Louise. Mark doesn't even know she's alive.* "Did your mother tell you that I bought myself a horse from Wes? A beautiful filly I named Sassy." April looked at Miss Margaret's daughters, then bit into the delicious homemade bread. Oh, but she loved hot bread and butter. It was the best thing this side of heaven.

"No, she didn't, but I saw Sassy in the stall when I went to feed the horses," Louise said stiffly. "I fed her for you too."

"Oh, thank you, Louise. I am so used to having our groomer do that that I totally forgot!"

"Tsk tsk, my dear. The horse is your responsibility now," Miss Margaret said, getting up from the table and helping herself to the coffeepot.

April looked at her and said, "Oh, and I fully intend to pay you for boarding her."

"And Mother would expect that," Louise said.

Miss Margaret looked at Louise sharply and said, "Louise dear, I am capable of speaking for myself."

April bit her tongue to keep from saying something she might regret. Did they think she wouldn't take care of her obligations? April liked it here and wanted to stay. She'd tell Miss Margaret her intentions after breakfast.

Natalie seemed to sense that April was uncomfortable. She passed her more hot bread and said, "What are your plans today, April?"

"I'm planning on going shopping for new clothes. I'm sure you all heard about the smell that got into my trunk. So I need to replace a few items." April hoped she could just charge her purchases on Josh's account until he returned.

Natalie and Louise both laughed. "We did, April, and we're

sorry for that. We weren't sure whether we should say anything or not," Louise said with a half smile.

"You'll need to dispose of them by burying them or burning them, April. It's the only way," Natalie said with all seriousness. "And you'll need to replace your trunk too."

April wondered if they knew that Wes had thrown her in the horses' water trough and hoped Miss Margaret hadn't said anything. She certainly wasn't going to tell them. It was so embarrassing and she didn't feel like reliving it again. Instead, she asked if either of them wanted to go shopping with her.

"Why don't you go, Natalie," Louise told her sister. "I need to work on the menu for this week and practice my piano."

"I'd like to if you can wait until I clean up the kitchen," Natalie said to April with a huge smile. "Cynthia will be here soon to start supper."

April noticed that Natalie was dressed in a charming dove gray skirt and white pleated blouse that only emphasized her shapely form. *She has good taste and would be able to help me choose the new outfits*, April thought. "I can wait. Maybe I'll go make up my bed today . . . or at least try." April got a chuckle from everyone with that statement.

"I'll look forward to it!" Natalie hopped up. "I'll meet you in the parlor in a little while."

When everyone had finished eating, April asked Miss Margaret if she could have a word with her.

"What's on your mind, April?" Miss Margaret asked, picking up her cane and walking in the direction of the parlor.

April followed Miss Margaret, who took a seat at her desk and indicated with her cane for April to sit. "I'll stand. This won't take but a minute," she said. "When I first arrived in Lewistown, I thought I'd be staying at the hotel. At first I wasn't thrilled about staying at the boardinghouse, but now I find myself enjoying it here, as well as the family atmosphere. Will my room still be available for another week or two?"

Miss Margaret's face was filled with relief. "Goodness, yes! Is that all? I thought something was wrong."

"Oh no, everything's fine. I find the accommodations wonderful, including the food. Now, if I can just iron my own clothes and remake my own bed for the next few weeks . . ." April's voice trailed off.

"That can be learned with a little patience. I must say I'm beginning to see the real April emerge, and I like her." Miss Margaret's eyes shone, and April couldn't tell if it was due to tears or just the older woman's aging eyes.

"I intend to pay for my room and board as soon as I get a transfer of funds from my bank. I didn't bring enough cash with me and had to spend more along the stagecoach ride. That was a poor oversight on my part."

"I'm not worried about the money or boarding your horse. I know you'll take care of your responsibilities. Why don't you go to Josh's, if that's what you want to do? I'm sure Andy and Nellie wouldn't mind."

"They did offer, Miss Margaret, but I can wait until Josh returns. I'm in no hurry. Plus I hardly know Andy and Nellie, and I would feel strange doing that." April turned to leave. "I'm going upstairs until Natalie's ready so I can do a few things that need tending to. Thank you for being so understanding about the money."

"Don't you worry about a thing, dear." Miss Margaret took April's hand in her own wrinkled one, giving it a motherly pat.

When Miss Margaret leaned close, April could smell her liniment but was surprised at how soft and warm her hand felt against her own. April's heart warmed. Miss Margaret had become like a grandmother to her in just a few short days. How was that possible?

Power Mercantile, Lewistown's general store, was located on the corner of Main Street and 3rd Avenue, and April noted that it was just across the street from the Bank of Fergus County. Farther down the street, written on the side of the building in bold white letters that could be seen a block away, was Phillips Drug Company. That must be where Miss Margaret got her liniment for her rheumatism.

The two-story brick and wooden structure of the mercantile boasted the finest of everything needed for a home or garden. The gleaming display windows exhibited a man's dashing suit and a lady's dress with matching hat on one side of its tall wood and glass door, and general merchandise on the other side.

April was interested in the bridle propped up in the window's corner. She heard Natalie gasp as her friend clapped eyes on the newest frock in the window. "Oh, isn't that lovely? They must have just put this out for fall." Natalie stared wistfully at the mannequin through the glass storefront.

April peered through the glass, seeing her own reflection. The sage green dress was indeed gorgeous, with fluffy leg-of-mutton sleeves ending just at the elbow. At the shoulders, velvet trim followed the neckline's edge, and along the inset of folded tucks, a bodice of cream fell in natural folds at the waistline. The gored skirt boasted a front panel in the center of a deeper shade of velvet continuing down the skirt, with narrow moiré satin panels on either side. A matching hat sat cocked to one side of the mannequin's head, complementing the outfit perfectly.

"Natalie, that dress would be perfect on you. You must have it." April looked at her friend, whose eyes were wide with desire for the dress. "Let's see if it will fit you." April yanked on Natalie's arm, pulling her through the store door.

"I can hardly afford that. Mother would have a fit!" Natalie sputtered.

"We won't know until we try, now will we?" April ignored her protest and walked straight up to the display to find the tag on the sleeve of the dress.

"May I be of help?" a voice behind them asked.

April and Natalie turned around. "Yes. My friend here would like to know what size this dress is or if you have another in her size." April eyed the clerk dressed from head to toe in jet black with her black hair pulled severely to the nape of her neck in a huge knot. She was middle-aged, thin with a dour-looking face. *I wonder if she's just come from a funeral.*

April smiled at her, but the clerk, with no expression, answered, "Let me see . . . I'll go check in the back. You may be in luck. It's one of our newest pieces that I just put out yesterday." She clasped her hands together. "Natalie, why don't you and your friend have a look around. I'll be right back."

"We'll do just that, Mabel," Natalie said. "But first, I'd like to introduce you to April McBride."

Mabel bowed slightly. "I'm glad to make your acquaintance. Any friend of Natalie's is a friend of mine."

April nodded to Mabel. "Hello."

"Josh is her brother, Mabel," Natalie added with a nod of her head.

"Is that so? In that case, I'm very glad to meet you." Her thin lips split with a big smile, exposing her somewhat large teeth. Then she hurried to the back of the store, her heels ricocheting against the waxed hardwood floor.

"Excuse me, Natalie, I saw a bridle in the window that I want to look at."

"But I thought you were here to pick out a couple of dresses?"

April paused. "Oh, I'll do that too, never fear. I can't be wearing this dress every day, now can I?"

"Where did you get that dress, April? It really is *old*." Then she quickly added, "I didn't mean that to sound insulting, it just seems a little out of style for someone like you."

April looked down and smoothed the folds of the rose calico with her hands. "Yes, I guess you're right—it's very simple, and I have no way of knowing how old it is, as it's on loan."

"On loan? From whom?"

April swallowed hard and wished she hadn't mentioned that. "Let's just say an acquaintance of mine."

Natalie arched an eyebrow. "You're being very mysterious."

"Here we go, Natalie." Mabel returned, keeping April from having to answer any more questions. "Take this to the dressing room and see if it fits." She handed Natalie the dress.

As Natalie took the dress, she looked at Mabel. "I'd better find out how much it is first, Mabel, or there's no point in me trying the dress on."

"If it costs too much, we can always hold it for you," she said when Natalie hesitated.

"I'll try it for size and then decide." Natalie went in the direction of the dressing room, and April asked the clerk if someone could assist her with the bridle in the window.

"I'll also be needing a new saddle and a couple of dresses," April told Mabel.

Mabel cocked her head to the side. "Let me go get Charlie to help you. I don't know much about saddles." She motioned to a gentleman who was wrapping a package at the counter.

April laughed. She just bet Mabel had never been on the back of a horse. Too straitlaced—and if she did, it certainly would have been sidesaddle.

"When you're through, I'll assist you with the other things," Mabel said.

Charlie was a big help, and soon April felt she'd made a wise choice in a good saddle, though he had very little to choose from. She realized by buying a horse and saddle that she'd unconsciously made a choice to stay awhile in Montana and wasn't sure why. She reasoned with herself that it was because she just didn't want to go back to a lonely house until her parents returned.

April was just about to go find Natalie and Mabel when she heard Wes's voice. She looked around to see Natalie chatting with Wes, who leaned against the long wooden counter. His hat was pushed back off his head, and April glimpsed the outline of a handsome, strong jaw. He said something to Natalie, who flushed prettily. April got a sudden knot in her stomach. Wes *was* handsome in a rugged sort of way that she found appealing, with his sandy brown hair sticking out from under his Stetson, and his long, slender legs encased in faded Levis that sported a silver oval buckle. Wes's leather gloves dangled from his back pocket, and April dragged her eyes away.

With just a hint of irritation, April strutted over to Wes from behind and tapped him on the shoulder. In a quick turn, he directed his gaze to her, then allowed his eyes to travel over her dress. *Please don't say you gave me the dress in front of Natalie.*

"Well, boy howdy . . . if it isn't Miss April," he said with dancing eyes. He said nothing about the dress, and April was relieved.

"I'm sorry to interrupt, Natalie," April said, then turning to Wes, "I just wanted to let you know that I'll be telegraphing my bank this morning as soon as we're finished here, and hopefully in about a week I'll have the money to pay you for the horse."

Wes cocked an eyebrow. "You did pay me, remember? A deal's a deal."

"You can't be serious."

"Oh, I am all right. Some little lady is sporting that belt and boots with pride." Wes's face was deadpan as he shifted on his boot heels.

"Whatever are you talking about?" Natalie interjected, looking from April to Wes.

But April continued on, looking up at Wes. "You *are* serious. Well then . . . I guess I'll need to add boots to my shopping list, Natalie. Did you get the dress?"

Natalie seemed only too happy to bring the topic back to herself. "Yes and no. I put some money down to hold it until I can get the rest. It was a perfect fit," she said, clapping her hands and beaming at Wes.

"And I'm sure you will look real good in it." Wes regarded Natalie with a softening of his features.

April took out her list, pretending to scrutinize the things she'd written down. Out of the corner of her eye, she saw Wes take Natalie's arm.

"We're about to walk over to Phillips Drug Company to have a soda water. Want to come along, April?" Wes asked.

April wanted to go but hesitated. "No, I have to finish my shopping."

"They have huckleberry soda. Sure you don't want to come along?" Natalie's plea seemed halfhearted. April knew she wanted to be alone with Wes.

"Thanks, no. I'd better stay here and finish, then go send that telegram." She forced a tiny smile. "But you two go and enjoy."

Wes drew Natalie's arm to his side. "You're going to miss out, April, and by the way, you should order another calico dress like the one you're wearing, instead of those men's jeans that you had on yesterday," he advised with a wicked twinkle in his eye. "More suitin' to a woman, don't you think?" He lifted his hat in a gesture of good-bye, then propelled Natalie to the front door.

April tensed, then called out to him, "I'd do that, but I'm no ordinary woman!"

14

Wes pulled out a chair for Natalie at the small round table in Phillips Drug Company and promised to return with two huckleberry sodas. While he waited for the sodas to be made, he wondered why he wasn't floating as high as the balloons attached to the string at the end of the soda bar. He had a fetching young lady at his side who seemed to be attracted to him. He couldn't ask for anyone nicer to have taken an interest in him. Something he'd learned from Josh about how to talk to a lady must be working, and he should be thrilled.

He shoved his hat back and scratched his brow. Any man would be proud to be seen with Natalie. Though he'd enjoyed Natalie's company the few times he'd been around her, he hadn't felt the spark inside he'd expected.

But I did with April.

Wes pushed that thought away and took a deep breath. Not that it mattered anyway. It was obvious that she held nothing but disdain for him.

The clerk set the sodas down and Wes paid for them. He carefully carried them to the table. Natalie's sweet face tilted up to look at him with a shy smile as he approached. Mercy! He felt guilty somehow. *Why in the world did I even ask her to come with me? . . . I guess because I felt guilty.* That was partly true. Natalie was so eager to find a beau that he'd felt sorry for her at Josh's wedding.

"Mmm . . . this is so refreshing. Thanks for asking me along." Natalie's eyes fluttered at him. "This will ruin my lunch and my figure, you know."

Wes swallowed after taking a big sip and looked at her dark, sparkling eyes. *What should I be saying now, Josh?* "Natalie, I don't think that's something you'll have to worry about." He saw her cheeks flush with his compliment. *A smile from a good woman is worth more'n a dozen drinks the bartender hands out. I could try to get used to that shy smile.*

"What a sweet thing to say, Wes." She smiled at him again. "Are you in town for the entire day?"

"No. I'll be heading back this morning. I had to come into town to buy coffee. A man can't be without his coffee," he said. "I become very grouchy without my first cup in the morning."

Natalie's head tilted to one side. "Oh, I hardly believe that."

"It's true. I'm not sure which is more important—my horses or my coffee." Wes chuckled and glanced out the drugstore window. He saw April walking down the sidewalk, her arms full of packages. He wondered where she was heading. To the bank, he supposed. There was a nice sway in her hips as the calico dress swished around her high-top heels with each step. She was different, no doubt about that, but he was drawn to her like a deer panting for water, and the thought stunned him. He drank his soda, allowing the coolness of the drink to flow over him.

Natalie interrupted his thoughts. "Wes, did you hear what I just said?"

"I'm sorry. What did you say?" Wes felt flustered that he should be pining for April when Natalie was right here in front of him wanting his friendship. He would gladly give her that. Lonesomeness was a disease that only friendship could cure. And he was lonely for companionship.

"April told me about the horse she got from you. But I didn't understand what she meant about the boots and belt."

"It's nothing. We just struck a deal, that's all. And she got herself a fine piece of horseflesh in the bargain." Wes took the last sip of his soda. "If you don't mind, I'm going to attend to one more thing before I head back to the ranch. I can walk you back to meet April, if you'd like." Wes pushed his chair back and stood.

Natalie did likewise. "No need to do that. Thanks ever so much for the soda. I'll walk out with you," she said as she picked up her handbag. "Will I see you at church?"

"Most likely. It's becoming a habit."

She giggled. "And a good one to have, I might add."

They parted ways on the sidewalk, and Wes strode toward the depot to talk to Morgan. He paused halfway to his destination and looked beyond the busy streets of Lewistown. It never ceased to amaze him each time he stepped outside how wide open the space of Montana with its distant purple mountains was. Seeing the cloud-flecked bowl of the bright blue sky created an urgency to hurry with his business so he could enjoy his ride back to the Rusty Spur.

On Wednesday he would be giving Miss Jane a riding lesson. He thought he'd seen just a bit of spark come back into her dull eyes when he'd talked to her about it. He was getting excited at the idea that the riding might help her legs, or at the very least give her something to do besides sit in her wheelchair all day.

Morgan was leaning back in a chair with his boot propped up on a whiskey barrel, his hat pulled down over his face to ward off the sun, and Leon was sitting on the steps whittling a piece of wood. They looked so peaceful that Wes hated to disturb them.

"What brings you to town, Wes?" Leon asked, his grin spreading across his bearded face.

Morgan dropped the chair legs to the floor with a thump. "Didn't I just see you yesterdee?"

Wes stepped up to the porch and took a seat in the rocker next to Morgan. "Yep, you did. I had to make a trip to the mercantile, so I thought I'd drop by and let you know that the mare I've been training for you is ready whenever you'd like to come get her."

"Good. I'll be ready for her in about a week," Morgan said.

"What are you planning on doing with the mare? Giving her to Billy?" Wes knew Morgan already owned six other larger horses for the stage.

"The mare will be for my wife, Lenora," Morgan said, his voice softening.

"Wife! I never knew you had a wife." Wes tried to think back if Morgan had ever mentioned that fact before, but couldn't recall it.

Leon stood up and spit a straight line of tobacco juice out into the dirt. "Well, now, Morgan don't always tell everything he knows, boy."

"She's been taking care of her ailing mama and papa and wouldn't leave Mississippi until now. We've been apart far too long." Morgan's voice choked.

"I see . . ." But Wes didn't see. If people were married, how could they be apart for several years? That seemed plumb crazy. "Then why is she coming now?"

"Because she buried her parents," Morgan answered matter-of-factly. "When she went to take care of them, she hadn't intended on staying. But things got worse. She just couldn't leave them. They were old and frail."

"I'm sorry. I didn't mean to pry," Wes mumbled. "I reckon I didn't know you then. I'm just surprised."

Leon snorted. "Don't feel too sorry for him. He's made a trip or two down South to see her."

Morgan looked over at Leon. "I think you should go see if Billy has everything ready for our trip tomorrow to Billings." Morgan got out of his chair, fished around in his leather vest pocket, and pulled out a piece of paper. "Go over this list with Billy to be sure everything's in order. I want the stagecoach in top shape, especially after our last wheel break."

Wes watched the older man give orders to Leon. He had come to admire and respect Morgan's wisdom. For the most part, as a black man he had earned his place in Lewistown by running the stagecoach line like a well-oiled machine. He knew that Morgan had made some good friends, and folks looked up to him as being wise.

The front door opened, and Will came bursting outside onto the porch, waving a piece of paper in his hand. "Boss, we just got a telegram for April McBride from her brother Josh. Do you want me to run it over to the boardinghouse?"

Wes immediately hopped up from his chair. "I'll be glad to drop it off on my way out, Will."

"That'll work. If she needs to send a reply, just tell her to give me a holler." Will handed him the telegram and went back inside.

Wes turned just in time to see Leon poke Morgan in the ribs, and they both grinned. "You can wipe the smiles off your faces. I'm just doing Will a favor. You should be happy about that." Wes thought they both looked like they'd been caught in the cookie jar.

Morgan beamed. "Whatever you say." He nodded in the direction of the street. "You won't have far to go. It looks like Miss McBride's heading this way."

Wes followed Morgan's gaze, and sure enough, April walked toward them, still juggling the purchases she'd made earlier. Wes moved with alacrity to April's side. "Here, let me help you with those." He saw hesitation flicker in her eyes, but after a moment, she handed him a couple of packages.

"Don't drop those in the dirt, Wes," she said. "I'm not looking forward to having to do laundry today," she whispered.

Wes didn't utter a word but followed her up to the depot office, breathing in a whiff of the rosewater scent she left in her wake. It was so much better than the skunk smell. He bet she had no idea of the effect she had on men. He could follow her to the ends of the earth if she belonged to him.

"Mr. Kincaid, good morning," April said, walking to where he stood. She nodded to Leon. Leon gave her an adoring look, then snatched the paper from Morgan's hand and scurried down the steps in search of Billy.

"Miss McBride, surely you can call me Morgan," he said, crossing his arms over his broad chest.

April smiled up at him. "Only if you call me April."

"I'd be pleased to do that." Morgan moved aside and gestured to his chair. "Won't you have a seat?"

"Thanks, but no. The clerk at Fergus Bank told me that the telegram office is inside your depot. What I really need to do is send a telegram to my bank in Colorado." She placed her packages down on an empty chair.

"He's right. I own the telegraph franchise here. You just had a telegram come in from your brother, and Wes was about to go locate you on his way out of town."

April shook her head. "Are you in the habit of letting him handle your business?" she inquired, casting a dubious look at Wes.

"Actually, no. Wes is a friend, and since he was going to ride right past the boardinghouse, I saw no harm letting him drop it off," Morgan said in a fatherly manner. "Now, did you want to send a telegram? My clerk, Will, can help you with that inside."

Wes pushed himself forward and held out the wire. "You may need to read this first."

April's eyes flashed. "Did you read it?" she asked, taking the paper from him.

"Of course not!" Wes wondered why she was in a bad mood. What had he done now? *See, Josh, there's just no pleasing women.* It made him wonder how Josh's honeymoon was going. Likin' women was one thing, living with 'em was another.

April's voice softened. "I just wondered since you thought I should read it before I sent my telegram." Her eyes held his briefly before she opened the folded paper and scanned it. Lifting her head, she puffed out a sigh.

"Is there something wrong, April?" Morgan asked.

"Not really. Josh writes that they're having such a wonderful time in Helena that they plan to take an additional week."

"Is that so? Doggone! They must be having a good ol' time," Wes said. A crestfallen look shadowed April's face, and he knew she was disappointed.

"I guess that changes my plans." April stared at the paper.

Morgan looked closely at her. "Does that mean you'll be leaving sooner rather than wait on their return?"

April's head snapped up. "No. I'll wait for them. Besides, my parents are in Europe for a couple of months. I told them to write me here when I notified them about Josh's wedding." Wes watched her pretty lips twist in a thoughtful expression. "I guess I'll have to find something to occupy myself until Josh and Juliana return."

"I have an idea," Wes said. "Maybe you could help me, April." He shifted from one leg to the other and his spurs jingled. "Remember little Jane? I'm going to be showing her how to ride this Wednesday. Since you're a good horsewoman, do you think you could be there to assist me? That way her mother wouldn't have to stay." He fully expected a resounding no from her, but she surprised him with her answer.

"That depends . . . Why don't we discuss it after I send my wire to the bank?" April lifted her skirt and walked inside to send her telegram, letting the door slam behind her.

"Looks to me like you may get to spend some time with the little lady," Morgan teased Wes.

"Don't start with me." Wes aimed a look at his friend while leaning against the porch's post.

Morgan threw his head back and laughed heartily. "I know that look," he said over his shoulder as he walked past Wes. "I'll ride over and get Lenora's mare next week. I'm on the trail this week."

"Okay. I'll see you when you return." Wes figured he'd just wait outside for April. He didn't think she'd want him to hear private information about her finances.

Moments later when she came back, he helped her gather up the packages. "I left my horse in front of the mercantile store, so I'll walk part of the way with you, if that's all right."

"So why are you planning on teaching Jane to ride?" She bristled. "I thought you were a horse trainer who liked nothing more than to dump women into water troughs."

So she was still angry with him for that! "Look, April, I'm sorry about the way I handled you at the ranch. I didn't mean any harm. Will you accept my apology?" He stopped on the sidewalk next to her.

His words hung in the air, and finally she answered. "Apology accepted. But don't go laying your hands on me again, you hear?"

"I promise. Not unless you ask me to." Wes locked eyes with her, and he could tell she meant exactly what she said.

"Not to worry . . . *that* will never happen."

She resumed walking and he fell in step with her. Wes decided that he'd better not comment back. Time would tell.

"What is your plan with Jane?"

"I had an idea that riding a horse could help her attitude and maybe stimulate her legs. The doctor can't find a medical reason that keeps her from walking since the accident."

Wes stopped again, excited about his idea, and looked straight into April's eyes. "My grandpa lived to be eighty-five, but there wasn't a day that he didn't get up and go ride his horse. He'd wake up stiff in the morning, but after a ride, his hips and legs moved more freely. So I figured if it was good enough for an old man, it might just help Jane. Being outside will help too, before our cold weather sets in."

April thought about that a moment. "Believe it or not, I had a similar idea when I talked to Mark a few days ago, but I had no basis for it. I just know that after I've had a vigorous ride, I feel better. I guess I feel sorry for her. I've never known anyone in a wheelchair before. That has to be so hard."

This close to her, he noticed that her face was a golden hue, probably from all the riding. He decided that he liked it. The color gave her a healthy glow. *Concentrate on what she's saying to you!* Wes mentally shook his head and said, "So . . . you'll come out to the ranch while she's there?" They continued walking like friends would on a normal day after shopping, with Wes carrying most of her packages.

April shifted the parcels to the crook of her arm. "I'll do even better than that. I'll borrow Miss Margaret's wagon and bring her myself. *If* Cynthia agrees. She doesn't really know me."

"Just ask her yourself. Cynthia works at the boardinghouse for Miss Margaret, so I know she'd really appreciate it, April."

"I'd forgotten she worked there." April pursed her lips together. "Hmm . . . I haven't seen her around, but I'm not an early riser. I'll see what I can do."

"Let's plan on day after tomorrow right after lunch. That'll give us the whole afternoon." They reached the mercantile, and Wes unwound the reins of Dakota, who patiently waited and snorted a greeting at his master with a toss of his mane. Wes reached for a carrot in his hip pocket to give Dakota and patted him lovingly on the neck. "Thanks for waiting, my friend," he whispered as he leaned close. He turned to April and asked, "By the way, how do you like your horse?"

"Sassy is wonderful! I intend to go for a ride this afternoon. Miss Margaret said I could board her in their barn, lucky for me. She is so good to me. I told Billy that he can ride her too. I've seen him ride and I trust him."

"Everyone loves Miss Margaret, though sometimes she really speaks her mind." Wes climbed onto his horse, moving aside the cloth bag that held his coffee. "See you soon," he said, looking down at the sun bouncing off her golden head. "And just for the record . . . my mother's dress looks mighty fine on you with your blue eyes."

Before she had a chance to respond, Wes gave a nudge to Dakota and they cantered down the dusty streets of Lewistown, kicking up the dust.

15

On Wednesday, it was all April could do to pass the time until the afternoon rolled around. She noticed that Louise was a very detailed person in everything she did, and April was itching to do something, so she helped Louise fold sheets and offered to help with the dusting. After April nearly dropped one of a pair of oriental dogs, Louise teased that April was better off grooming her horse than helping around the house. Luckily April managed to catch the figurine before it hit the hardwood floor. They'd both laughed in relief.

The two were becoming fast friends. Finally April decided to take a chance on asking her about Mark. "Louise, I got the feeling at supper the other night that you may have feelings for Mark Barnum. I saw how you reacted when he was here attending to Willard."

Louise's face showed complete surprise. "What do you mean?" She continued with dusting the windowsill without looking up.

"I wonder if you like him more than just a friend."

A small sigh escaped Louise's lips. "And what if I do? It's apparent that he can see only Cynthia, and I have to work with her every afternoon."

April chose her words carefully. "It could be that he's not even aware that you care for him. You might need to give him a hint."

Louise stopped with her dusting and said, "Ha! He doesn't know that I exist!"

"That's my point. When you're around him, you never even make eye contact with him or even stop. You're always fretting about your next chore. You wouldn't even know if he was looking at you because you're too preoccupied with running things perfectly around here."

Louise put both hands on her hips and remarked, "Are you trying to tell me that he has actually appeared to be interested in me?"

"Well . . . maybe. I have seen him watching you from a distance. It could be that he thinks you don't want a relationship with *any* man." April laid her dusting cloth down and reached for Louise, turning her to look her squarely in the eyes. "I do know this. You need to relax a bit and give men a chance to approach you. And"—April hesitated, then forged ahead—"you could soften your look a bit."

"What?" Louise straightened her shoulders.

April chewed her bottom lip. "You dress like a matron or a spinster who couldn't care less one way or the other. Try wearing something more suitable for your age and perhaps do your hair in a different way. Let go a little bit and have fun. You aren't doomed, you know."

Louise reached up and patted her tight chignon and fingered her hair. "I . . . I don't know what to say."

"I'm not trying to hurt your feelings, Louise. I only want to help you." April gave her new friend a quick hug.

Louise's eyes glittered with unshed tears. "I've always felt such a responsibility after my father died to take care of my mother and maintain the boardinghouse. There's never been much time for me."

"And you've done a great job. I know how proud your mother is of you and Natalie, but you *can* make time to care about yourself, or no one else will." April sighed. "I should know because I've cared more about my own wants than I should," she admitted.

"Will you help me? I'm afraid I don't know where to begin," Louise said.

"I'd love to! How about after supper? I'll come to your room and see what can be done."

Louise giggled. "You almost say that like I'm a lost cause."

April laughed, picking up her dusting rag again. "Not at all. Underneath that severe appearance lies a soul of passion and ideas. I'm sure of it. You just have to be yourself." Her answers seemed to appease Louise, and they zipped through the rest of the chores in record time.

April hitched Sassy to the wagon right after lunch and hurried down the street to Cynthia's. Billy had volunteered to meet her there to help lift Jane and her wheelchair into the wagon. She was glad for that since it would be hard for her to do it alone. Cynthia would leave when they did in order to get back to her job. The arrangement for her to work at the boardinghouse in the afternoons until supper was working out perfectly with her schedule for her daughter.

Pulling up to the gate, April set the brake and climbed down.

Billy was already on the porch chatting with Jane. It appeared that they were getting along quite well. April had never seen Jane so animated. It seemed having someone close to Jane's age was good medicine for her, and she was lapping up Billy's chattering like the hummingbird sucking up nectar from the flowers near the front porch. Well, good for her! This might turn out to be a fabulous day.

Cynthia hurried up the pathway to meet April. "Good afternoon, April," she said. "I can't thank you enough for doing this. Jane has been rather cantankerous with me this morning. She's in one of her moods."

April took her hand and said, "Now don't go worrying, Cynthia, Wes and I will get her right out of that mood, you'll see. This is going to be so good for her." She smiled, nodding toward the porch. "It looks like she has a new friend too."

Cynthia turned in time to see her daughter give a wide smile to Billy. "Hmm, you're right . . . but we don't know much about him, do we?"

They started for the porch. "You don't need to worry. I know him, and now he is working for Morgan Kincaid at the stage depot. Do you know Mr. Kincaid?"

"Indeed I do."

"Then that settles it. You have nothing to fear if you trust Mr. Kincaid's instincts."

Cynthia regarded her with a pensive look. "I suppose you're right on that point. Let's get Jane in the wagon so I won't be late for work."

When Cynthia picked up her daughter to carry her to the wagon, the blanket fell away, exposing April's specially made boots

Maggie Brendan

on Jane's feet and her belt firmly holding her jeans in place. April drew in a quick breath.

"Is something wrong?" Jane asked.

April recovered. "No, no . . . I just got a stitch in my side, that's all," she lied. Why didn't Wes tell her that he was giving the leather goods to Jane instead of letting her think he had a lady friend? Was it to make her jealous?

April put on her best smile. There was no need to take it out on the little girl. It wasn't her fault that she owned them now.

Once Jane was settled in the wagon with a blanket around her legs, she waved to her mother and Billy, who promised to come back some night and play a board game. April urged Sassy forward in a trot down the road toward the Rusty Spur. She was glad to have something to do outside, especially since it involved horses.

April kept her eyes on the road ahead, carefully guiding Sassy, who was a bit frisky. "Jane, are you excited about horseback riding?"

Jane turned in her seat to look up at April with her large, piercing eyes and beautiful bouncy blonde ringlets framing her small face. "I *have* ridden before, you know," she snapped. "It's just been since this accident, I've not had an opportunity, and then no one would care if I wanted to or not." Her face twisted into a frown.

"I'm sorry about that. But someone cares now," April said, and she turned her head in time to see Jane's face soften.

"It will be nice to do something besides sit around the house. The only time I get out is to go to church."

April could hear the pain in Jane's voice. "Maybe today will change that. Wes said his grandfather had terrible pain in his joints, but when he'd go riding, his joints moved easier. There

177

may be something to that. Maybe it will help you to move your legs and help you to walk again."

Jane shifted on the seat, crossed her arms in her lap, and became quiet. April tried to draw her into conversation, but she only muttered one- or two-word answers until they neared Wes's ranch. April figured that it was because she didn't know her very well. She wondered how Juliana had been able to break through that exterior. At least Billy had brought out a few smiles today.

Wes stood with his arm propped up on the fence post next to the corral in anticipation of their arrival. "Howdy! Nice afternoon, isn't it, ladies?"

If she didn't know better, April could have sworn his hair beneath his hat was combed and he wore clean britches. His normally scruffy jaw was clean-shaven. She wasn't sure why, but April was pleased with his overall appearance and couldn't help but notice the twinkle in his eye when he winked at her. "Good afternoon," she said with a half smile.

Jane murmured hello. Wes lifted her wheelchair out of the back of the wagon while April climbed down and stood nearby, ready to assist.

"April, why don't you turn Sassy loose in the pasture while we have our riding time with Jane?"

"Good idea." April began unhitching her horse, and once Wes placed Jane in her chair, he came to assist her. Sassy seemed to know that she was home again and raced to the pasture. To April's surprise, Jane laughed.

"I think she wants to be free, Miss April."

"Could be you're right, Jane." April watched her horse romp

with several other horses in utter abandon. "But this isn't her home anymore."

"Well, let's get started." Wes pushed the wheelchair over to the corral. "I see you wore those nice leather boots. Do they fit all right?"

"They're only a tiny bit long," Jane answered, looking down at her feet. "But they are so nice. I'm wearing the belt too."

Wes chuckled. "Then I'll be sure and tell the lady who donated them how pleased you are." He turned his gaze to April and winked again. Thankfully, Jane couldn't see him wink since he was behind her. He stopped her wheelchair and knelt down in front of her. "Before I get a horse for you, have you ridden before?"

Jane stammered, "No, I haven't."

"But you told me—" April frowned as Wes interrupted her.

"I thought so . . . Jane, you have to do as I tell you, understand?" Wes studied her face.

"I will. Honest." Jane placed her right hand over her heart, grinning at Wes.

"Then I have just the horse for you. I'll go get her and we'll be all set." He stood up. "I'll be right back."

April waited until he was out of earshot before she spoke. "Jane, why did you tell me you'd ridden horses?"

"Because I felt like it," Jane said with irritation in her voice. She pulled the blanket off her legs and draped it over the wheelchair in readiness to be lifted.

April knew what she wanted to say but didn't reply. Besides, she'd promised God she would watch her words.

Wes came back leading a beautiful mare. "This is Cinnamon. She's 'bout the gentlest mare around and will do whatever you tell her to do just by the touch of your knee or a gentle tug of the reins." He led the mare into the corral while April pushed Jane's wheelchair inside and stopped next to the horse.

"She sure is pretty! I hope she likes me," Jane whispered to April anxiously.

"I'm sure she will." April patted Jane's shoulder.

"Okay, ladies. April, I'll pick Jane up if you'll go around to Cinnamon's other side and put Jane's leg over the saddle, then put her feet in the stirrups."

April could feel Jane's shoulder tense underneath her hand. "You're going to be fine. See how still she stands waiting for you?" Jane bobbed her blonde curls in response with a nervous look. April knew that a horse seemed very powerful and big when one encountered it for the first time, and Cinnamon was *big*. April might have chosen a smaller horse to start with.

Wes scooped Jane up into his arms and carried her to the mare, and April guided her leg over to the other side of the saddle.

"How's it feel?" Wes stood with his hands on his hips.

"Gosh . . . like I'm way up high."

"Are you scared?" April asked, looking up at Jane.

"A little." Her voice shook.

"Well, don't be. I'll keep hold of the reins and lead you around the corral," Wes said.

"Hold on to the saddle horn, Jane." April handed Wes the reins.

"What's a saddle horn?" Jane looked down at Wes.

"It's what we call the point sticking up on the saddle."

Jane put both hands around the saddle horn and held tightly.

April climbed up onto the top rung of the fence and watched as Wes led the mare in a walk around the dusty corral. When Cinnamon tossed her mane with a snort, it made Jane jump and nearly lose her seat, but Wes was right there to guide Cinnamon and reassured Jane that her movements were normal for a horse. A couple of times around the ring and Jane was smiling.

"May I hold the reins now?"

"If you want to. When you want to stop, just pull back slightly. If you want to go left or right, since you have no feeling in your legs, just give a tug with the rein in the direction you want to go. That's all there is to it." Wes handed her the reins.

"Will I ever be able to ride like April?" Jane's eyes were shining like a starlit night.

"Could be, but we may have to tie your legs in place somehow. We'll think about it." Wes rubbed his chin thoughtfully.

Not wanting to leave Jane by herself, Wes walked alongside the horse. April watched the pair from her perch on the fence. She was impressed that Wes showed so much patience with Jane. He was a calming presence, and his long fingers gently guided Jane's on how to hold the reins. April also noticed how his jeans hugged his backside and long lean legs and were tucked into his black leather boots. His plaid shirt brought out the green flecks in his eyes, and as he neared her, April decided that no man should have lashes that long.

"Look, April," Jane yelled, "I'm riding by myself!" Jane's face was glowing with delight, and April was glad to see how much difference there was from the girl's previously sullen countenance.

April clapped her hands. "I knew you'd love it! Would you like me to take a walk alongside Jane for a bit, Wes?"

"No, I'd rather be right here since Cinnamon knows me." Wes paused and glanced over at April.

His look said he was pleased to be doing exactly what he was for now, and he gave her a small smile. "In a while we'll stop and have some huckleberry pie."

"Pie? Yum!" Jane smacked her lips as she came close to where April sat. She tested her ability to stop the mare. Cinnamon obeyed and Wes stopped too, standing close enough to touch April's leg.

April reached out to give the horse a loving pat on her withers. "Don't you just love being on a horse's back?"

"I don't know about love, but I do like being way up here," she answered. "Cinnamon is huge. I could get used to doing this every day."

"Wait until you learn to let her trot, then it becomes more fun. But you'll have to feel really confident in the saddle for that to happen." Wes pushed back his hat to see the little girl better.

"Do you mean we can do this again?" Jane's eyes were wide with delight.

"I think that can be arranged. Maybe April can help us out again," Wes said as he curved a look at April.

April shrugged. "I have nothing else to do until my brother arrives, although I don't see that I'm much help to you."

"'Course you're helping. We need your help, don't we, Jane?"

Jane gave April a sweet smile. "Yes, because I'd like to learn to ride like her. Billy told me all about you."

"He did, did he?" April laughed. "Who knows, if you learn to ride well enough, I might let Billy ride Sassy with you and Cinnamon, if that's okay with Wes."

"Fine by me. Now go ahead and have a few more laps around and then we'll have that huckleberry pie."

Jane was only too happy to comply but didn't know how to get the mare moving, so April told her to make a clicking sound with her tongue or say "giddyap."

When the girl was out of earshot, April looked down at Wes. His shirt was open at the throat and his neck was tanned from long hours outdoors. When he smiled, she noticed that he had a slightly crooked tooth, but his lips were nice with a natural lift at the corners. She wondered if he'd ever kissed Natalie. It had been a long, long time since April had been kissed by Luke, and she found herself wanting to feel the taste of Wes's lips against hers. *Am I crazy? He's just an average horse trainer. He owns a few measly unkempt acres, and I'll inherit a ten-thousand-acre ranch. He doesn't have any family. I have a father to answer to.* These thoughts jumbled her mind and she couldn't think straight, especially with Wes standing so close.

"So, did you bake the pie yourself?" April asked.

"I did. Picked the huckleberries myself. Here, let me help you down," he said, reaching for her. April slid down off the fence rail, his hands supporting her at the waist until she was touching him leg to leg. They were so close she could smell his soap and see his mouth twitch.

Wes backed away, turning to look at Jane on the other side of the corral. "One more circle and then we'll stop for today, Jane."

Jane made a face at him, and Wes just laughed. April stood next to him with sweaty palms, her heart thudding hard against her ribs. Was it just the September sun that made her feel so warm?

Wes ushered April and Jane into his sparse home and took them to the small kitchen. He knew his home was not like either of theirs, but it really didn't matter to him. Material things didn't impress him much. Still, he could see the disappointment in April's eyes after they entered the house. As long as he was comfortable, had food and shelter and his horses, he felt like life was good. It wouldn't hurt to have someone to share his life, but it would have to be a compromise. He always wondered why women wanted doodads and knickknacks in the first place. They were just another thing to keep track of.

He pushed Jane up to the kitchen table, still littered with a couple of plates and a glass from lunch. "I was just about to clean this up when you gals arrived," Wes said, hurriedly picking up the plates and carrying them to the sink.

"Do you live alone?" Jane twisted in her chair to see him.

"Yep. My pa's been gone now for about four years," Wes answered as he placed a pie on the table.

"It must get pretty lonely here, then." April stood next to the table. "May I help with anything?"

"Nope. You just sit there and act like company while I dish up the pie. I make good huckleberry pie and picked these berries just yesterday," he bragged. He cut three slices and placed them on old rose china plates. "I'll take the chipped plate. You gals get the nice ones."

Jane giggled. "You're funny, Wes."

He looked at April, who was a little quieter than normal as she took her fork and tasted the pie. He waited for her reaction while she chewed.

"Wes . . . your skill as a cook surprises me." April licked a crumb from the side of her mouth. "A horse trainer who can cook. Now there's a story for you. I wonder what other skills you have hidden." Her blue eyes seem to flirt, and Wes's heart thumped. He swallowed hard.

"I'm a man of many talents, but I try not to show off too much," he replied. Her nearness earlier at the corral had made his hands shake, but he pretended she had no effect on him now as her gaze flittered back to him across the table.

Jane finished off her pie. "I can't wait to tell Mother what a delicious treat we had. I love huckleberries."

Wes shuffled toward the sink with his empty plate, his spurs jingling, then walked to the cupboard to take out a jar. "Here, Jane. Take this jelly home for your breakfast. It's my mother's special recipe. It's mighty fine on hot buttered biscuits."

April rose and took the other dirty plates to the sink. Wes liked the way she looked in her jeans, but he'd liked the soft feminine side of her in the calico dress too. Not to mention the beautiful gown she'd worn to Josh's wedding. His throat went dry just remembering how she'd looked that night with her shoulders bare. But maybe it was the pie that made his throat dry.

"Would you ladies care for some water now? I'll go draw some cold water from the well." He walked back to the cupboard to retrieve the glasses. As he reached to open the cupboard door, his hand brushed against April's. Wes felt a sudden rush of heat. "Sorry."

"Excuse me, but . . . er . . . Wes, I need the necessary room." Jane looked around.

"All I have is the outhouse, Jane. Maybe April could help you." Wes felt the heat rising in his face. He sure didn't want to offer her the slop jar in his bedroom.

"Not a problem," April said, grabbing hold of the arms of Jane's chair. Wes led the way back outside.

"April, I'll pick her up if you'll just push her chair down the back steps." He reached down and picked Jane up. "Girl, you're light as a feather."

Once they got Jane to the outhouse and opened the door, Wes sat her inside. When Jane told them she could take care of the rest, he was relieved.

"Give us a yell when you need us, Jane," April said. She followed Wes to the well. "I'm sorry about that. I wasn't thinking about dealing with that aspect."

Wes wanted to change the subject. "I thought Jane did all right on her first lesson. What'd you think?" They'd reached the well and he dropped the bucket down, then let his eyes travel to April's.

"She seemed like a natural and caught on very quickly. You were very gentle and calm with her. Another side of you I hadn't seen," April replied, pushing the hair back from her brow.

Wes pulled the bucket back up and handed her the dipper and a cup that sat next to the rim of the well. "Thank you. It's what I enjoy most—being outside doing what I love to do." His eyes swept over her, and her eyes skittered away as she brought the cup to her lips.

April drank the entire cup in one gulp, then handed it back to him. Wes wished his own thirst could be so easily satisfied.

"I guess I'd better go see if I can talk Sassy into coming back with me," she said, looking at the pasture.

"I'll walk with you. It looks to me like the horses are at the farthest end of the pasture with the other horses. But do you think Jane will be all right by herself?"

April gave him a half smile. "She'll be fine. A minute or two will teach her patience."

As they walked with the sun beating down on their backs, Wes resisted the urge to hold her hand. A gentle breeze floated through the cottonwoods and rippled past through the high grassy meadow. When a jackrabbit hopped across April's foot and ran away in the tall grass, she grabbed Wes's hand and gave a nervous giggle. "I wasn't expecting that."

They were nearly under a tall shade tree, and he pulled her out of the sun, still holding her hand. "It's cool under here."

"I'm not complaining. It's a lovely day," she said, her gaze searching his.

Wes's gaze bore through her. "It is now with you here," he said hoarsely, watching her face flush. She lowered her eyes, and he noticed how long her lashes were. Her small nose had a little tilt to it that he thought was charming, and when she smiled, a dimple formed near her mouth. Wes couldn't resist the urge to touch it and ran his thumb across the side of her face. He couldn't tell if she was shocked or pleased from the look she gave him, but she didn't let go of his hand.

Wes felt brave, so when she leaned against the tree, he stretched his arm against the tree trunk for support and leaned over her. She looked up at him, and he felt almost weak. *It's now or never.* He moved closer, tilting his head down, and with the lightest touch, he kissed her waiting lips. A spark of fire shot through him, shaking him to his boot heels. April's lips were still parted, and when she didn't resist, he kissed her harder, tasting the sweetness of her lips. He felt her catch her breath and go weak, laying her head against his outstretched arm. The kiss was better than he'd even imagined, but when he reached to stroke her face, she pulled away.

"Wes, don't. This won't work," April whispered.

Wes's smile faded. "Why not? You haven't given us a chance yet." He dropped his arm, allowing her to move away.

"We're from two different worlds. I don't live here and I intend to go back to Colorado."

"You may change your mind after a month or so."

Her gaze skittered away. "I don't think so, Wes."

"You can't deny that you have feelings for me—you enjoyed the kiss." Unease swept over him. Was he wrong, and she was repulsed by him? He'd even taken a bath, washed his hair, and made a huckleberry pie to impress her!

"Wes, I can't live the way you live."

"What's that supposed to mean? What's wrong with the way I live?" Anger flooded his chest. "I didn't even say anything about living with me."

April blushed and stared at him after a moment of silence. "For you, nothing's wrong with the way you live, but it is for me," she said. "I shouldn't have let this happen."

"But you did," Wes said flatly.

"*April! Where are you?*" Jane's yell could be heard clear down to the pasture.

"April, can we talk about this later?" Wes pleaded.

"There's nothing to talk about. I must go help Jane back into her wheelchair," she said, hurrying through the tall grass. "Would you bring Sassy when you come, please?"

Wes just shook his head and watched her walk away.

16

April's head was pounding from Jane's incessant chatter on the entire way back home. April huffed but was able to lift Jane to carry her into the house, wishing she had told Billy to be waiting. She put Jane down on the settee until she could go retrieve the wheelchair. April quickly said her good-bye, promising to remind Billy to come back and play checkers with Jane.

Jane's riding lesson had gone better than she expected, but allowing herself to be kissed by Wes—what was she thinking? April's face burned at the memory. How was she ever going to look him in the eye again? The truth was she'd been thinking about kissing him from the time they drove up to his place, but she shouldn't have let it go that far. There could be nothing permanent to their relationship. Their lives were just too different. April's father had given her a college education, travel, everything she ever wanted. She figured that Wes had never been any farther than Lewistown. April might appear wild in her jeans on horseback, but she was well-acquainted with the finer things in life. From the look of his house, Wes didn't care about any of those things.

April laughed and Sassy's ears twitched at the sound. It was not as if he'd even thought that far ahead. She must be careful. She would not give her heart lightly again and wasn't planning on another man breaking it.

While the afternoon shades lengthened, the stagecoach depot came into view, and April decided to stop in and inquire as to how long it would take for the bank in Colorado to send her money. She knew from her own ride on the stage that Morgan also carried the US mail on his route. Perhaps he could shed some light on it.

She turned the wagon into the yard to see Leon and Morgan doing a thorough inspection of the coach's rigging before their trip to Billings in the morning. She yelled out a hello, and the two paused, waiting for her to climb down from the wagon. Morgan pushed his brown hat back, giving her a broad smile. Leon swept his hat off in greeting and held it to his chest, his hair a matted mess where the hatband had flattened it.

"Hi there!" April walked toward them.

Morgan nodded slightly. "What brings you here so late, April?"

"You know that I telegraphed the bank in Colorado for some cash. Do you have any idea how long it takes to arrive here? My bank said they would transfer funds to the bank in Billings, since my father had done business with them before, and then they'd be sent to the Fergus Bank."

"Then it should be in a strongbox waiting on us when we get there," Morgan answered. "It's just a matter of travel time."

"I see . . . Well, I'm kind of at loose ends for a while until Josh comes back. Without funds, I won't be doing much of anything until my money is deposited."

Leon stuck his hands in his pockets and rocked back on his heels. "Say, Miss April, why don't you just go for the ride? This trip's a quick turnaround."

"Have you lost your mind?" Morgan sputtered, looking at his partner. "We don't need another rider. Besides, I'm bringing Lenora back. She'll be waiting in Billings for me. We may be cramped for room with the mail and all."

Leon harrumphed. "Boss, you know there ain't nobody signed up on this particular run, unless we pick up a passenger in Billings," he said, a wad of tobacco filling his cheek. "Besides, you can ride in the stage with your wife and give your arms a break. Miss April can handle those horses and I'll keep my eyes peeled to protect the strongbox."

Morgan looked more closely at Leon. "I might take you up on the offer."

April studied both men, instantly interested in the offer. "I'd like to go on the route with you since it'll be a quick trip. I have nothing to do around here but wait," April said. "Is Lenora your wife, Morgan? She might enjoy some female company." She could see that Morgan was hesitant to answer. April supposed that she had done a lot of complaining on that long ride, but she reasoned it was only because she hadn't wanted to miss Josh's wedding.

Morgan crossed his arms and stood with his feet apart. He exhaled slowly, apparently giving in to Leon's crazy idea. "We leave at 6 a.m. sharp." His blunt gaze swerved to her. "Can you get those blue eyes of yours open that early? I refuse to wait around for you, April."

April knew he was serious, but she batted her eyelids and smiled. "I'll be here, but don't expect me to be wearing a dress.

If I'm going to sit on the bench, then I'm dressing sensible to the position." April lifted her chin with a reassuring look at Morgan. "I think it will be a great adventure to drive the team."

Morgan roared with laughter. "You would think of it as an adventure! We'll see what you think after tomorrow—and you'd better grab something to eat before you come." He went right on inspecting the axle wheels and left her with Leon.

"Better get to bed early, Miss April, he means what he says," Leon said as he turned to leave.

"Oh! That reminds me of something I have to do tonight. I must run. I'll see you in the morning, never fear. By the way, thanks for suggesting that I go along, Leon."

He gave her a sheepish grin, and the thought occurred to her that he really liked her. Somehow on the trip to Lewistown, she had apparently impressed him with the way she'd handled Gus. The thought made her heart warm. *I've made another friend.*

After a wonderful meal of roasted chicken and some of Margaret's canned green beans and carrots, April began helping Natalie and Louise clear the dishes while they chattered away like they'd known each other for years. Margaret looked on as the three worked together, trying to hide her surprise. May had shared a tray with her husband in their room, and Beth retired to the parlor away from the noise to give Anne a bottle while she enjoyed Margaret's rocking chair. Margaret was so tickled that Beth was beginning to feel more comfortable around them and had even allowed her to rock baby Anne sometimes. It was almost like having her very own grandchild. *Ahh . . . maybe someday.*

"Josh is going to stay at least another week on his honeymoon," April told them with a long face.

"Is that so? My, they must be having a wonderful honeymoon," Natalie said, picking up the half-empty bowls. "We, on the other hand, can only dream to be as happy as they are." She stared off wistfully.

"It'll happen in God's timing, not a minute earlier and not a minute too late," Margaret said.

Louise wiped her hands on her apron. "Listen to you, Mother. You're the one who's so worried you'll never see it happen."

Margaret knew that was true. "Well, maybe, but it never hurts to be reminded that things happen when they're supposed to happen."

"Speaking of which . . . Louise and I have to scoot out. We have something we need to tend to tonight, because I'll be out of here before daylight." April paused with a stack of plates still in her hand.

"And where might you be going so early? Are you going off to see Josh's ranch?" Margaret asked. She hoped April wouldn't think she was being too nosy, but April had quickly grown to become like her own ward, and she wanted to protect her until Josh returned.

April's eyes twinkled. "I'm going on a stagecoach run with Morgan. When I get back, maybe I'll ride over and check out those despicable little creatures that my brother is so fond of."

Natalie took the dishes from April. "Why in the world would you want to go along on a stage route?"

"For the adventure of it. I don't have a whole lot to do until Josh returns."

"I thought you were teaching Jane to ride," Louise said.

"Oh, I am, but not every day." April walked to the door. "Come on, Louise. There's not much left to do here."

"No, there isn't, unless you count *washing* the dishes," Natalie snipped at her sister.

"Natalie, Louise let you go off shopping on Monday, remember. Besides, Louise never allows herself any free time," Margaret reminded her.

"Oh, all right . . . Go on, you two. I'll handle the dish washing, though no suitor will want to hold my poor dishpan hands." Natalie stared down at her hands, feigning sorrow with a pout.

Louise and April left the room, and Margaret couldn't help but wonder what they were up to. With April, one never knew. Natalie carried the dishes back to the kitchen for washing, and Margaret decided to lend her a hand tonight.

April was amazed when she stepped inside Louise's spotless room, which smelled of lemon beeswax and just a hint of vanilla. She drew in a sharp breath. Beautiful voile sheers crisscrossed the bedroom window, allowing slants of waning sunshine to touch the highly polished wood floors. A simple white matelassé coverlet adorned the bed, with muted green linen-covered pillows plumped against the cream-colored iron bedstead. Simple, but very inviting and relaxing.

"You approve, I take it?" Louise waited just inside her room.

"It's lovely. Did you make this coverlet?" April ran her fingers across the tiny, flawless stitches.

Louise's face beamed at the compliment. "Yes, I did."

"That must have taken you a very long time to do." April marveled again at how detailed Louise was in all of her work.

Louise shrugged. "I guess so, but I enjoy being busy."

"I believe that to be a fact. However, we must help you find time for a little fun, or Mark will never even know that you're available," April said. She took a seat on the edge of the bed, and Louise cringed. "Relax, Louise, my sitting here will not destroy your bedcover." April laughed. "Now, we don't have much time, so show me what clothes you have."

Louise turned on her heel, and April followed her to the wardrobe where she flung open the doors. April stepped up next to her and peered inside. There were two dark brown dresses and one navy serge traveling suit. The only others in the closet were a gray dress and two more nondescript dresses that April had seen Louise wear to church. "Heavens above! Louise, is this all you have?" April asked.

"It's sufficient," she answered meekly.

"It may be serviceable for work, but it's hardly sufficient." April touched the fabric of a couple of Louise's dresses and just shook her head. "How is it possible that Natalie dresses stylishly, and you wear clothes suitable for a matron, which you are *not*!"

Louise's face turned pink. "Who would look at me no matter what I wore? Just look at me—I'm tall and bony without the womanly curves or the beautiful head of hair you have. Natalie is vivacious and pretty, and people are drawn to her." Louise looked down at April, her bottom lip trembling. "You even look feminine in those jeans!"

"What! I can't believe you're saying that." April reached up and touched Louise's hair. "You have gorgeous thick brown hair with hints of auburn, but you have it so tightly wound up from the front of your forehead to the base of your neck that I wouldn't be surprised if you have terrible headaches every day. I think you carry yourself with the regal look of a true aristocrat."

"But I—" Louise sputtered, fingering the back of her chignon.

"No buts. Just keep quiet and listen to me, my friend." When she saw the look of apprehension cross Louise's face, she softened her tone. She didn't want to hurt Louise's feelings. "You are not old—no need to look that way. First thing we're going to do is style your hair and make it appear softer."

"Why? I'm not going anyplace tonight."

"Doesn't matter. We're going to practice. You can always pull your hair back out of your way when you're doing chores. But you can leave a few curls framing your face, even if you pull most of it back." April hoped she wasn't wasting her breath. "I'll loan you something to slip on for now so we can get the full effect. Come Sunday or the next time you go out, you'll have a new look. I think a little shopping is in order when I return from Billings."

"I don't know if Mother will agree to this . . ."

"Just leave that to me. Something tells me that Miss Margaret will be pleased," April said while she began taking the pins from Louise's hair. "Oh, and we will need to order you some different shoes for entertaining. Those brogans won't do. I'll even see you wearing jeans before you can blink. Then people will say, 'Mmm, Louise is very modern!'" April stood with her hands on her hips, pretending to be a typical observer on the sidewalk.

Louise giggled nervously and sat down at the dressing table. "I don't know about that," she said, but she succumbed to April's fingers as they worked their magic on Louise's hair.

April and Louise walked into the parlor a half hour later, and Natalie's jaw dropped when she saw her sister's new look. April had to nearly drag Louise into the room with her timid modesty. She wore one of April's new frocks with tiny white sprigs of flowers on a background of deep lavender moiré, with a neckline dipping below the collarbone. The sleeves of the dress ended just below the elbow with two rows of delicate lace edging. A light dusting of powder gave Louise's face a softer look, and April had rubbed just a hint of rouge on her high cheekbones. Louise didn't look like the same person who'd left the dining room earlier.

"Louise, is that you?" Natalie asked, rising from her chair and slowly walking to her.

"It is. What do you think?" Louise twirled around for all to see. It seemed her attitude had changed along with the clothes and new hairstyle.

Miss Margaret left her chair and touched her daughter's face while leaning on her cane. "My . . . but you are so pretty, Louise. Let me look at you," she said, holding her daughter at arm's length. "Did you just buy this dress?"

Louise giggled. "No, Mother. It belongs to April, but it would be nice to own something like this and these heels too." She lifted her skirt up just enough to show them her borrowed shoes. "These are a bit tight, different than what I'm used to."

Natalie was so excited that she gave her sister a swift hug. "April, you have done wonders and brought out my sister's natural good looks."

Footsteps sounded in the hallway, and they all turned to see Dr.

Mark Barnum and Beth walk into the room. Mark drew up short when he saw Louise. "I'm sorry . . . am I interrupting something?" he said as his eyes swept over Louise. He seemed embarrassed that he was caught staring.

Louise almost bolted from the room, but April stayed her with a firm hand on her arm. "No, we were just experimenting with my hair for the next social event," Louise stammered. She stared at her toes, which peeked out from the edge of her skirts.

"That's too bad. You look stunning!" Mark continued to gaze at Louise with open admiration. April watched Louise's face, and her look seemed to say, *For the first time I'm proud of who I am.* Her cheeks flushed, and she murmured a "thank-you" that was barely audible.

"I have to agree," Beth said.

Mark cleared his throat and said, "I was just leaving. I came to see how Willard is doing, and he's getting a little stronger every day." He bowed to Louise and then to the others, then bade them good night. April gave Louise a push, indicating that she should walk him to the door.

"Let me walk you out," Louise said, following Mark to the front door.

April and the others stood motionless and listened to the couple's brief conversation.

"I meant what I said in there, Louise," Mark said.

Louise took his hat and coat from the hall tree and handed it to him. "I'm afraid I'm a little embarrassed to have you see me all dressed up with no place to go." Her voice sounded weak.

He laughed good-naturedly. "Think nothing of it, Louise. I assume that all ladies practice with that sort of thing, and there's no harm in it, especially when they turn out like you." He plunked his hat on. "Well . . . I'll see you around."

"Good night, Mark," Louise whispered and closed the door behind him. She leaned back against the door with a dreamy look.

Four heads peeked from around the door's edge. "Were you all eavesdropping?" Louise scolded with a silly grin.

Miss Margaret pushed the door open wide to expose all of them looking guilty but laughing. "I guess we were at that." She tapped her cane. "Looks like Mark got an eyeful tonight and will be back for more."

Beth tilted her head sideways at them. "I talked to him about being his nurse today, and I got the impression from the lady he was with that he's courting her."

Louise's face fell. "Oh, do you know who she was?"

Beth tapped her chin with her finger. "Let's see . . . Cindy, no Cynthia. She looked familiar to me."

"Cynthia works for me in the afternoons, helping in the kitchen, if indeed that's the same person," Miss Margaret said.

"Was she a redhead?" Natalie asked.

"She certainly was, and she had her daughter with her in a wheelchair."

"Then that's Cynthia Hood," April said. "Doesn't mean a thing, Louise." April hooked her arm in Louise's. "Don't you start worrying now, you hear?" But April knew that her words rang hollow, for Louise lost the playful smile she'd had just moments earlier.

It was all April could do to roll out of bed before dawn, but a promise was a promise. She staggered over to the water pitcher next to the sink. *Mother wouldn't believe it if she saw me now, getting up with the chickens.* She pulled her jeans and boots on, then slipped on a chambray shirt over her camisole and threw extra clothes into a saddlebag. Plucking her hat off the bedpost, she decided she'd need her duster since the early mornings were cool. She paused momentarily and then stuffed her Bible in her saddlebag. Never know when one might have need of it, although when, she didn't know. They would be driving the coach for long hours to get to Billings in two days. She carefully tiptoed down the stairs, trying not the make any noise, but as she passed the kitchen, she smelled bacon and heard Miss Margaret humming.

"April, is that you?" Miss Margaret called out.

"Yes, ma'am," April answered. She poked her head through the doorway to see Miss Margaret holding out a cup of coffee and a hot biscuit filled with bacon for her. The kitchen was warm with a fire burning in the grate.

April took the biscuit and coffee from her. "I had no idea that you were up this early, Miss Margaret."

Miss Margaret gave a sweet smile. "I have always been an early riser, and I like to start my day enjoying the quiet. I thought you might need something in your belly before you take off on that long, harebrained ride."

April took a bite of the fluffy biscuit and savored the taste of bacon inside. "Miss Margaret, you are just too good to me." She smiled at the older lady, then drank some of the coffee. "Don't you worry about me. I'll be careful," she said, polishing off the biscuit. April donned her duster, then hoisted her saddlebags over one shoulder.

"I hope so, or Josh will be angry with me for not watching out for you." Miss Margaret gave her a stern look, one hand on her hip, the other one on her cane.

April gave her a quick peck on the cheek, thoroughly surprising Miss Margaret, then hurried out the door.

Leon climbed up to the seat of the stage toting his shotgun, and Morgan glanced around once last time, looking for April. *She said she'd be here. I'll bet she's still sleeping.* "Billy," he said to his young helper, "when April shows—"

Billy touched the sleeve of Morgan's arm and pointed to the sidewalk. April, holding her hat on, was practically running to reach them.

"Well, I'll be danged." Morgan let out a low whistle. "I really didn't think she'd show." Then he climbed atop the stage to wait for her.

"Aw, if Miss April said she'd be here, then I knew she would," Billy said as April drew closer. "I'd rather be the one going with you."

"Son, you will, and soon. But I like the idea that someone is back here in charge while I'm away. You and Will keep watch over everything now, you hear?" Morgan said, looking down at Billy's shiny black hair.

"Yes, sir." Billy looked down, dragging the toe of his boot in the dirt.

Breathing hard, April pulled up short and dropped the saddle-bags from her shoulder to the ground. "Sorry, I'm exactly two minutes late by the boardinghouse clock. Miss Margaret made me wolf down a biscuit to hold me until lunch."

Morgan pulled out the pocket watch tucked into the top of his vest and squinted to read it in the moonlight. "By my watch, you are five minutes late!"

"Quit splitting hairs, Morgan, and let's get going," Leon said, handing the reins to Morgan and laying his shotgun across his lap.

"I thought I was going to ride up there with you, Morgan." April's brow furrowed in her forehead.

"I never said when, April. Have a seat inside the stage and we'll talk about it when we stop for lunch."

April rolled her eyes at Billy, shaking her head.

"Just be glad you get to go, while I stay here," Billy said. He picked up her saddlebags, then opened the door and threw them inside.

April got in and Billy shut the door. Leaning out the window, April said, "I'm sorry, Billy. I wasn't aware that you weren't going on the trip this time. I'll be glad to teach you everything I learn."

"It's not your fault, Miss April. See you in a few days."

"If you two will quit jawing, we can leave now," Morgan said, hoping he sounded friendly. Then he cracked his whip, the team of horses leaned into the riggings, and the stagecoach jerked forward. April waved at Billy as he jumped back out of the way. Morgan had a twinge of regret that he was leaving Billy behind, but logic told him the boy had a lot to learn, even with his knowledge of horses. It was better this trip that he didn't come because they would be transporting the strongbox of cash from Billings to Lewistown. No place for a kid to get in the way.

Morgan could hardly contain his joy that Lenora would be waiting for them in Billings. He missed her so badly that many nights he lay awake thinking about her lying next to him. But he understood that she'd needed to be in Mississippi for a while to take care of her parents, and then later to settle their affairs. He'd savored every letter from her, reading it over and over. He hoped she was missing him as much, and the thought brought a smile to his lips.

The rocking of the stagecoach with its heavy springs had put April to sleep three hours later. She'd stretched out the length of one side and propped up her boots heels on the window frame, placing her hat across her eyes. The only companion in the coach with her had been the huge bag of US mail that occupied the seat across from her.

The coach stopped and April stiffly sat up. Leon's head popped in the window, and he gave his naturally warm, contagious smile, showing his tobacco-stained teeth. "Are you 'bout ready for lunch, Miss April?"

"My goodness, Leon, I think I've been asleep since we left the station." April stepped through the coach door that he held open for her and glanced around, recognizing the familiar stop from her first trip to Lewistown.

Morgan hopped down from the top seat, rubbing his hands together. "My stomach is about to eat my backbone. I hope they have some good vittles cooked up today." April and Leon laughed at his comment. "We still have another four hours to go before we stop for the night," he continued.

"Something smells good," Leon said, leading the way.

A couple of folks hung around the rest stop, waiting for the stagecoach to arrive, but thankfully there were no babies this time. April hoped that she would be sitting outside on the next leg of the trip.

The lunch fare was tolerable—beans that needed salt and sourdough bread with canned peaches for dessert. No sense complaining, but April missed Natalie's crusty homemade bread and fresh churned butter. Leon drank so much coffee that the cook made another pot.

"April, this afternoon you can ride outside on the seat with me. Leon can get a little siesta," Morgan informed her as they walked back outside in the spectacular sunshine.

"Okay. I slept almost the entire way here. Your coach can rock one to sleep when there's no one to talk to." April followed him to the front of the stage, and he gave her a hand up while Leon climbed inside.

"You're right about that, April. But it sure can make a body stiff after weeks of riding." Taking a seat next to April, Morgan lifted the reins.

"Morgan, do you think you could show me how you do this? It seems a bit complicated."

"Pay attention and I'll explain to you how to handle the reins. We call them ribbons because you thread them through the fingers of your left hand like so." Morgan demonstrated placing the reins through the fingers of his thick leather gloves. "Now you keep your right hand free to let off the brake as needed." He reached down to where the break was set and pulled it free. The team of six horses made a slight movement when they felt the break's release but stood awaiting Morgan's orders.

"The right hand also stays free to handle the whip. Just nice and gentle-like will get the team moving." With a flick of his wrist, Morgan touched the whip to the horses' backsides, yelling, "Git up there, now!"

April was exhilarated to be riding up high behind such magnificent horses, their manes flowing in the wind, their ears laid back, and their hooves moving in smooth, connected rhythm. She had no idea that this could be so much fun. April felt a pang in her heart that Billy wasn't here to experience this, but she knew he would be soon. It was just a matter of time.

It was hard to have a conversation without raising one's voice above the din of hoofbeats on the hard-packed road. Morgan glanced over at her, the whites of his eyes large with pleasure, and April knew he loved his work.

"Would you like to give it a try for a bit a little later?" Morgan asked.

April couldn't believe she'd heard correctly at first, but he continued to look at her with a question in his big brown eyes. "You mean it? I guess I would like to see what it's like to control that many horses at one time."

"Did you bring a pair of gloves with you? You're gonna need 'em," Morgan said.

April pulled her gloves out of her duster and held them under his nose for inspection. "These are the only ones I have. Do you think they're thick enough?"

Morgan narrowed his eyes to get a good look, then said, "They'll have to do. Mine will be way too big. You don't want to get blisters. Maybe after you've watched me awhile, I'll give you a chance to see how you'll do the driving."

April could hardly wait to give it a try, but for now she was content to observe Morgan's skill with the team and learn as much as she could. She wondered if these were some of Wes's trained horses. What would he think of her handling a team?

When they pulled up to the station to stop for the night, April's back was stiff, but what an experience. Morgan had given her the reins for a short time on the drive, and though she was a bit apprehensive at first, she concentrated and was beginning to get the feel of the horses straining against the ribbons, as Morgan called them. The rush of power was hard to describe. She felt like she had to strain with all her might in order to keep the several thousand pounds of horseflesh from jerking her clean off the seat.

Now April began to feel a steady burn between her shoulder blades and wished Tilly would be at the station with a warm bath and a rubdown. But April wouldn't dare complain to Morgan. No sirree! Right now she would be grateful just to lay her head on the pillow.

The next morning, two businessmen joined the stage ride on the last leg to Billings. Part of the time, April was in the coach with them, but they weren't inclined to talk other than to exchange pleasantries, so April remained quiet and leaned her head against the side of the coach and rested. She and Leon traded off again in the afternoon, and Morgan gave her another lesson on driving the team. The feel of horsepower coupled with the fact that she controlled their speed gave her a rush.

"I'm impressed with how well you catch on, April." Morgan looked at her with such favor that April felt her face turn pink.

"I'm having a good time with this, Morgan. Thanks for letting me spend time with you doing this. My mother and father will never believe it."

"You could be a real Stagecoach Mary, though you're a mite lighter in weight—and color too, I should add." Morgan chuckled.

"Who might that be?" April asked.

"She delivered the US mail by a mule named Moses in rain, sleet, blizzard, or heat, and she was called Stagecoach Mary because she was always on schedule." Morgan paused. "Yep, she was a large black woman, hard-drinking, cigar-smoking, tough as any man. She stood about six foot and weighed around two hundred pounds. I wouldn't want to get on her bad side, that's for sure."

"You're teasing me, right?"

Morgan quirked an eyebrow. "Would I tease you?" He laughed. "Yes, I would, but not this time. It's the truth."

"Did you know her? Where is she now?"

"I met her once, and Lenora gave me the evil eye just for looking.

But I couldn't help myself. I've never met another soul like her. I heard she opened a laundry service over in Cascade."

"Humph. I'm not sure I want to be compared to a tough woman the likes of her." April glanced sideways at Morgan with a teasing grin.

Morgan grinned back at her. "Too bad her laundry service wasn't here when you had need of it." He chortled.

"All right, now you're being funny!" April laughed. "Thank goodness Wes had the nerve to tell me how I smelled."

"Do tell!"

April told him how Wes had tossed her over his shoulder and threw her in the horses' water trough.

Morgan hooted until tears were in his eyes. "I wish I'd been a fly on a horse's back." He paused. "You know, April, Wes is a good man. His daddy was really hard on him, especially after his mother died." Morgan wiped his brow with his big bandana, then stuck it back into his hip pocket. "His ranch lacks a woman's touch, and he's a little brash at times, but really his heart is in the right place. I'm so glad he and Josh are friends and respect one another. It wasn't always that way."

"Are you taking up for his behavior?" April slowed the horses as they came to a big curve in the road. She didn't want to flip the coach on its side.

"Nope. Just telling it like it is," he said, turning his eyes back to the road ahead. "Very skillfully maneuvered there, April. Guess you're not afraid of nothin'. You catch on fast."

April was pleased that he admired her skill. "Tell that to my brother. I was just a little pest to him growing up."

"Not from what I hear. Josh thinks the world of his little sister and has nothing but good things to say concerning you, though he *did* mention a time or two that you were a mite spoiled by your daddy."

April snapped, "That's not my fault, you know. I guess I was just trying to please him." She didn't want to think about the many times she'd whined to or manipulated her father to get her way against her mother's word about something. She felt ashamed. Now that she wasn't at home and around her parents, she could see herself in better focus. Especially since she wasn't the center of everyone's attention in Lewistown.

Morgan shot her a look. "Why not start pleasing yourself instead?"

"That's exactly what I'm doing now," April answered.

"Then it's a good start." Morgan gave her a quick pat on the shoulder.

Morgan's face was serious when she looked over at him. April would never have thought she'd be driving a team of horses for a stagecoach in Montana of all places, and having a real friendship that had started off shaky with an older black man, who now treated her like a daughter. She just shook her head, wondering what the Lord was up to now.

"It's time I took over, April," Morgan said, reaching for the reins. He kept a steady hand as he extracted her fingers woven through the leather straps. "It doesn't take long for a body to start hurting in places you didn't know you had after pulling against these powerful horses."

April didn't argue. The pain between her shoulder blades burned sharply, and her hands and arms were cramping, but she would never let on. Though she was sure the beads of perspiration along her upper lip and her flushed face were a dead giveaway.

Morgan was itching to reach Billings before sundown, so he pushed the team hard. His sweet Lenora would be there waiting, and he couldn't wait to hold her in his arms. Everything had gone as smooth as glass on this trip, and he'd been impressed with April, who was probably asleep now.

Another hour later, just before dusk, Morgan rumbled into the busy town of Billings, and there she was. *Lenora!* He was so overcome with joy that he almost forgot to set the brake. He and Leon hopped down. Lenora was standing off from the rest of the passengers, looking with wide eyes for Morgan. When she saw him, she dropped her satchel and rushed up to him. He lifted her off her feet in a tight embrace and spun her around, covering her face with kisses. Lenora's large eyes were brimming with tears as he set her down. Suddenly realizing where they were, they pulled apart shyly but still held hands.

April was standing with Leon, watching their reunion. Leon gave Lenora a friendly nod. "I sure am glad to see you. Maybe now we can stand to be around him," he joked, nodding in Morgan's direction.

Lenora beamed. "And I'm happy that I'm back with my man, Leon," she said with a Southern voice as thick as honey. Lenora's striking stature complemented her husband, and her smooth, coffee-brown face split with a wide smile, exposing white, even teeth. She was dressed in an olive green tweed traveling suit that set off her beautiful color. April thought she must be a few years younger than Morgan.

"April, this is Lenora," Morgan said.

Lenora stretched out her hand. "I'm happy to meet you. I didn't realize my husband had hired another driver," she said with a slight frown as her eyes swept over April.

"Oh, heavens, no. I don't work for Morgan." April giggled and saw the relief flood Lenora's face. "I'm just along for the ride."

Lenora looked at her husband, one eyebrow raised, and Morgan said, "It's a long story, Lenora. Why don't we all get settled in for the night?"

"I'll go take care of the horses and see you for supper quicker than you can spell Mississippi!" Leon said.

Lenora gave a short giggle, and Morgan harrumphed. "That'll be the day. Can you even spell Mississippi?"

"Go on with you," Leon said, then waved them off and traipsed back over to the stage to tend to the horses.

By morning's light, they'd hit the trail bound for Lewistown with the latest bag of US mail and the strongbox from the bank. April had gotten to know Lenora during supper the previous night and found her to be pleasant and very much in love with Morgan, which she thought was sweet. Morgan returned her affection, squeezing her waist several times during their meal. He hung on to every word Lenora had to say about her stay with her folks and tales of their friends back home. Her speech was educated and she had excellent manners, which overshadowed her shyness. Before long, they excused themselves, with Morgan reminding Leon and April to be ready early.

April was surprised by how much she'd enjoyed their company. She was used to fancy dinner parties that her mother hosted and the best cuisine prepared by their cook, followed by board games or an occasional dance with a string orchestra. Here, meeting people with everyday problems in a relaxed atmosphere made April feel included in something bigger than herself. Maybe she'd try to express her thoughts in a letter to her parents later. Or, better yet, maybe she could convince them to come to Montana to see Josh.

The second day of the trip back, April sat opposite Lenora in the stuffy stagecoach. It was an uneventful, breezy day that Leon said would bring cooler temperatures by nightfall.

"If you don't mind me asking, what brought you to Montana, April?" Lenora asked.

April smiled. "My brother Josh's wedding. I couldn't miss that for anything. My mother and father are in Ireland for their anniversary, so I really wanted to be here for Josh."

Lenora smiled, showing off her perfect teeth. "I'm glad that you and your brother are close. Family is so—"

Lenora's words were cut short when gunshots suddenly rang out. Her eyes were wide with fear as the coach sped up and the shots continued. April wanted desperately to look out the window but feared she might face a bullet.

"It must be robbers. They might know that we have the US mail and the money in the strongbox," Lenora cried. "Oh, Lord, help us!"

Fear shot through April. "Maybe we can outrun 'em!" She hoped that would be true, but when she felt the stagecoach slowing down and the sound of the rings and riggings as the horses halted, she heard voices.

Suddenly the door of the stagecoach was yanked open by a cowboy with a bandana over his face, holding a six-shooter. "Get out!" he yelled.

April and Lenora did as they were told. April looked up and saw Morgan slumped down on the seat, a red stain on the front of his coat. She heard Lenora suck in a breath and cry, "Morgan!" But he didn't move. Leon, who'd been riding next to Morgan, now lay sprawled out on the roof, but April couldn't tell if he'd been shot and if he was alive or dead. She feared the latter since he wasn't moving. Alarm filled her, and though she was terrified, she knew she must do something. Lenora reached for her hand, but April's eye was on the shotgun that lay next to Leon.

"Just you be quiet and don't move an inch," the robber said. From the front of the coach, another rider still on his horse ordered his cohort to get the strongbox. His face was covered as well, and he seemed nervous. The first one reached in the stage and yanked the strongbox down to the ground. He fired one shot at the lock, and the women jumped back, startled. April's heart beat furiously against her ribs, and her hands shook.

"Well, don't just stand there, get the money and let's go!" the man on horseback yelled.

"Give me time, Boss," he said, lifting the heavy metal lid. "What the—" His jaw dropped. "There's only a bunch of government documents in here!"

April and Lenora didn't move a muscle for fear of what the men would do to them. But what had happened to her money and the bank's? This had to be some terrible mistake! April wished that

Morgan and Leon hadn't been shot. She wasn't sure what to do. Any sudden move and the bandits might shoot. *Think!*

"You fool, you said that the transfer from the bank was on this stagecoach!"

"Like I said, I *told* you that's what I overheard at the station yesterdee," he spat out at his boss, then turned to the women. "Where's the money?"

"I have no idea what you are talking about," April said. "I'm traveling with my maid from the South. We've been on the stage since Billings."

Lenora picked up on April's game. "Yes'm. That's shore 'nuf true, mister. I's only jus arrived. Please don't hurt us none—"

"Shut yore mouth!" The boss regarded her with disgust from his perch on horseback while the other one snickered. Lenora lunged at him with fists raised, her eyes flashing with rage. April pulled her away just before his arm came down to hit Lenora.

April held Lenora as she sagged against her, crying. "You're a sorry excuse for a man! Why don't you leave us alone? There's no money on this stage," April said. She prayed silently that she sounded confident and that they would leave. She couldn't bear to think about Leon and Morgan. "You've already shot two people, what good will two more do? There is no money!"

The man on the ground searched the inside of the coach again, dumped out the mailbag's contents, then climbed up behind Morgan and poked around under the seat.

"Empty your handbags!" the boss shouted at them. Lenora did as she was told and dumped out a few bills.

"I don't carry a handbag, as you can see," April spat, which seemed to infuriate the bandits further.

The second man stood with his feet apart, his eyes slowly looking her over from head to toe. "I shore can tell that's a fact, with you in men's britches." He started toward her, and April backed up.

"We've been duped! All for nothin'! Git on your horse and let's scatter," the boss ordered. "You two, git on back into the coach and close the door. You best stay there for fifteen minutes, or else!"

Lenora pulled April toward the coach with fear in her eyes. They'd barely stepped foot inside when the two highwaymen galloped out of the clearing. Immediately, April sprang out again, scrambled to the top of the coach, and picked up Leon's rifle, bringing it up to her shoulder. Her heart thumped like crazy in her chest from the adrenaline rush. She barely had time to aim at the moving target before firing. One of the men, the boss, jerked in his seat and grabbed his shoulder. She could've killed him if she'd wanted to—her father had taught her to shoot when she was thirteen—but at least she knew he'd been hit. He'd be easier to track. Not too many people walked around with a bullet hole in the back of their shoulder.

She turned back to Leon and noticed a gunshot wound in his right temple. Sudden nausea clenched her gut, and she felt weak. She closed her eyes momentarily and took in several deep breaths to control herself. April reached down to his neck and felt no pulse, so she pulled his eyelids down. She'd have to get him down somehow.

"Lenora, what about Morgan?"

Lenora was already in the front checking her husband. "He's badly wounded, April. He needs a doctor. We must do something fast." She looked over at Leon hopefully, but April just shook her head.

18

Together, Lenora and April were able to pull Leon's body to the edge of the stage's roof and roll him over. Between the two of them, they picked him up and laid him on the seat inside. Lenora covered him with a lap robe left there for travelers when it was drafty. April's hands were shaking and she was sick at heart. She had lost a good friend. Why had this happened? But she didn't have time to think about it now, while Morgan lay wounded.

They hurriedly scooped up the strewn mail, stuffed it back into the mailbag, and placed it and the strongbox on the floor of the stage. April stopped long enough to push her hair out of her eyes. "I'll drive the stage, Lenora. We still have a few hours before we get to Lewistown. You sit next to Morgan and hold on to him. At least he's breathing."

"Please hurry, April," Lenora pleaded, her voice cracking.

"Don't you worry about a thing. Can you get Morgan's gloves off for me? Since I'll be driving longer, I'll need the extra padding."

Lenora removed the gloves, and Morgan groaned. "Baby, everything's gonna be just fine. I'm here with you," Lenora said, her tears splashing onto her hands as she held him close.

April let off the brake and yelled "Giddyap!" Then she laid the whip across the horses' backsides, spurring them into an all-out run down the worn wagon road, with rocks and dust flying in all directions.

Hours later, exhausted and feeling as though her arms would fall off, April roared into Lewistown, turning a few heads as she flew past townsfolk in the streets. Instead of going to the depot, she drove straight to the doctor's office and stopped the stage, blocking one side of the street. She jerked the brake back and nearly fell as she climbed down. Ignoring a man who asked what the trouble was, April flew to Mark's office door and banged hard enough to shake the glass panel. A bystander looked up, saw Lenora, and hurried over to help get Morgan down as another citizen walked over to help. A crowd started to cluster around, buzzing with questions.

"Did she drive that stagecoach all by herself?" a woman in the crowd asked.

"Yep, she sure did! I saw her coming down the street. I wonder what happened."

Mark hurried out to assist. He told the men where to place Morgan as he followed close behind then shut the door. He looked at Lenora, whose eyes were red-rimmed, and led her to the waiting area with a firm hand.

April turned to the men for their help. "Leon's been shot and he's in the coach," she said. "Better go for the sheriff . . . and the undertaker. Leon didn't make it." Her voice choked and her eyes stung with unshed tears. She collapsed into a chair next to Lenora, her shoulders slumped forward.

The two men shuffled back outside. April hoped they would send for the undertaker. How had the beautiful reunion earlier with Morgan and Lenora been shattered so tragically? She reached over and grabbed Lenora's hand, giving it a squeeze. Lenora sat stiffly in the chair as if at any given moment she would spring up.

"Don't fret, Lenora. Mark is a good doctor." Then, surprising herself, she added, "We just need to pray and ask God for His mercy."

Lenora slowly lifted her head and looked at April through her tears. "Yes. I know Mark, but thankfully we haven't had need of a doctor before, although Morgan has been complaining about his rheumatism in his letters to me. I just hope the doctor can stop the bleeding." She sniffed into her handkerchief. "Morgan loved Leon, you know. It didn't matter that they were different colors or different backgrounds. They completely accepted each other. Morgan will be lost without him."

April leaned toward Lenora. "He has you, and you'll like his young helper he recently hired. His name is Billy."

"All I can think about is Morgan right now."

April looked down at Lenora's bloodstained hands clasped in her lap. "We need to wash your hands, and mine too. That'll make us feel a lot better. Follow me to the washroom."

When they returned, the sheriff was waiting for them. "Evening, Miss Lenora," he said, then his gaze swept over April, a strange look passing over his round face. "Are you the young lady who drove the stage in?"

"Yes, I am." April stuck out her hand and gripped his big palm in a firm handshake. "I'm April McBride."

"You don't say. Josh's sister?"

She nodded. It seemed everyone knew her brother, but she wasn't surprised. People liked Josh's easygoing, good nature.

"I'm Ben Wilson, the sheriff here. Can we go sit down and talk about what happened?"

"I need to see about the horses—"

"No need to worry, ma'am. One of my men drove the stage on over to the depot. They'll help Billy see to that."

"Okay then." She turned to Lenora. "Will you be all right for a few minutes?"

Lenora waved her off. "You go ahead and tell him everything. I'm not moving from this spot until Mark comes through that door with news of my husband," she said, her voice faltering.

By the time April had given a statement to the sheriff, Mark had emerged from the operating room and closed the door behind him. Lenora popped out of her seat to meet him. "Dr. Mark—"

Mark reached out and touched her shoulder. "He's lost a lot of blood, but he'll pull through. The bullet just missed his heart. Morgan's tough and he'll bounce back, but I sure am glad you're here to nurse him, Lenora." Mark paused. "I'm sorry about Leon. He was a good man."

Lenora grabbed his hands in hers and held them in gratitude. "Thank you! When will I be able to take him home?" Her eyes were shining with tears.

"Let's leave him here a few days. He's over the worst of it. We just need to make sure no infection follows." Mark ran his hand through his dark hair and added, "You can come tomorrow and check on him. I have a nurse now, Beth Reed. She'll be here with him when I can't be."

"I can't leave him tonight, Doc."

April touched her on the arm. "Lenora, we both need to get some sleep and rest. I know Beth, and she'll give him good care until you arrive in the morning."

"She's right, you know," Mark said. "You won't be much help to him if you're exhausted."

Eventually the two of them talked Lenora into going to Morgan's apartment over the depot. "May I see him before I go for just a few minutes?" Lenora asked.

"By all means," Mark answered, then moved aside to let her pass. Once she was behind the closed door, Mark looked over at April, his voice tender. "That had to be a terrifying time for you. I'm sorry you had to deal with all of it."

She smiled at him, still feeling a little shaky. "I'm just thankful I could handle those horses. I was only going for the ride out of sheer boredom, you know. But now I'm glad I did. I'm not crazy about staring down the barrel of a gun," she said with a nervous giggle. "I'm more at home at the other end of the barrel."

"Well, I'm proud of how you handled it, and I'm sure Morgan will be too."

Mark's praise warmed her heart. It felt good to finally do something worthwhile, but never had April expected to save someone's life.

Lenora emerged with sagging shoulders but managed a weak smile after having seen her husband. "You'll come and get me if there is any change at all?"

Mark smiled at her. "You know I will. Try to get some sleep. I promise I'll be right here and I won't leave him."

"God bless you. I'll be here bright and early," Lenora assured him, looking worn out. She allowed April to steer her to the front door.

When April walked through the door of the boardinghouse, the word had already spread about the stagecoach robbery. Miss Margaret was pacing the hardwoods, tapping her cane and waiting for April to arrive.

"Thank God you're all right!" Miss Margaret rushed toward her. "If my hair wasn't already white, it certainly would be turning now!" Miss Margaret continued to cluck like an old hen. "I never should have let you go on that trip, not that I have any power over what you do."

April was too tired and frazzled to even laugh at her comment. "I'm all right now that it's all over with, though I left Billy with a heartache at the depot. He'd taken to Leon immediately when he first arrived in Lewistown, and poor Leon . . . he . . . I just don't want to think about it now, Miss Margaret. It's just too sad . . ." April's voice trailed off.

Louise and Natalie came hurrying downstairs, already dressed for bed in their robes. April almost laughed when she saw the white cream on their faces. "April, we heard what happened. You look a fright!" Natalie said.

"You would too if you'd just driven a team of horses with an injured man all day and into the night," Louise admonished her sister. "How do you think we must look with our faces covered in thick cream?"

"Well . . . thanks for the compliment, I think," April said. "But if you don't mind, I really must go to bed now."

Miss Margaret stopped her. "I've kept a plate warm for you on the stove. Don't you want something to eat?"

April looked at the older lady, patting the hand that rested on her cane. "I really couldn't eat a thing right now . . . You understand, don't you?" Without waiting for a response, she wearily climbed the stairs, grateful for her own room and somewhere to lay her head. April pulled her boots off but didn't even bother to remove her clothes. She dropped onto the bed facedown and let her aching muscles slump in exhaustion. Right before she closed her eyes, she wondered what Morgan could have possibly done with the money.

Margaret prepared a tray with hot tea and toast with a bowl of oatmeal and placed the tray on the dumbwaiter. Her daughters were busy attending to chores. Louise was at the market for tonight's supper, and Natalie was cleaning the Wingates' room. May had taken Willard out for a visit with their daughter and grandchildren.

Margaret carefully climbed the stairs to the end of the hallway where she unloaded the tray onto a cart Louise had left there. She almost hated to knock on April's door. The poor dear had been through so much. Certainly life had been an adventure for her since arriving in Montana. Margaret had promised Josh she'd watch over April until Josh returned, and she intended to keep her promise as best she could.

Margaret knocked softly, and April answered the door, looking less enthusiastic than the person Margaret had come to know. April's eyes were swollen—from crying or lack of sleep, Margaret wasn't sure. "Good morning, April. I've brought a little nourishment for you." April murmured hello, then waved her arm for her to enter.

"Are you feeling rested? As if I even need to ask. One look at you and I know the answer." April was still dressed in her dirty jeans and shirt, and Margaret made a clicking sound and shook her head. "Have a seat over there next to the dressing table." Margaret rolled the tea cart next to it, lifted the teapot cozy, and began pouring the steaming brew into a china cup.

April watched and accepted the cup of tea. "Miss Margaret . . . why do you treat me so well? I'm certainly not worth all your attention."

Margaret lifted her eyes from the tray and looked at April. "Oh, but you are, my dear. Everyone has value and worth. Just look at what you did. If you hadn't been along on that route yesterday, we may have lost Leon *and* Morgan. And you drove that stage safely to Lewistown."

"I don't know . . . I only did what anyone would have done." April sipped her tea.

Margaret adjusted the spectacles on her face before responding. "I don't believe that for one moment. You kept your head and were able to think clearly about what to do, and you gave support to Lenora. I think that was God-ordained."

"Mmm . . . don't count on that, Miss Margaret. I still didn't return with the strongbox full of money, only the mail. So I'm afraid that I'm still going to be beholden to you awhile longer. I'll understand if you want me to look for another place to stay." She reached for the toast and took a small bite.

"You'll do no such thing. I thought the sheriff said no one made off with the money?"

"That's true. They didn't, but I don't know what became of it. I guess we'll have to wait until Morgan wakes up and tells us."

"Then that's what we'll do." Margaret reassured April with a quick hug. "I wanted to personally thank you for giving Louise just the right push that she needed with her appearance. She would never listen to her mama. Since you took her in hand, Louise has a bounce in her step and a smile most of the time now. I wish I knew if the kind doctor was really interested in her." Margaret knew she couldn't interfere, but she wanted to see her daughters happy before she died.

April shrugged. "Time will tell. We mustn't let her run after him. He has to see what he's missing."

"Spoken like someone who's had some experience with love." Margaret's interest piqued, but she simply opened the curtains and pretended to look out at the street below.

"Only a little, yet enough to know that I forced my love on someone who had a hard time saying no, but he loved another," April blurted out.

Margaret jerked around to look at April, beginning now to understand what made April tick. "April, I'm so sorry."

April tossed her hair. "Don't be. I'm finally over him now, but I won't be letting that happen again."

Margaret watched as April added sugar to the oatmeal and poured cream over the mixture. Changing the subject, she asked, "How did the riding lesson go with Jane?"

"Ha! It was really something, I'll tell you. I've not had much experience with children, but she can be a little conniving."

"I thought as much. I believe Cynthia needs to be firmer with her. Tell me about Wes. Was he good with her?"

April squirmed in her chair. "To a fault he was. He was very tender and encouraging with her, and she caught on quickly."

"Were you able to get to know Wes a little better?" Margaret watched April's face for clues, but she stared down at her bowl of oatmeal.

"You might say that . . . but I hardly think we're a match just because we share a common love of horses. I already told you my father would never approve." April stirred the oatmeal before scooping a spoonful to her mouth. "This is so good."

Margaret wouldn't be deterred. "You're very lovely, April, and I know he's attracted to you. So what did he say to you? That he wanted to court you?"

April smacked her lips, then blotted them with a napkin. "He did more than that—he kissed me!"

Margaret pretended shock before suppressing a smile. She poured another cup of tea for April. "Did you like his kiss?"

"Miss Margaret, do you *really* think you should be asking me that?"

Margaret smiled and said, "Probably not, but I'm an old lady with nothing else to be concerned about except other people's welfare. And Wes and you, my dear April, are at the top of my list."

April gave her a funny look. "I suggest you take me *off* your list. I couldn't care one whit what you do about Wes. He hasn't two pennies to rub together and lives in a run-down ranch on a few meager acres."

Margaret looked at her sharply. "May I remind you that you

don't have two pennies to rub together either?" she said, poking April gently in the side with her cane. "If it wasn't for the kindness of Wes, you wouldn't have even had a clean dress to wear."

April blushed to the roots of her blonde head. "If it wasn't for Wes, I wouldn't have lost my boots and belt to a spoiled child either. My situation is temporary and you know it," she snapped back.

Margaret walked to the door and opened it. "Forgive me if I was a bit too inquisitive. I'll leave you to finish your breakfast now. But everything in this world is temporary, April. Try to remember that."

April sighed, her shoulders lifting in resignation. "How well I know that after yesterday . . . but thank you for breakfast, Miss Margaret."

Margaret nodded stiffly, knowing that she'd been too meddlesome, then slipped through the doorway and down the hall. In her own way, she wanted to help April be the best she could be. *If only she'd see Wes for the nice young man that he is . . .*

19

The clear October sky beckoned to Wes while he was out mending breaks along the property line. He was grateful for the barbed wire that kept his few steers from wandering off, but he'd snagged a hole in his shirt as he did the repair, and he had a small cut on his finger for his trouble despite his leather gloves. The weather was still warm but comfortable, and the brilliant sun was high in the sky.

He'd been working longer than he realized. He paused, removed his hat, and wiped his brow with his handkerchief, gazing at the trees along the edge of the mountain ridge. They were just beginning to change from green to a hint of subtle gold beauty. The wind stirred through their boughs, making them sway like dancers along the horizon.

Fall was Wes's favorite time of year. He loved the pungent smell of firewood burning on a leisurely afternoon. He enjoyed sitting on the front porch, a cup of coffee in his hand, or raking leaves while the delicious smells of simmering soup and corn bread in the oven tantalized his senses. In fact, he looked forward to the day he would be sharing the scene in his mind with someone close to his heart.

From the looks of things, it wouldn't be April. Wes felt a rock in his chest when he recalled what she'd said about the way he lived. He knew he was frugal and hadn't worried about keeping the place up. But now that she'd pointed it out, he realized that he'd neglected the ranch too much. Instead, he'd spent most of his time training horses and, if he was honest, at the saloon in Lewistown.

But that was before Wes started seeing life differently. He was grateful for the change in his heart. He'd always thought no one would look at him as a possible love interest in the first place. He knew he wasn't what a body would call handsome, so he'd relied on his wit and humor to get attention from the ladies. Except he had to admit it hadn't worked in the past . . . or at least not for any long-term relationships with the opposite sex. And it sure hadn't worked on April.

This week he'd taken a critical look around him and decided that his ranch had little to be desired in the way of welcoming a woman, so he'd gradually started cleaning up the place. Since he tended to get distracted easily, he made a list of things that needed to be done. He removed the pile of extra lumber from a repair he'd made on the porch last year and discarded items that until now lay covered in tall grass. He needed to replace some shingles and knew a trip to the hardware store for supplies was necessary. He knew nothing of how to make his house inviting. Maybe he should ask Juliana's advice about the inside of his home when she and Josh returned. Even Josh had asked her for suggestions on building his kitchen before the terrible fire.

Thankfully, Wes's place had been spared from the fire. Had that been just a short time ago? It seemed like years now. He smiled, thinking how God had given back so much to Josh after all his losses. He wished Josh were here to give him insight into his sister—what she was like and what made her tick. *There you go again, Wes, thinking she's gonna give you the time of day. Would you stay if you had a sprawling cattle ranch in Colorado?*

Wes just shook his head and gathered up his tools. This kind of thinking was getting him nowhere. He threw his tool bag across Dakota's back and headed back to the house to change his shirt before riding into town. He planned on taking the horse Morgan had ordered for his wife since he was going into town anyway and could save Morgan a trip.

He wondered when April would be going back to Colorado. Maybe he'd run into her somewhere around town. *Best not to get my hopes up. She made it very clear that she wouldn't live in Montana. Maybe she has a beau back in Colorado waiting on her return.* That'd make perfect sense since she was pretty and well-to-do.

He gave Dakota some oats to eat while he washed his face and hands. He stared at his reflection in the mirror as he patted his face dry. Just an average cowboy with sun-streaked hair and light stubble on his jaw, with a tinge of sunburn on an already tanned face in spite of wearing his hat. A slow smile spread across his face. He may not be the best-looking man around, but he was certain April had shared the spark between them when he'd kissed her.

He stopped, recalling the taste of her sweet lips. Had his breath smelled okay? He sure hoped so. Wes tried to be scrupulous about that because of all the times he'd smelled alcohol on his dad's breath.

Time to get going. He slicked his hair down, then donned a clean flannel shirt over his undershirt, quickly tucking it in with a cinch of his leather belt. He suddenly remembered that he needed to check on an order he'd placed at the general store too. He sighed. His list was growing. After he delivered the mare to Morgan and went by the hardware store, he'd check on little Jane before going home. Maybe she'd be ready for another lesson, and Cynthia should be home from work by then.

The town was bustling more than normal in the late afternoon when Wes rode Dakota down the street to the depot, the mare trailing behind. He wasn't expecting the stagecoach to be parked outside. He assumed Morgan was going to be gone most of the week, but he must have misunderstood him. Before he could tie the reins around the hitching post, Billy came running out and in a breathless voice told him Morgan had been shot.

"What do you mean, Billy?" Wes asked, taking the steps two at a time.

"He and Leon was robbed! Somehow the bandits knew he was carrying a strongbox with the money from the bank." Billy's eyes were big and animated.

Wes reached past Billy for the door. "Is Morgan all right?"

"He's going to be okay," Billy answered.

"Let me talk to Leon then," Wes said, striding through the door. When Billy didn't follow him and was quiet, he turned around. "Well, what are you waiting for? Tell me where they are—are they upstairs in the apartment?"

"No." Billy looked down at the floor, his voice choking. "Leon didn't make it."

Wes stopped dead in his tracks. "What? Leon was shot too?"

There was a moment of silence. "Are you telling me that Leon is dead?"

Billy's brown eyes misted as he stared up at Wes. "That's what I'm telling you," he said, his face solemn.

"Morgan's at Dr. Mark's place," a voice answered. A woman walked down the stairs and stood before him. "And you are?"

"Wes Owen, ma'am," he said, removing his hat. "You must be Lenora. I've heard some good things about you."

"I'm glad to meet you, even under these sad circumstances. I'm about to go over to see my husband. He's lost a lot of blood."

"Mind if I come along?" Wes's fingers absentmindedly rubbed the felt on his hat. "I brought Morgan's mare for you."

Lenora pulled her shawl around her shoulders and shrugged. "Suit yourself," she said, then turned to Billy. "I may not be back until late. I'm not sure when the doctor will let him come home."

"I'll stay right here, Miss Lenora. Tell Morgan not to worry about a thang!"

Lenora reached out and tousled his head affectionately. "I'm sure he'll thank you himself when he returns."

Wes followed Lenora, then pulled Billy to the side and spoke quietly. "Billy, think you could take Dakota's saddle off? I'll just leave him here and walk with Lenora. Take Lenora's mare to the barn out back. She can take a closer look at the mare when she's got her mind on it."

Lenora was polite, but they talked little on their short walk to Mark's office. Wes thought her gentle personality seemed well-suited to Morgan's. When Wes pushed open the door, a bell jangled, and he was surprised to see Miss Margaret and April talking with Mark.

Mark walked toward Lenora. "Morgan's doing well and asking for you. He's still weak and spiked a fever during the night. Beth is in there tending to him now."

Lenora's shoulders drooped in obvious relief. "I'm so glad to hear that, Mark."

"You can go on in and see him." Mark gave her a nudge.

"I just want to thank April for her quick thinking. If she hadn't been driving that stage, I don't know what I would've done," Lenora said, reaching out to take April's hand. "You're the kind of woman we need here in Montana."

April blinked her eyes and seemed embarrassed but squeezed Lenora's hand. "Just doing what came naturally to me."

"Maybe, but you are our hero, like it or not." Miss Margaret thumped her cane against the floor for emphasis and winked at Wes.

"Excuse me," Lenora murmured, and slipped past them to the room where her husband lay.

Wes stood as if his feet were nailed to the floor. He was seeing a different side of April. Softer . . . more caring. He wasn't sure why he was surprised, but he was. What did he think—that she was always looking after herself and speaking her mind? Well . . . maybe so.

"Well, boy howdy! I guess this deserves a celebration of sorts." Wes captured April's hand in his, pumping it in a firm handshake. "You'll have to tell me all about it." She was the picture of creamy churned butter in her beige homespun dress, which gave her a more feminine look than the jeans she'd worn to his ranch. Wes found her delightful and wanted to crush her to him in an embrace. Could she feel the tension in his body? He swallowed hard and blinked to clear his thoughts.

April's gaze never left his face. "You'll have to pick up the afternoon edition of the *Gazette* and read all about it. I've said about all I have to say."

"You're being modest, April, but if you folks don't mind, I have other patients to check on today," Mark said. "Morgan's in good hands with Beth and Lenora. Perhaps tomorrow he'll be up to going home when he's a little stronger."

"Don't let us keep you," Miss Margaret said. "We won't be staying. We just wanted to see how Morgan was this morning."

"Oh." Mark paused and turned back. "I almost forgot, April. Morgan told me when he woke up that he hid the money in one of *your* saddlebags, because he knew if they were robbed, the bandits would be looking for the strongbox."

April drew in a sharp breath. "So that's what he did with it! I never thought to check my own saddlebags. How clever! I guess I'm not entirely broke after all."

"In fact, he said he was wearing it over his shoulder when the bullet hit him. Even though it went through, that might have saved him from considerable injury. Anyway, the money is probably over at the depot, or Will deposited it today. Check with him about it."

"Then why didn't the robbers see it?" Wes asked, finally directing his gaze to Mark.

"I reckon they didn't figure anyone would be crazy enough to stow the money in a bag right out in the open while he was driving," Mark answered. "Either way, it turned out to be a timely idea."

Wes shifted his weight, one hand on his hip. "You got that right!"

Mark stepped up to the door. "See you folks later."

"Wait," Miss Margaret called out. "Why don't you all come to dinner tonight at the boardinghouse? It'll be good for Lenora, and we can welcome her back home."

"Excellent idea." Mark smiled. "See you all then."

Wes wasn't sure if Miss Margaret had included him or not.

"I expect you to come too, Wes," Miss Margaret said, tapping him on the arm with her cane. "Seems like you could use a home-cooked meal from the looks of those baggy jeans."

Wes jerked around at her remark, and April let out a giggle, then quickly covered her mouth. He almost said something to her but instead said, "I'd love to have dinner with everyone tonight. I have nothing better to do at home."

"Good, we'll be expecting you." Miss Margaret turned to April. "Are you ready to go now and see about your money?"

April took a step toward the door, and Wes could smell the sweet fragrance of rose water as she walked past him. His gaze flew to her eyes, which showed a momentary flicker of softness when she turned around. Or did he just imagine that?

"Yes, let's go," April said. "I've got a lot to do and I'm sure Natalie and Louise could use some help with extra guests."

Wes plopped down in a chair and waited for a chance to speak with Morgan when Lenora emerged from his room. The image of April tucked into the corner of his mind gave him a chance to daydream.

Wes hoisted the box of shingles to his shoulder and walked in the direction of the depot where he'd left his horse. He'd already checked on his order at the general store, and Earl told him it was due in any day from Texas. Wes couldn't help his excitement and could hardly wait for the package to arrive, but then he wondered if he'd jumped the gun with his idea. No time to think about that now. He'd worry about it later.

When he saw Morgan earlier, he'd been propped up in bed and smiling weakly at him, teasing him about having dinner with Miss Margaret and the girls. Wes knew it was a good sign when Morgan had his sense of humor back.

"I can tell you're better. Lenora can't wait to get you home." Wes grinned at his friend. "I brought the mare over for you since I had to come to town to get shingles for my roof."

Morgan squinted at him. "You finally gonna fix the roof? You have a burr under your saddle?" His unshaven face split with a wide smile. "Or might you be trying to impress somebody?"

Wes slapped his hat on his thigh as he stood up. "Now don't go speculatin' about things. Could be I decided it was high time to tend to chores I've neglected lately, that's all."

Morgan took a sip of water left on the bed table. "Have it your way. Just remember . . . it's easier to catch a horse than to break one."

Wes had left soon afterward, not wanting to tire Morgan—or endure more teasing about April. Now he saddled up Dakota and left Billy a tip for taking care of him, then went to Cynthia's Victorian house two blocks away. It wouldn't be long before he had supper at the boardinghouse, and the prospect of seeing April again enlivened his steps as he walked to the front door.

He stopped short when he saw movement through the curtains that covered the living room window. It looked like Jane, but that couldn't be because she was walking across the room. He couldn't believe his eyes, so he quietly drew closer to the window and peeked in. Sure enough, Jane was putting a record on the gramophone. He stepped back. He felt like an intruder, but what was she doing walking around? She wasn't even using a cane. How could that be? Wes removed his hat and scratched his head, then slapped it back on. Had she been faking it all these months? He'd soon find out.

He rapped on the front door and heard Jane's high-pitched voice cry out, "Who is it?"

"It's just Wes, Jane." Now what was he going to say? Tell her straight up that he caught her walking?

"Just a minute, please," she answered.

Wes crept to the edge of the window and saw her settle herself in the wheelchair, and moments later he heard movement in the hallway. The door swung open and Jane smiled up at him.

"Come on in. Mama will be home from work in a few minutes."

"Why don't we just sit out here on the porch instead? It's so nice outside."

"Good idea. I love sitting outside, but it's not fun by yourself." Jane adjusted the robe over her lap. "Are we going riding tomorrow?" she asked eagerly, her freckled face looking innocent.

"That's why I dropped by. I wanted to see if there's been any improvement in the feeling in your legs or not." Wes took a seat in the rocker facing Jane, anxious to hear her answer.

Jane fumbled around with her response. "Well . . . I . . . I think maybe a little tingling in my legs sometimes—"

"Really? Well, goodness, Jane! That's great. Have you tried to stand at all with your cane?" He watched the expression on her face as she seemed to struggle with her answer while picking at the threads in her lap robe.

"Not yet . . ." She wouldn't meet his gaze.

"Why not? I should think you would be excited at the prospect of any feeling in your legs. Have you told your mother or Dr. Barnum?" *Okay, Wes, go easy on her.*

"I'm not ready to say anything because I still can't walk."

Wes cleared his throat and plunged right in. "Jane, I saw you through the window just now as I was coming up the steps. You were *not* in your wheelchair—you were walking around the room."

Jane's face blanched. The silence hung between them. "You were seeing things, Wes!" she sputtered.

"Is that so? Then why do you look like the cat that ate the canary?" Wes stared at her, leaning toward her so they were at eye level.

Tears sprang up in her eyes. "Please don't tell anyone. I'll be in big trouble," she pleaded.

Wes shook his head and picked up her small hands in his. "Jane, Jane . . . why are you lying about this?"

Jane shrugged. "I don't really know. At first I really couldn't move my legs. Then everyone started being nicer to me, noticing me. Or giving me gifts." She paused as tears started rolling down her face. "When I realized that I could walk, I didn't want anyone to know. I've never had so much attention since my father was alive." She hiccupped. "I miss him so much, and with Mama working, I'm all alone." Wes handed her his handkerchief, and she wiped her eyes. "Are you angry with me?"

"No, I'm not angry, just trying to understand all of this. How long were you going to let this go on?"

Jane blew her nose loudly. "I don't know. If I tell Mama, she's going to be so mad at me that she'll hate me."

"No, she won't. She'll be so happy that her little girl can go run and play and do things for herself. I know because once I fell off an ornery horse and broke my arm. I enjoyed all the attention from my mama, so even when it felt better, I lied and pretended I was much worse. Mama would read to me and bake special cookies for me. I didn't have to do any of the zillion chores on the ranch before and after school that my daddy made me responsible for." Wes laughed and sat back in his chair. "Yep! I thought I had it made until the other boys at school started playing baseball when school was out. That's all it took for my 'miracle.' Suddenly I was cured! But you know what? Now that I think about it, I believe she knew all along that my arm had mended before I let on, but she protected me. If my daddy had known, he would've whipped me something terrible."

Jane's eyes were wide. "Really? Do you think my mother knows?"

Wes narrowed his eyes and answered, "I don't know, Jane, but you have to tell her. It's not fair to your mother. She adores you, and I've noticed sometimes you don't speak kindly to her."

Jane sat with downcast eyes. "I don't know how I can do that. She's gonna skin me alive."

"I have a little idea." He had Jane's full attention now. "You said you were feeling more in your legs after riding. You could start with that. Tell her tonight and then let her warm up to the idea that you are getting better; then after our lessons in a couple of days, you can try standing."

"But isn't that lying?"

"No more than what you've been doing, Jane. I'm just giving you a way to tell the truth slowly. Or you could just tell the whole truth. It's not my story, but you do have to do something about it." There was silence between them, and a bird chirped loudly, calling to its mate.

Finally Jane said, "You aren't going to tell Mama?" Jane looked baffled and handed him the dirty handkerchief.

"No, I won't. You have to do that, however you decide." Wes could see that Jane was filtering this information in her head.

"Okay." She sighed. "I'll decide tonight. But why are you doing this? You should be mad too, teaching me to ride and always running over here checking on me for Josh and Juliana. I've lied to them too, and to my friend Marilee, I guess because she has wonderful parents and she's so pretty. She has the nicest things and prettiest dresses."

"I'll say a little prayer for you," he said softly. He gave her shoulder an affectionate pat, then stood. "I've got to leave now. Don't compare what you have to what Marilee has, Jane. Things are nice to own, but they don't always mean you'll be happy." He started down the steps and stopped next to Dakota. "If you want, tell your mother that I dropped by and we'll do a lesson on Wednesday. Maybe April can join us."

"Wes, thanks for being my friend," Jane said.

Leather squeaked as he pulled himself into the saddle and gathered the reins. Wes smiled at the girl. "You have many friends, Jane. All you have to do is look around you."

April was anxious to get to the depot and retrieve her money. It tickled her that Morgan had the foresight not to use the strongbox. Thanks to him, her money as well as the bank's was safe. She walked a little slower than usual with Miss Margaret with her, but April enjoyed her company. "I really like Lenora," she commented.

"Oh, so do I. She's been so good for Morgan," Miss Margaret agreed.

"It's unfortunate that she's been away so long," April said as they drew closer to the stage depot. She could see Billy up ahead sweeping off the waiting area.

"Yes, it is. Sometimes we have no control over the hardships of life. We just have to be able to deal with them with the Lord's help."

"Mmm, perhaps you're right, Miss Margaret. I've been trying to talk to Him about things that I've been wrestling with, and I think it's helping me."

As they strolled along, April admired the trees. "Have you noticed the leaves are just beginning to change?"

"I have indeed. Our nights are getting colder too. I just love autumn. It's a time of reflection for me when I see the dazzling colors of fall, before the trees lie dormant and winter sets in and the leaves turn to dust. Much like Leon will." Her voice was reverent.

April cast a glance at the tiny lady with curiosity. "Do you think that even if we turn into dust, we'll go to heaven?"

Miss Margaret stopped on the sidewalk, placing both hands on her cane. "Indeed I do, April. Scripture says believe on the Lord and you *shall*—not *might*—be saved. I don't know whether or not Leon believed in the Lord, but I hope so. He did show up from time to time at church, and none of the Lord's words are ever wasted. But we can't always know someone's heart based on whether they're in church every Sabbath." She sighed deeply. "When you have time, look up 1 Thessalonians. I believe it's in chapter 4 that Scripture tells us the Lord will descend from heaven one day. Those who've passed on and those who are still alive and believe in the Lord will be taken up to heaven." Miss Margaret looked wistfully up at the blue sky, and April followed her gaze. "I long for heaven when I can be with my dear, dear husband. But I know that right now my work on earth isn't done."

April was quiet a moment. "I wish that everyone had that confidence in their hearts."

"Me too, April. It's pride that keeps men from humbling themselves to their Creator. But we get the opportunity to show that assurance every time we share with people who are hurting or hungry. It's mainly taking our focus off ourselves and placing it on how we can best live out our faith in love."

"Miss Margaret, I guess you've lived long enough to learn how to figure people out from experience. You've taught me so much in the short time I've been here. About life and how to give consideration for others before I reach my own conclusions."

"And you, my dear girl, are making me proud to be looking after you while Josh is gone."

April marveled how she was able to be her true self with Miss Margaret. She surely would miss her when she returned to Colorado.

They continued their walk in companionable silence. Billy stopped sweeping to greet them. "Two of my favorite ladies!" He beamed, leaning against his broom handle.

"Now where'd you learn such flattery, Billy?" Miss Margaret teased.

Billy grinned and shuffled toward the door to open it for them. "From Wes," he said with a lopsided smile.

"Of course!" April rolled her eyes at him and grinned.

"Follow me inside and I'll go get Will for you. He figured you'd be coming once you found out what Morgan did with the money. That was a smart idea. I heard that if it hadn't been for you, Morgan might even be dead by now."

April shook her head. "I hardly think that's true, Billy. I just drove the stagecoach. You could have done it yourself."

The two ladies entered the office area, and Will walked over. "Miss April," he said, handing her the saddlebags that she'd taken on the trip. "There's a nice round hole right through one of your bags, which probably saved Morgan's life, the doctor said. He'd draped it across his shoulder on the ride, and the bullet went right through the bag then ricocheted upward into his shoulder instead of his heart."

"Oh my goodness!" April took the saddlebags from him and reached inside one of them. She pulled out her Bible and ran her hand over the smooth leather. There was a gaping hole in the dead center of the "H" in the words "Holy Bible." A slight shiver went down her spine as she thought about the danger they'd been in. "God protected him," she whispered.

"He sure did, but He used you to do it, and we must be grateful," Miss Margaret said, touching April on the sleeve. Turning to Will, she asked, "Who's going to drive the stage while Morgan heals?"

"I'm not sure. For now tickets have been suspended, since we've lost a good driver and Morgan's laid up." Will's face saddened, then he looked at April. "Unless, of course, you want to drive the stagecoach?"

"I could do it!" Billy's eyes were wide with enthusiasm. "But not alone."

April smiled affectionately at her young friend. "I'm not sure I want to." April shoved the Bible back inside and looked through the other bag. It was empty, so she threw it over her shoulder. "Right now, I'm looking for the money that was probably in this bag, Will."

Will raised up his hand. "Just a moment." He scurried back behind the ticket counter and handed her the envelope of money. "Here ya go, Miss April. I checked the manifesto for the money and counted yours out. I took the rest of the deposit to the Fergus Bank. I'm sure they'd want our 'hero' to be paid. It's all been squared away." He paused and scratched his head. "Shoot! There ought to be a reward coming."

"Thank you, Will." April put the money in her handbag.

"Miss April, will you let me know the next time you take Jane for her riding lesson? I'd love to come along." Billy stood with his hands in his pockets with a sheepish smile. "I think Jane's a nice girl. In fact, she beat me at chess while you were gone, but I bet I can outride her."

April laughed. "I bet you can too." April's skirts swished as she walked to the door with Miss Margaret following her. "Sure thing. I'll be seeing Wes tonight, so I'll ask him when he wants me to bring Jane back out. I'd like to know how she's doing too. Tell you what—you can ride Sassy if Miss Margaret will loan me a horse for the wagon to take Jane."

"Of course. Anytime you have need of a horse is okay with me."

Billy was clearly happy. "Oh goodness, I can hardly wait. Since my horse died, I've been without my best friend in the world." He hurried to open the door for them, and as he did, a gust of wind billowed around their skirts.

April held her palms against her skirts, exclaiming, "I believe fall has arrived, Miss Margaret." She turned back to Billy. "Sassy will love the attention, I'm sure. I'll have to help you figure out a way to get your own horse so you'll have a friend once again," she said with a wink.

Back outside, Miss Margaret told April that she wanted to pick up some embroidery thread at the mercantile. "Would you like to go with me before we return to the boardinghouse? I think Louise and Natalie will have everything under control for supper. We have just enough time before Earl closes his doors."

Instantly April had an idea. "Miss Margaret, I'd just love to."

April took her arm, pretending she hadn't seen the questioning look on Miss Margaret's face. "I may have a thing or two to buy."

The two hurried to get to the mercantile before Earl locked up. "You ladies are in luck. What can I do for you?" he asked.

"I need some scarlet embroidery thread for a piece I'm working on," Miss Margaret said.

"Right this way. I'll see if we have any in stock."

Miss Margaret followed him to the other side of the store. April cast a glance around the store until she saw Mabel and rushed over to her.

Mabel was getting ready to leave and was tidying up the sales counter. "Why, Miss April. It's you again. How can I help you?" She seemed a bit more cheerful than the last time.

"Do you remember the dress that Natalie had you hold for her?" When Mabel looked thoughtful and then nodded, April continued. "Could you go get it for me? I wish to buy it."

"I don't know about that . . . Natalie has her heart set on it."

"I know she put some money down for you to hold it, but I'd like to pay off the remainder of the balance for her as a gift."

Mabel hesitated. "I guess I could let you do that. That would be a nice surprise for her." She moved to go to the back.

"I'm in kind of a hurry, if you don't mind."

"I see. I'll be only a moment." Mabel scooted behind the curtained doorway to the storage room.

April looked around nervously. She didn't want anyone to see her purchase the dress. But true to her word, Mabel was back in a flash with the dress.

"Could you please ring it up and wrap it for me before Miss Margaret walks back over here?" April chewed her bottom lip.

245

"Yes. Step this way, Miss April." Mabel folded the sage green dress, laid it between sheets of brown paper, and wrapped it up, then tied a sturdy string around it. April paid for the purchase and thanked her, hardly waiting for Mabel's reply. She was so pleased that she could afford to buy the dress now. She hugged the package to her chest as Earl and Miss Margaret came to the counter and prayed they wouldn't ask her what it was.

Dinner was one of the most enjoyable meals April had had since becoming a boarder. Miss Margaret's big dining room table was filled with all her newly found friends. From the looks of the table laden with roast beef, potatoes, peas, rolls, and apple pie for dessert, one would have thought they were celebrating a holiday. Willard and May were able to join them, and some of the color had returned to Willard's cheeks. April watched the affection May bestowed—she constantly patted him on the arm and listened intently to everything he said. Before his heart attack, their constant display of affection had nauseated April, but now she understood why. They were soul mates, and May had been so afraid of losing him. Miss Margaret had said that God spared Willard for a little while longer. April would consider herself lucky to be married as long as the two of them and have someone still be so in love with her.

Wes sat directly across the table from her, with Natalie to his left. Watching Natalie, April had no doubt she had her eye on Wes, who was polite but didn't seem to return her fondness. His eyes caught April's and he winked at her, making her heart race. His rugged, tanned face spoke of hours working with his horses under Montana's wide-open skies, and when he lifted his water glass, the backs of his hands were as bronze as his face. April recalled how his hands had gently guided the mare for Jane and how his fingers had tenderly stroked April's face. She could almost feel his touch now, and she hoped her face didn't reveal just how flustered she was. She picked up her fork and knife and attacked the roast beef but found herself no longer hungry, the meat forming a lump too big to swallow. She sensed Wes's eyes on her.

Willard paused in his eating to press his napkin to his lips and looked over at April. "Young lady, you are the hero of the day!"

April could feel the heat in her cheeks. "I only reacted as anyone else probably would in the situation. Lenora did her part too."

Willard smiled back at her, then directed a question to Lenora, who sat between Louise and April. "I hear from Miss Margaret that Morgan is doing well, Lenora?"

"Yes, he is doing well, and he may get to come home tomorrow. Thank you for asking," Lenora said. "But I really do have to thank April for her quick wit—I'm afraid I couldn't think straight and only got angry." Lenora directed her gaze to April.

April laughed unabashedly. "Lenora was quite the actress. And you should have seen her trying to attack the bandit."

"Let's toast to April, shall we?" Mark said, lifting his water glass. Everyone at the table did likewise, and he said, "Here, here! To April, for her ability to handle not only a bad situation but a team of six horses as well." Mark finished his toast, then clinked his glass against Louise's, and the others did likewise. Happy chatter filled the room, and April felt that she was truly among friends for the first time in a long while.

"All right, enough of that now. I'm thankful that Morgan survived, but I'm very sorry about Leon." April saw that Natalie had leaned in close to Wes, touching his arm as they toasted. April quickly looked over at Miss Margaret. "Did Leon have any family?"

"He has a sister still living in Bozeman, and his remains will be sent there to be buried," Miss Margaret answered.

"He was a nice guy and always friendly. I believe Billy took it kinda hard." Wes looked in April's direction, his face somber.

April laid down her fork. "I have to agree. I want to talk to you later about how we might cheer him up." She beamed at Wes, but he made no comment, nor did he give her one of his usual wide smiles.

Natalie suddenly sat up straighter. "Let me know if there's anything I can do to help."

Lenora changed the subject and glanced over at Beth. "Beth, you are doing wonders with Morgan. He listens to your instructions better than mine."

April listened to Lenora's pleasant-sounding Southern voice, which brought to mind another Southerner she knew, Crystal Clark . . . which also reminded her that Luke had married Crystal and not her. But that was all in the past now, and she didn't intend to look back.

Beth gave a nervous laugh. "I do what I can. I'm afraid my father left no wiggle room when it came to his instructions on how to care for the sick. I find your husband has a great sense of humor, Lenora."

"Oh, he does, all right. He keeps me in good spirits, yet he's the one wounded." Lenora's laugh was soft, just like the gentle tone of her voice.

Louise, who had been unusually quiet, stood up. "I'll make a fresh batch of coffee and we can all retire to the parlor. Perhaps Willard might be a little more comfortable there."

Mark rose. "I'll come help," he said, surprising Louise.

"There's no need," she said nervously, moving to clear the dinner plates.

Mark wouldn't be deterred. "I can help with the cups and saucers."

Louise, let him help. April wanted to use Miss Margaret's cane to nudge her. Louise glanced over at April, who gave her a quick look without being too obvious.

"In that case, I could use your help," Louise said. "Come with me."

Miss Margaret caught April's eye and winked, a smile on her wrinkled face.

"I think I'll pass on the coffee if you don't mind, folks," Willard said, pushing back his chair. "But May, why don't you go ahead without me?" He gave her a pat on the hand.

May got up and hooked her arm through her husband's. "You can't get rid of me that easy. I'll get you comfy and then read you some more of the adventures of Sherlock Holmes." They said their good nights to everyone and strolled arm in arm down the hallway to their bedroom.

Lenora thanked Miss Margaret for the meal and left to go check on Morgan. The rest moved to the parlor while they waited for Mark and Louise to bring the coffee.

"It's a bit drafty in this room. Wes, would you build us a nice fire so we can be comfortable and chat?"

"I'll be happy to do that for you." Wes bent down to start the fire.

April watched him scrape ashes into a bucket, then place several logs on the grate. Her eyes went directly to his taut muscles beneath the flannel shirt tucked into his jeans, and April got a good view of his trim waistline and slim hips. His hair nearly reached his collar, but it was nicely trimmed. He took a match from the tin box and struck it on his boot heel, making the spurs jingle. Moments later, a bright fire flickered, lending a soft ambience to the room and casting shadows along the walls. It felt cozy and comfortable to April. If someone had told her a few weeks ago she'd be enjoying a quiet evening in a boardinghouse in Montana, chatting by the fireplace with people of all backgrounds, she would have laughed in their face. It made her wonder why her father was so snooty when it came to his acquaintances. All she knew now was that she didn't want to be just like her father anymore.

Natalie sat on the settee, and from her pining look at Wes, April knew she wanted him to sit with her, but he stood instead, one arm propped across the mantle, watching the blaze burn with a thoughtful look. April took the chair next to Miss Margaret.

Beth sat down next to Natalie and heaved a weary sigh. "I didn't realize how tired I was." She leaned her head back against the settee's wooden trim. "I guess I'm not used to standing as much as I did today."

Miss Margaret, who was happily settled in her rocking chair, gave Beth a sympathetic look. "I'm sure it was hard on you, after not working for a while since baby Anne's birth. Mark is glad to have you working for him."

"Yes, I didn't realize how much I missed it. And Nellie's sister has agreed to watch Anne while I work. My life hasn't been the same since my husband died from pneumonia." Beth's bottom lip trembled.

"I'm so sorry, Beth," April murmured. "I can't imagine raising a child alone."

Beth dabbed her nose with her handkerchief. "Thank you. It will be difficult, but I know the Lord will provide. But I felt I had to get a fresh start in a different town, against my father's wishes. Little Anne was only a month old when my husband took sick."

April's heart twisted. *How terrible to lose your husband so young and be left to find work with a baby to raise.* "I can only imagine."

Natalie patted Beth's wrist. "You have us now, and we are all more than willing to help in any way we can."

Miss Margaret nodded. "You can count on us. Anything you need, just let us know. We all adore little Anne, so it won't be hard."

"Thank you all so very much," Beth said with a smile.

April looked up to see Louise and Mark enter, chatting amiably. He held a tray of teacups, and she carried a tray of coffee, sugar, and cream. Louise's countenance seemed to have heightened, judging by the pinkness of her face. She filled the teacups, and Mark started to hand them around.

"Is everyone going to the mayor's event in the square this weekend?" Mark asked.

"My son was telling me about that." Miss Margaret stirred her coffee. "He said it's something to do with land, I think."

"Mmm . . . I believe it is." Mark reached across the tray, taking another cup from Louise.

"I'm sure it must be newsworthy if Albert was asked to cover it in the newspaper." Margaret sipped her coffee, pleasure filling her round face.

"When are they doing this?" Wes asked. He moved to take a cup from Mark as he expressed his thanks.

"It'll be Sunday afternoon and should be like other political events. Usually the band plays anthems, and there are typically other speakers besides the mayor. It'll be held on the square and decorated with red, white, and blue flags. The ladies usually set up lemonade and cookies for refreshments." Mark's hands seemed to be at home handing out the china cups. "It makes the entire event very festive," he added. He followed Louise across the room to the vacant overstuffed chairs with a small table between them. April was so glad that Mark *did* seem interested in Louise and caught Miss Margaret watching them once or twice.

"Well then, we should all attend as citizens. It may affect us." Wes strolled nearer to April's seat.

"I agree. Now my interest is piqued." Miss Margaret turned to Beth and asked if she knew how to play chess.

"I do. Would you like to play a game?" Beth answered.

"No, not me. I've never cared for the game, but Natalie likes it, don't you, dear?" Miss Margaret smiled at her daughter.

"I'm no expert, but I do enjoy the game." Natalie rose to retrieve the board game and pieces from the secretary. "We can sit next to the fire, Beth. Drag your chair up close."

"All right. I can play a short while before I'll have to go check on Anne. She was fast asleep earlier, but I'll have to listen for her in case she wakes." Natalie took a seat and they set the pieces up while Miss Margaret looked on.

April was acutely aware of Wes's nearness. She held tightly to her cup and saucer, afraid that her trembling hands would betray her. What had happened to her this last week? Hadn't she sworn that another man would not own her heart?

Wes leaned down and whispered in April's ear, startling her. "Would you care to go for a walk, April? We can discuss your idea on how to cheer up Billy."

April was caught off guard and looked up at him in surprise. "I'd like that very much." She rose from her chair and caught Natalie's deflated face when she looked up from the chessboard. "I'm sorry," April mouthed.

"Better grab your wrap. It's chilly." Wes strode past Louise and Mark and followed April into the foyer, where she donned her woolen cape. Wes wore his brown duster and cowboy hat. He placed his hand on the small of her back when she walked through the door to the porch. She felt a tingle down her spine and took a quick breath.

The glittering stars filled the velvety black sky like a million diamond fragments, and the moon shone brightly. It was the perfect night for an intimate stroll. Laughter and music could be heard from the saloon down the road on the other side. April drew her cape together against autumn's chill as she and Wes walked toward the quieter streets of town. Except for a passing wagon or the few people out walking to various destinations, all was quiet, punctuated only by Wes's spurs jingling with each step on the sidewalk.

After a few minutes, Wes broke the silence. "I wanted to tell you how proud I was of how you handled the robbery situation and the stagecoach, April. But I'm not surprised at all. You're strong as well as a good horsewoman." He paused and looked down at her face. The moon lit one side of Wes's face, making his light-colored hair appear as blonde as hers. His square jawline was clearly outlined, and April controlled the urge to reach up and touch it.

"Everyone is making it a big deal, Wes, but honestly, I just reacted." She laughed. "Maybe I'm better under pressure."

"Nah, don't think so. Just look when I pressured you the other day with that kiss. I'm afraid all I did was aggravate you, and that was not my intent, I assure you," he said hoarsely.

April felt a twinge of regret. "Wes, I . . . I really like you, a whole lot. But what good would it do to be more than friends? You already know that I intend to go back to Colorado. There are some big differences about us too."

"Meaning, you're from a wealthy family and I'm just a would-be rancher and horse trainer?"

She directed her gaze to his, and their eyes held. Her heart sped up. "That's partly true, but I don't want to hurt your feelings." April moistened her lips, and his eyes narrowed. "Wes, don't you see that Natalie's set her heart on you?"

Wes leaned against a hitching rail and folded his arms across his chest. "I did notice, but I don't feel that way about her. Anyway, I want to talk about you. Are you telling me I don't even have a chance with you because you're looking for a rich man?" His face hardened.

"That's not what I meant at all, so don't get your spurs all tangled up. I never said that I was looking for anyone," April said. "There would have to be lots of compromises for both of us to deal with."

Wes let his arms drop to his sides. "So you have given this some thought, or you wouldn't have said that. We can work those things out." He gave her an endearing half smile that charmed her, and she saw a dimple in one cheek that she hadn't noticed before.

"I'm very neat and like things simple but nice," April reminded him.

"I'm a clutter bug, but I would try harder."

"I want a home large enough to have friends or family stay over." April waved her hands.

"I can add on to the ranch house."

"My father won't like you."

"I'll respect your father."

"I want to train horses too."

"We'll be partners."

"I can't cook."

"I can."

"I'm spoiled."

"I'll rein you in."

"But I love Colorado."

"You'll grow to love Montana and we can visit Colorado." Wes shifted on his feet.

"Hmm . . . that sounds like a proposal to me." April licked her lips, then pressed her hands into the folds of her cape.

Wes reached for her hands and pulled her to him. He smelled clean but manly as she felt the taut muscles in his arms. She liked the feel of them wrapped around her, and her gaze flew to his lips, which were curled in a sensuous smile. "I'd like to work on that, April," he said huskily.

April's heart beat wildly against her ribcage. Tenderly he reached out, stroked her cheek, and moved a strand of hair from her face, and she heard his breath quicken. His gaze bore through her, and she tilted her face up to his with a clear invitation. That was all he needed. He tightened his grip around her and leaned down to press her upturned lips in a tender, deep kiss.

April's eyes drifted shut, enjoying the moment. His kiss overwhelmed her very being. Nothing else seemed to matter, and she melted into him. Wes shuddered. He hesitated, then repeated the kiss, stroking her shoulders and back until she felt a deep longing she thought she'd put away forever after Luke. He folded her into his arms, and she rested against the soft flannel of his shirt and closed her eyes. Wes kissed the top of her head and then rested his cheek against it, expelling a deep sigh.

After what seemed a very long time, April pulled herself from his embrace, though she longed to stay there forever. "Wes . . . there's just one other thing that's been bothering me."

"What is it?" Wes's brow furrowed with a questioning look as she stepped back.

April took a deep breath to calm her ignited feelings for him. "That day I saw you going to the saloon—"

"Don't worry about that," he said with a wave of his hand.

"I'm not so naive that I don't know what goes on there." She pressed on. "That's another difference between us. It's one that I just won't tolerate from any man."

He looked as though he'd been slapped in the face, and April was sorry for that, but she had to tell him what that meant to her. She'd already loved one man who'd been in love with another woman, and she wouldn't let it happen again.

"April, that was only—"

April held up her hand. "Please don't deny that you frequent there, Wes. I've heard other people say so."

"Don't say that." Wes took a step toward her, but she backed away. "You would listen to gossip before asking me?" His temper flared, but he waited, shoulders stiff.

"Well, I know what I saw that day. You *did* go into that saloon, and I can't help but wonder why you haven't married before now," April scoffed.

"What are you saying?" He implored her with his eyes.

April's throat closed, and she was unable to speak.

Wes looked at her with hurt in his eyes. "Think what you will." He clamped his jaw shut, then wheeled around on his heel with spurs jangling and headed down the street, leaving April rooted to the spot.

"Well, I never," she sputtered and stomped her foot. "The saloon's still open, you know," April yelled at him, but he never stopped. She watched as he strode back to where he'd left Dakota, shoulders slumped, head down. The sight made her sad, and her anger melted. She lifted her skirts to hurry after him, but by then it was too late. He had disappeared into the dark night.

Miss Margaret was the only one in the parlor by the time April returned to the boardinghouse. She sat by the fire dozing, her fingers curled loosely around her Bible in her lap and her mouth slack. She looked so old tonight, and April felt a tug in her heart for the older lady. April started to tiptoe past the doorway, but Miss Margaret stirred.

"Is that you, April?"

April really didn't want to stop and talk right now, but to be respectful, she paused at the doorway. "I didn't want to disturb you. Where is everyone?"

Miss Margaret motioned for her to come in. "Come warm yourself by the fire," she said, pulling herself up. "Louise and Mark picked up all the dishes and they're still in the kitchen. Beth has gone to bed, and I think Natalie went to her room." She frowned. "Natalie seemed perturbed when you left, and I have a good idea why."

April plodded over to the fireplace and stood with her back to the low-burning embers not offering much heat now. "It's Wes, isn't it?"

"I'm afraid it is," Miss Margaret answered. She pushed her wire spectacles up on the bridge of her nose. "I don't want to see her hurt, but it's as plain as the nose on your face that Wes has no real interest other than friendship with her, and never has. But that hasn't stopped her from caring for him."

April plopped down in the chair opposite Miss Margaret. "Well, he might be interested now." She stared into the fire as if the answer to her dilemma could be found there.

Miss Margaret leaned forward, her watery eyes big. "You don't say? What happened on your walk?"

"I hurt Wes's feelings again." April's voice cracked, but she would not cry. Even now she could remember how wonderful it had felt to be in his embrace.

"How so? It's plain to me that he cares for you, April."

April felt sick to her stomach. "Our walk was wonderful until I asked him about the time I saw him go into the saloon. I think he took it all wrong, and I'm afraid I didn't give him a chance to explain. Then he clammed up and wouldn't say another word and left." April felt her eyes sting behind her lids. "But Miss Margaret, it won't work between us. We both have terrible tempers. I'm afraid that we'll never agree on anything. We're as different as day and night." April bit her bottom lip and looked at Miss Margaret, who shook her head and made a "tsk tsk" sound with her tongue.

"That's not true and you know it. I think you're afraid to let someone love you, but I'm not entirely sure why."

The truth of her words pierced April. She shrugged. "I was once very much in love with a man. His name was Luke, and we were engaged. I made all the wedding plans. Trouble was, he loved someone else and had a hard time telling me the truth. He let me go on believing a lie. Then I felt like a fool and was embarrassed to show my face in Steamboat Springs." She sighed, letting her shoulders sag, and stared at her hands in her lap. "Josh was in love with the same woman Luke loved—Crystal. After Luke finally told me how he felt, it took me two years to get over him, but I finally realized that I wouldn't want someone who doesn't love me totally and completely."

Margaret leaned in toward April, intent on catching every word. Tears spilled out and ran down April's cheeks, and Margaret's heart ached along with April's.

"Wes makes me feel like a woman whose heart is eager to love, but tonight when I asked him about going to the saloon, he told me that it wasn't anything to worry about. We argued. I don't want to share him or feel the pain that I did with Luke. Can you understand?" April sniffed.

Margaret got up and stood next to April, then placed an arm around her shoulders and handed her a handkerchief. She waited quietly as April shed her tears. Crying was good for the soul sometimes, and maybe April had never truly let out the pain of losing Luke. A few minutes later, she lifted her head and wiped her nose.

Margaret chose her words carefully. "Dear one, love is always a risk, and sometimes there is a high price to pay for true love. Luke was probably never meant to be the one for you. We frequently make bad choices when it comes to life's biggest decisions, based on how we think things should be, and when our expectations fail, we think somehow it's our fault. But you must not blame yourself. Lean on the Lord's unfailing love for guidance. It was unfortunate that Luke couldn't admit his true feelings sooner, but don't let that keep you from trusting again."

Margaret returned to her chair, and April straightened. April's pretty eyes were red-rimmed, and her face reflected her pain.

"I see you much stronger than you see yourself," Margaret said. "You were the gal who rode into town looking like a man and confronted Wes. You kicked up the dust like a cowboy heading into the stockyards when you arrived for Josh's wedding. And though you were used to the finest things in life, you decided to stay with us instead of moving to the Stockton Hotel." Margaret chuckled, and April forced a smile. "You're also the sweet gal who's kindhearted to Billy and Jane. When people laughed at you behind your back, you shrugged it off. You brought my daughter Louise out of her shell, and I'm so grateful to you for that. You stayed calm in a difficult circumstance and brought Morgan, Lenora, and the bank's money home safe and sound. That's something to be proud of, April. I don't think of you the same way I did when I first met you at the wedding. You're becoming more tenderhearted in spite of yourself," she said with a little chortle.

"You can see all that?" April's eyes widened in disbelief.

"I certainly can. You don't give yourself much credit, but that's okay. I suggest that you talk to Wes. Give him time to think and then go to him. Unless I'm a doddering old woman, he'll come around. His pride was wounded. But most of all, give him a chance to explain. I have a feeling you'll be surprised at the answer."

April blinked at her. "I guess I was accusatory at the very least. I'll think about what you said."

"Why don't you and Sassy take a ride over to Josh's ranch in the morning? Andy and Nellie will be happy to see you and show you around before Josh and Juliana return. It'll take your mind off things, and the ride will do you a world of good." Margaret rose and laid her Bible on the table next to her chair. "Let's go up to bed now, shall we?"

"I just remembered. I have a gift for Natalie." April's face brightened.

"You do? See, you're already thinking outside yourself." Margaret smiled and thought Josh would be very pleased at the new April when he returned. Margaret's prayers were being answered. She'd never had a doubt that they would.

The moon lit the trail back to the Rusty Spur. Dakota knew the way, and Wes let him poke along and stop for a drink from the stream. The moon's silvery light glittered across the water, which rushed over the rocks, its soothing sound peaceful on this cool, autumn night. He was in no hurry to return to his lonely house. Maybe he should get a dog. One just like Shebe. She was a friendly dog. At least a dog would be someone to come home to and sleep near his feet on a cold Montana night.

April's face was uppermost in his mind, and he tried to push it aside. She was right. They *were* different, but the difference was that he was willing to test out his love for her. He would risk it because he was sure he loved her. He sighed and admitted that he was smitten with her. Her very presence, her feistiness, her long legs in her jeans, that silky blonde hair, and those luscious eyes made him go weak in the knees. The way she walked and talked and softened in his arms . . .

Oh, Lord, help me. She doesn't want me. I'm not good enough for her. Maybe I'm not good enough for any woman, or I'd be married by now. I've been talking to You now for a while, and I guess I don't see Your answer for me. I don't want to make her unhappy, but I can't give her everything she has in Colorado. I'm in the dust now, completely discouraged. Please revive me with Your Word.

He decided he'd just back off and let April go back home. He'd put her totally out of his mind except as a sweet memory he could pull out from time to time, like he did his mother's cedar chest.

April hurried to her room to get the dress for Natalie. Everything always made more sense to her after talking with Miss Margaret. She was usually right about everything. April thought about her own mother and missed her. She hoped she was having a wonderful time on the anniversary trip and could hardly wait to see her again. The thought made her stop short. Since when had she thought about her mother that way? Usually it was her dad she was dying to talk to.

Since you started talking to Me and Miss Margaret.

April felt a strange tingle go down her back, but it was true. She was beginning to see her mother in a completely different light now.

She picked up the package in her room, rapped on Natalie's door, and heard the padding of feet crossing the floor. The door opened, and Natalie stood there in her nightgown, her long dark hair in a plait down her back and a book in one hand.

"What do you want, April?" Natalie's tone was curt. "I'm busy reading."

"I can see that. What book do you have there?"

Natalie gave her a cool look. "If you must know, it's *Little Women.*"

April stood in the doorway and wondered if Natalie would ask her in. Apparently not. "That's a wonderful book. Mind if I come in?" This wasn't going to be easy, she realized.

Natalie shrugged. "I guess." She stepped aside to let April in.

"Natalie, I'm really sorry if your feelings have been hurt where Wes is concerned. Wes and I took a walk tonight, that's all."

Natalie took a seat on her bed, tucking one bare foot under her, and gestured for April to have a seat. "What makes you think I care? It's none of my business what you do." She placed her book to the side.

"I don't want to hurt your feelings because you're my friend, but I need to be honest with you. I do care about Wes. That's no lie. I think he cares for me too, but I don't see a future for us. I know that you like him—"

"Not anymore. It's obvious to me now that he was only being a friend to me, nothing more. How could I have been so blind?" Natalie plucked at a thread on the blanket.

"Natalie, you weren't blind, you just saw what you wanted to see. Sometimes we do that when we don't have control over another person, hoping that the feeling is mutual." April reached out and touched Natalie's hand. "I'm truly sorry, but let's just say I have a little experience with loving someone who didn't love me in return. I don't want the same thing to happen to you."

"I know it's not your fault, really. I guess he wanted to be friends and I misread that. I shouldn't have snapped at you. I'm sorry."

"There is no need to say you're sorry. Believe me, I do understand." April handed her the brown paper package. "Here, I bought something for you."

Natalie took the package. "What's this? A peace offering?"

April bit her tongue to keep from snapping back. The old April would have, regardless of Natalie's feelings. "No, give me a little credit. I'd already bought this before I knew you would be upset with me. Open it."

Natalie untied the string and ripped the paper away, revealing the sage green dress. "Oh, April! It's that dress I wanted," she exclaimed, blinking away tears. "You shouldn't have done this. It know it cost a small fortune!" Natalie jumped off the bed and held the dress up to her body.

"Call it an early birthday gift. I know you have one coming up in a few weeks, but I'll be back in Colorado by then, I'm sure." April slipped off the bed. "You could turn any man's head in that dress. It suits you."

"You think so?" Natalie twirled around, her eyes shining with hope. "Of course, I have to find an eligible man to flirt with first." She giggled.

"You will. Don't worry. Anyone as pretty as you and as nice . . . Well, the right one hasn't come along yet. But he will. Just wait on the Lord, Natalie."

Natalie gave her a serious look. "Sounds like you've been talking to Mother."

"I have. Talking to her has helped me so much. She's been a great encourager to me. You have a precious mother, and that has made me miss my own."

"Yes, Louise and I are very blessed. But I'm blessed with your friendship too. Are you sure you won't stay, April?"

April shook her head. "Only until my brother returns, then I'll stay a few days and visit with him before I leave. My parents will be home soon."

"We'll miss you."

"Then you'll have to come and visit in Colorado," April said as she walked to the door to leave.

"I'd love to. Thank you so much for the dress." Natalie followed her to the door. "I'll have to do something special for you sometime."

April leaned in and gave Natalie a quick hug. "Your friendship is enough. Now get back to bed, because that's where I'm headed."

"And Louise put fresh sheets on everyone's beds today. See you tomorrow."

"Ooh, fresh sheets sound heavenly. Good night," April said. She slipped out the door and down the hallway to her room.

23

April saddled Sassy and headed in the direction of Josh's sheep ranch with instructions from Miss Margaret on how to get there. A stiff breeze blew over the majestic mountains this morning, whispering that cold weather wouldn't be too far away. There wasn't a cloud in the sky, and just above the timberline, April could see snow-capped peaks that seemed close enough to touch but were really miles away. She was always amazed at the beauty around her, and here in Montana the bitterroot flower flamed brightly, waving in the wind. The trees showed signs of Chinook winds—they were bent over permanently from the constant onslaught. A bushy-tailed black squirrel and its mate scampered nearby, looking for food for winter storage. There was no place she'd rather be than on the back of her horse, surrounded by nature's incomprehensible splendor. Only God could have created such magnificence and wildlife.

She heard the bleating and smelled the sheep before she even saw them. The furry creatures in thick groups appeared as a white ocean rolling before her. April still had to wonder why Josh gave up cattle for this, but she knew he would have thought it over long and hard.

As she drew closer, she saw Andy amid the sheep and a dog running alongside them. She reined Sassy in and slowed her to a walk as Andy approached.

"Well, hello there, April. Fine horse you got there." He removed his hat, wiping his face with the back of his sleeve.

April slid off Sassy and greeted him. "Thanks, Andy. I got him from Wes."

"Well, I hope he didn't charge you too much. Some of his horses go as high as five hundred dollars. He raises some fine horseflesh."

"Let's just say we came to an understanding on the price," April said with an evasive smile. The dog ran up to them, barking.

"It's okay, Shebe. April's our friend," Andy said to the dog. To April, he said, "She won't hurt you at all. She just wants to say hello. If you hold out your hand, she can pick up your scent and remember you."

April did as Andy requested, letting Shebe lick her hand. "So this is the wonder dog Josh wrote me about." She chuckled as Shebe wagged her tail in delight while April continued to pet her through the thick fur. "She's a beautiful dog."

"What brings you out on this gorgeous fall day?" Andy asked, putting his hat back on his shaggy brown hair.

"I needed to be outdoors today and thought I'd come check out Josh's place. I guess I should tell you that they've decided to stay away a few more days."

Andy laughed. "I can't say I'm surprised. I figure he'll get back eventually."

A few woolies wandered over, and April moved away, but they continued to be curious.

"Sheep are the gentlest of God's creatures, April. Maybe dumb, but gentle."

April couldn't resist touching the woolly lambs' backs and was surprised at their softness. "I've never been near sheep."

"Most people haven't. Josh told me your daddy raises prime beef cattle," he said. "Let's walk on up to the house. It's not far. Nellie will be setting out lunch about now. We'd be happy if you'd stay." He turned to hold Shebe's face in his hands. "Shebe, you stay," he commanded. Shebe's brown eyes looked directly at him, then she responded with a yap.

April trailed Sassy behind her and walked alongside Andy. Though he smelled of sheep and the outdoors, she struggled not to turn up her nose. "That would be nice, Andy. I'm enjoying getting to know the people who live around here."

"If Josh had his druthers, he'd have you stay."

They chatted as they walked through the meadow, and April learned that Josh had made certain his house was large enough to have a separate area for Andy and Nellie. April saw evidence of trees half-burned and new grass in the field amid areas charred from the recent fire Josh had written about. They'd weathered some tough times together, Andy confided.

Eventually, Andy and April started up a gradual incline until Josh's ranch house, rebuilt after the fire, came into view at the foot of the mountain. The house was hewn out of rich ponderosa pine with a front porch that ran the full length of the house. A split-rail fence on either side of the long, wide driveway was flanked by spruce trees leading right up to the front door. A fat calico cat that lay curled up in a rocking chair hopped down and ran when the two approached. Something wonderful wafted on the breeze, making April's stomach growl.

"That's Prissy, Juliana's cat. She just had to have her. She can be a little snooty sometimes," Andy said.

"She's a pretty cat," April said, following him through the door. "I've never had one."

"Stick around long enough and Juliana will see to it that you will," Andy said with a wink.

Nellie came from the kitchen, her beautiful, ivory skin flushed—from the oven's heat, April assumed. She beamed when she saw April with Andy and wiped her hands on her apron. "What a pleasure 'tis to be seeing you again! And just in time for lunch. I've just taken a shepherd's pie out of the oven to cool," Nellie said in her jolly British accent. She stretched out her hand to clasp April's, giving it a firm shake.

April liked Nellie's warm smile, and the freckles sprinkled across the bridge of her nose and cheeks made Nellie all the more charming. Her hair was pushed up into a bun, but now the curls escaped their pins. "It smells wonderful in here. I'd love to stay, if it's not a bother," April said.

"Lovely! Andy, show her the washroom. We can eat in the kitchen since it's just the three of us. No sense in being too formal, don't you think?" Without waiting for an answer, Nellie bustled off to the kitchen while Andy showed April where she could freshen up.

April was impressed with the large expansive living room and heavy furniture carved in ponderosa pine. A heavy leather chair flanked the fireplace, and a smaller rocker, which must have been made for Juliana, sat kitty-corner from the chair. Her brother's home was simply decorated, warm and inviting just like he was, but it lacked a woman's touch. April was sure that would change as soon as he and Juliana returned from their honeymoon.

Entering the washroom, she removed her hat, then hurriedly washed her hands and stared at her reflection in the mirror. Her face was a golden tan, and the sun had lightened her hair to a flaxen color that only complemented her features. April smiled at her reflection and decided that she liked her looks. She paused, wondering what Wes was doing right now. She blinked hard. What did it matter? Yet she couldn't keep from thinking about it.

She scurried to the kitchen, dying to taste Nellie's shepherd's pie. What a treat that would be!

After a second helping, April blotted her mouth, and when Nellie would have put more in her dish, April held out her hand, stopping her. "I couldn't eat another bite, Nellie. Andy has himself a wonderful cook."

Nellie turned pink with pleasure. "'Tis Andy who does most of the cookin' around here. I've learned a thing or two from him myself." Nellie looked at Andy with pure love, and he blew her a kiss across the table. They had a good time talking about Josh, and April learned a little more about Juliana. They made it clear that Juliana was a favorite of theirs.

"Josh has found himself a good wife," Andy said with a grin. "They had a few battles to work out, but once they did, nothing could've kept them apart. Juliana is totally devoted to your brother."

"I'm glad to hear that. True love is hard to find or keep." April set her water glass down and smoothed the tablecloth with her hand.

Nellie frowned with a questioning look. "I should think you'd have the men eating out of your hand. How many beaus do you have? I'll wager a few, no doubt." Nellie beamed, leaning toward April as though she was about to be let in on a secret.

April laughed. "Hardly. I don't have a beau at the present time."

Nellie's face was full of surprise. "I find it very hard to believe that there isn't a man in Colorado waiting to snatch you up!"

"No, really." April shook her head. "There isn't."

"What about Wes? I heard him talking to Earl at Power Mercantile the other day and thought maybe you two were courting."

April drew in a sharp breath. "He did? Well, that was wishful thinking. I'm not sure we could ever get along. He's hotheaded, you know."

Andy roared with laughter. "He said the same thing about you."

"He did, did he?" April arched an eyebrow. "What else did he say?"

Andy's eyes twinkled. "Just that he thinks you're the best thing that's happened to him since he got Dakota, and that's saying something. Hard to get between a man and his horse."

The rest of lunch was pleasant, but April couldn't stop thinking about what Andy had said. Had Wes really talked about courting her? It made her pulse quicken.

Afterward, Andy and Nellie showed April around the ranch and their adjoining living quarters, which were connected to the main house by a passageway. It pleased April that Josh would provide them a place to live. It was just like her brother to be mindful of others' needs. *Unlike me . . . I'm just now learning to think that way.*

By the time April rode away on Sassy, she knew she had made good friends in Nellie and Andy. The kind she could always count on.

The sun burned high in the cerulean sky now dotted with a few fluffy clouds, and the heat began to build again. April stopped her horse in the wide-open field to watch a magnificent eagle soar effortlessly, the updraft of the wind carrying it on its flight. The sight made her hold her breath as it dipped down for its prey and plucked a rodent from the ground in its long talons, then flapped its wings and flew away. She could hear Big Spring Creek gurgling downstream past the deadfall, where she had stopped once before.

The wind had ceased along with the clouds, giving way to a warm afternoon. She hoped this pristine land with its wildlife would still be this beautiful when she had grandchildren. *Ha! That's funny . . . you have to be married first to have children before you have grandchildren*, she chided herself.

She had nothing but time today, and Miss Margaret's words about going to talk to Wes and hearing him out echoed in her mind. Besides, she had the rose dress in her saddlebag to return to him.

April's insides began to quiver at the thought of just dropping in on Wes. What would he think? Would he tell her to leave, or would he want to talk to her? *He'll probably be gone or out riding or training a horse anyway. But I guess I could go by.*

When April arrived at the Rusty Spur, Wes was standing next to the water pump by the barn, shirtless, his muscular tanned chest wet with perspiration as he drank water from a metal cup. His damp, sandy brown hair clung to his head just above the neckline, and his jeans and boots were covered with dirt and grime. His long, lean torso was without an ounce of extra flesh, and his muscles rippled when he moved his arms.

April stopped Sassy at the edge of the yard and crossed her arms over the saddle horn as she watched him. She had a funny feeling in her stomach, seeing him without his shirt. *I shouldn't be looking* . . . But April couldn't help herself. Wes was unaware that she was there, and he stared up at the roof of his house, hammer in hand. What was he looking at? April's eyes traveled upward and saw a stack of shingles on top of the sloped roof. He must have been patching the roof, which would explain why he was sweaty.

April slid off Sassy's back, still holding the reins, and started over to where Wes stood. A snort from Sassy caused him to turn around. She couldn't tell from his expression what he might be thinking. His jaw was set in a hard line, and his eyes narrowed when they locked with hers.

"April." He nodded a greeting. "What brings you all the way out here?"

She stopped a couple of feet away from him and tried not to stare at the place where his waistline met the top of his jeans loosely cinched. She leveled a gaze at him directly. "I . . . rode over to Josh's place and wanted to drop this by." She moved to the saddlebags on Sassy's haunches and pulled out the dress wrapped in paper. "I wanted to thank you for lending it to me." As she held it out to him, their fingers touched. April drew her hand back. His touch had caused a stirring in her heart, and her mind became befuddled. She didn't know what else to say, but he needed to put his shirt back on. Now that she was closer, she could see streaks of dirt on his tanned face and arms.

An uncomfortable silence ensued while they stood eyeing each other. His lids were heavy over his normally bright hazel eyes. From hard work, or lack of sleep?

Wes laid his hammer down next to a stack of shingles and put the dress aside, then cleared his throat to utter, "You're welcome." He turned back, washing his hands with a bar of soap as though she wasn't still standing there.

April felt dismissed. "Is that all you can say?" She took a step closer to him, staring at his back with her hands on her hips. Phew! She could smell his perspiration now.

He snapped back up and gave her a blunt stare. "What else is there to say?"

"I don't know. How about 'hello' for starters?" She glanced down at her boot and dragged the toe through the dirt.

"Why? I'd just be wasting my time, now wouldn't I? I'm about to wash up and put away my tools for the day," he said in a clipped tone.

April opened her mouth to protest but said instead, "Good idea, I can smell you from here. You're about as popular as a wet dog at a parlor social." She let out a tiny giggle. His mouth twitched, and she knew he struggled to keep from smiling at her comment.

"Humph! Then it's a good thing I don't have any intention of that this evening." He continued to lather the soap and wash his face, then he looked up. "I guess it's my turn to smell, huh?" His eyes twinkled.

She took a step closer, watching as soap suds slid down his face and neck, creating streaks down his back. His muscular back . . . the back she longed to touch. He sure was a sight for sore eyes!

"Let me help you," she whispered, surprising herself.

Wes blinked. "What?" His brows became two angled peaks that jutted upward in surprise.

April firmly took the soap from his hands, telling him to lean over the water pump. He obeyed, and she pumped the cool well water over the soap and began to lather his hair, gently massaging his head. Her fingers moved across his scalp with ease, then moved down to rub his neck and shoulders.

Wes expelled a deep sigh, closing his eyes to her gentle massage. Never had a head washing felt so good. Just as he was beginning to feel content, April shoved his head sideways under the spigot and pumped the handle up and down, rapidly covering his face and head with water. Wes gasped for air. "Mercy, woman! Are you trying to drown me?" He straightened up fast, cut her a hard look, then lunged to grab her by the wrists.

Her jaw dropped in surprise, and she squirmed against him, but it was no use. "It's just payback, Wes, for what you did to me when I barely knew you!" She continued to fight against his strong handhold.

"Well, you wicked little tease . . ." Wes yanked her close to him and kissed her soundly on the mouth, then released her none too gently. She staggered back in surprise. "You deserve a spanking instead of a kiss." *Well, now I've done it . . . I've made her mad.*

What would he do when she left? Same old thing as before. Nothing . . . just emptiness with no one to share his dreams or his bed.

April stood there, her mouth open, breathing raggedly. She

touched her fingers to her lips but was silent, her eyes full of emotion. He could get lost in her beautiful eyes.

With his hair still dripping water down his chest and back, Wes reached for her, but she lifted a towel that was draped over the pump's side and handed it to him. He took it, his eyes never leaving hers. "I really wouldn't spank you, but you sure can infuriate a man and make him consider the possibility," he said huskily, wiping his face and chest, then rubbing the towel through his hair. "About our conversation last night . . . can we talk about it? Will you let me explain?" He watched her face for a reaction and saw her face soften, and the sweet curve of her lips made him optimistic.

"Wes," she said quietly, "I really came here to apologize. The dress was just an excuse. I have a bad habit of having the last word and then acting like a spoiled little girl, or so I've been told. I'd like to talk, if you want to . . ." Her voice trailed off, and her eyes skittered away to look beyond the barn.

His breath caught. Wes could feel joy coursing through him straight up to his heart. Maybe there was a little ray of hope for them. He wouldn't push his luck. "I'll finish up here. How about staying for supper? I was going to fry a steak and panfry some potatoes. You like steak, don't you?"

Sassy pawed the ground and tossed her head to get their attention. They both laughed. "I'm a cattleman's daughter, remember? Of course I like steak." She picked up Sassy's reins. "I need to take her saddle off and give her some water, Wes. I hadn't planned on being out late."

"If you'd rather do it another time—"

April gave him an encouraging smile. "No. Tonight is fine and I'm hungry. And I'll get to test out your cookin'."

"You won't be disappointed. Let's get Sassy settled with some water and oats and corral her with the rest of my horses, and then I'll get started on supper."

He moved to lead Sassy to the corral, but April touched his arm. "Wes, could you please put your shirt back on? It's hard to take you seriously without your shirt and your hair all sticking straight up!"

Her smile said more than her words, and Wes felt his heart lift. *Maybe I'm not as homely as I thought.* He whistled a tune as he led Sassy to the corral.

24

Together April and Wes stacked the empty plates in the sink while he poured hot water from the teakettle over them to soak. "Don't you want to wash them now?" April asked.

"No," he said, laying down the dish towel and taking her hands in his, "I can do this later. It'll give me something to take my mind off you." His eyes strayed to her face.

"The steak was delicious. I'm afraid that by splitting it between us, you didn't have enough to eat." April smiled back at him. "I think you're a man with a big appetite, in more ways than one," she teased.

"I'll live off your smiles," he said, lifting her hands to kiss her fingertips. "That'll be enough for me. How about we go sit on the porch before you have to get on back to the boardinghouse?"

"I'd say that's a good idea. It's a beautiful night." They passed through the living room and out the front door to the porch. April took a seat in a rocker, and Wes sat next to her. She'd been surprised at how fast he whipped up their meal with all the deftness of a chef. She asked him how he learned to cook like that.

"When my mom died, cooking duties fell to me. So did a whole lot of other chores."

Something about the way he answered made her think he'd had a miserable childhood. Without his cowboy hat, his face looked more vulnerable and younger somehow. She controlled the urge to soothe the crease in his forehead, not wanting to interrupt his thoughts.

Wes continued as she rocked back and forth, causing the floorboards to squeak. "The truth is, my father was an alcoholic, but he tried to keep it hidden so most people didn't know. He was lazy and left most of the hard work for me. I worked from sunup to sundown, but I learned to cook mostly out of necessity. Then I began to actually like cooking." He stretched his long legs out in front of him, leaned back in his chair, and turned to look at her while he talked. His face was serious, and his eyes showed deep emotion as he recalled his childhood. His hands curled around the arms of the rocking chair, and April noticed them again. Nice, capable hands.

"Was he ever mean to you?" April dared to ask.

"Only verbally, but I don't blame him. I forgave him a long time ago before he died. And since we're talking about it, I want to tell you the night you saw me at the saloon—you're right, I did go in, and that wasn't my first time." Wes paused and took a deep breath.

April could feel her pulse speed up. Was he going to confess something she didn't want to hear?

"I used to go there a lot before I asked God into my life, but I've changed. That particular night after you left my place, I was so lonely, and I thought it wouldn't hurt to go have a drink to get you off my mind. Something changed the minute I was inside. It was like everything suddenly became clear to me—how uncomfortable I was—and I knew I'd left that life behind." Wes reached over and picked up April's hand, rubbing her palm with his thumb. "You must believe me. I'm not like my father. I left when the bartender brought me my drink, but you weren't there to see that. There's not another woman in my life and hasn't really ever been, until you."

It was exactly what April wanted to hear. But should she believe him? *Lord, I want to believe him.* Her hand felt small in his large, calloused one, and April felt sad that his childhood had been so hard. Her own had been such a happy one. "Wes, I'm sorry I didn't give you a chance to explain." Her voice shook. "And I'm sorry that your father mistreated you. My life was so different from yours."

Wes shrugged. "It wasn't all bad. I had a wonderful mother, but after she died, I learned to be independent and look after myself, and I stayed out of my father's way. As I said before, that was her dress you were wearing, and I might add, you looked beautiful in it."

"You'll have to show me her photograph sometime. You must really miss her." April paused, thinking about what his mother must have been like. Perhaps she had been a lot like her own mother. "I guess I should leave now, so Miss Margaret won't worry," she said, pursing her lips together. "It'll be dark soon."

"Can you come back tomorrow? Jane will be here for another lesson, and I think she really likes you. Cynthia is bringing her." Wes rose from his chair. He pulled April to her feet, and they stood nose to nose.

"I guess I could . . . if you really want me to," she answered softly. A bird landed on the porch railing and warbled, but they paid it no mind, lost in each other's eyes.

"I *do* want you to," he whispered.

Her arms prickled with goose bumps as she gazed at his lips, her hands still in his.

"Are you cold?"

"No, it's just that . . . I . . . will you hold me close again?"

Wes enveloped her in his arms. "It'd be my greatest pleasure, sweet thing."

She snuggled underneath his chin, breathing in his scent of the outdoors mingled with horses and leather, and sighed content-edly. How had she let go of her heart like this? She could feel the rhythmic beat of his heart against her ear.

"April." Wes's lips touched her hair, and he ran his fingers through the silky strands. "It feels so right holding you like this. I'm in love with you, you know, and I don't want you to go back to Colorado."

She relaxed into his arms. Somehow she knew it before he'd said the words. She knew she loved him too, but could she stay? She pulled back and looked into his eyes. "Wes . . . I don't know what to say . . ."

"Say you'll stay awhile longer. I won't pressure you. You can think about whether you can live here or not. I don't want you to stay unless that's what you really want. Unless there's another man waiting on you in Colorado?" His brows furrowed.

She gave a lighthearted laugh. "No, there's no one, but there was once. I don't want my heart broken again, Wes. I couldn't take that."

"So that's why you don't want to trust me. I'm not like who-ever broke your heart. Just give me a chance to prove it to you. I'll never hurt you intentionally. I want us to grow old together on this porch . . . well, maybe on a new and improved one." He chuckled. "One that'll meet your standards."

She loved how his eyes crinkled at the corners when he smiled. Looking around the yard, she muttered, "Mmm . . . we'd have to work on that, wouldn't we? Is that why you started repairing the shingles?"

He gave her waist a tight squeeze. "Yes, among other things. I've bought new paint to spruce the place up too." His hazel eyes twinkled, and his smile was endearing.

"I *did* notice you cleaned up around the house. That's a good start."

"You approve then?" he asked.

She stood on tiptoe and planted a quick kiss on his lips. "I approve, but now I really need to go."

Wes stopped her with a kiss, capturing her face with both of his hands, and April felt a flash of heat sweep over her. She swallowed hard, and he kissed her again. "I could kiss you until the cows come home, April McBride, but I guess this'll have to hold me for now." He touched the tip of her nose with his finger, and emotion flickered in his eyes.

She laughed, and he released her from his grip. "Do you have any cows?"

"No, but that can be arranged, if you want them." He laughed heartily, exposing the dimple in one cheek.

"For now, I'll settle for just you. Eventually cows would be nice." April started down the steps.

"I'll ride back with you." Wes lifted his hat from the porch's fence post. "It'll get dark soon, and you can't be too careful around here with bears and such. I don't want you out there alone."

"Really? Have you seen one?" April hadn't thought of that possibility, and a tingle of fear went down her spine. "I've only glimpsed a grizzly from a distance back home."

"I've seen one a time or two. But I keep my distance. If it's a mother and her cubs, it could be dangerous. Let's go get Sassy and Dakota saddled up." He clasped her hand, directing her toward the barn. "I'll need to put the rest of the horses in the barn before we leave."

"I can help with that," she said, following his long strides.

They pushed their horses, now saddled, in the direction of Lewistown and chatted along the way. Wes told her he'd discovered by sheer accident that Jane could walk.

"What? You can't be serious." April knew Jane could be a little manipulative, but that was going a bit too far. April had been guilty of being calculating more than once as a child, and now she was embarrassed by her actions. "Why would she do that?"

Wes tried his best to explain what Jane had told him. "I told her she'd have to confess eventually and gave her a couple of options. I don't know what she decided, but we'll find out tomorrow. Just don't mention it or let on that you know. She feels badly enough about lying all these months."

"Mum's the word." April held her finger to her lips in agreement.

Wes rode all the way to the boardinghouse with her as darkness fell. When they stopped outside the house, lights from the windows gave a welcoming invitation. Wes followed April to the barn and helped her unsaddle Sassy. He volunteered to give her a quick rubdown, but April wouldn't let him.

"I appreciate it, Wes, but you have a long ride back home," she said, brushing Sassy's shiny coat while he put away her saddle. Sassy nudged April's shoulder, looking for a treat. "You spoiled lady," she cooed, but dug a sugar cube out of her pocket. "I shouldn't let you have this before your dinner." April patted Sassy's nose affectionately. The glow from a lantern Wes had lit gave the barn's interior an intimate feel, and April felt right at home amid the horse smells and fodder.

Wes stepped around the horse to stand next to her, placing a bucket of oats down in front of Sassy. Straightening, he said in a low voice, "Then I'll say good night until tomorrow afternoon." He reached out to lift a lock of her hair that lay across her shoulder, caressing it between his fingers. His eyes smoldered.

"Good night, Wes," April whispered.

He took a step closer and lightly brushed her lips, then kissed her brow. "Sleep well, my sweet one," he said tenderly, then left.

When April finished grooming Sassy, she dreamily sauntered inside, her feet barely touching the ground. She started up the stairs, her mind on Wes. Natalie was carrying clean towels and paused on the stairs to peer down at her. "You're back!" she called, her voice echoing throughout the foyer. "Mama was getting worried. You missed supper. Did you have dinner with Nellie and Andy?" Her impulsive chatter reflected the personality of a younger woman, and her smile was so bright that April had to smile.

"No, I had lunch with them but supper with Wes," she answered, going up the stairs to where Natalie leaned against the railing. Instantly Natalie's bright countenance fell.

"Oh. I see." She shifted the pile of towels that she carried to her side.

"Natalie—" April felt like she had to apologize.

"It's okay, April." Natalie drew her shoulders up and took a deep breath. "I've worked it out in my heart. Honest. Did you have fun? Tell me about your afternoon."

"Yes. Wes cooked us a steak—well, we divided it. He wasn't expecting someone for supper, least of all me." April tread carefully, not wanting to rub Natalie's nose in her wonderful afternoon. "He's a pretty good cook. Good thing, because I'm not."

Natalie blinked. "Sounds serious."

April pursed her lips. "I think maybe it is, Natalie."

"Does that mean you'll be staying here?" Her dark eyes twinkled.

"I'm not certain yet, but it's a strong possibility—"

Natalie rushed over and gave her a hug. They banged foreheads, laughing as Natalie dropped the stack of clean towels in her enthusiasm. Her eyes shone with tears. "Oh, I hope so, no matter what the reason. You've become like a sister to me and Louise!"

April was stunned. "Really?" She looked hard into Natalie's dark eyes. "I've never had a sister, and I'm honored to hear you say that, Natalie."

Natalie shook her head. "I'm not at all angry with you. I mean that. It's not your fault he loves you instead of me. What kind of person would I be if I got in the way of that? No, no, no. I must have my man devoted to me entirely." She winked and smiled. "Whenever I find him!"

"What's going on up there, girls?" Miss Margaret stood at the end of the hallway with Louise right behind her. "A celebration?"

"Something like that," Natalie answered.

"What are we celebrating?" Louise asked.

April felt a little uncomfortable now that they knew about Wes.

"She and Wes are seriously courting!" Natalie said.

Miss Margaret clapped her hands. "Oh, goodness! So you were with Wes."

"Yes, ma'am," April responded with a shy smile.

Louise touched her sleeve. "Will you be staying longer, or will this be a long-distance romance?"

April laughed. "We haven't talked about all that yet."

Louise hooked her arm through April's and started downstairs. "I have no doubt that you will. Let's all go downstairs for a dish of huckleberry cobbler," she called over her shoulder to Natalie and her mother.

"Sounds good to me," April agreed. "You're all becoming like my family, you know."

Louise beamed at her. "Good! Maybe that'll help convince you to stay." The others chimed in their agreement with loud chatter and laughter.

They all trooped back to the kitchen, and Louise dipped up the cobbler. Sitting around the kitchen table, April looked around at their familiar faces and surmised that she hadn't really thought of home or missed anyone there since she'd arrived in Montana. Well . . . maybe Tilly. Tonight she would write Tilly and try to talk her into coming out here. She could just see her now, rolling her big eyes in her round black face and fussing, saying "Lawsy!" at the quick turn of events.

25

Cooler temperatures crept in while the community of Lewistown slept. A light frost lay on the ground and covered the sidewalks while north winds blew across the Judith Mountains, making it feel colder than the thermometer's reading. As usual every fall, the fabulous weather energized folks with fervor to prepare for the coming winter. The streets were congested with wagons and carriages, street vendors, and people shopping by the time April completed her self-imposed chores and saddled her horse. She wanted to stop by and check on Morgan and find out how he was doing since Lenora had brought him home. Billy must be running the stage line, but who was driving the stage? Billy wasn't old enough.

She wondered how they were doing without Leon around. Sheriff Wilson had a posse out looking for the robbers, but nothing had turned up yet on their trail as far as she knew.

She let Sassy take her time clopping down the couple of blocks to the depot. When she spotted the mercantile store, a thought struck her, so she turned Sassy toward the store, and Earl waved to her. He was wiping down the glass display window.

"How are you, Earl?" April said as she slipped off the horse and looped the reins over the hitching post.

"Just fine. A beautiful day. And you?" He paused with his rag, hands on his hips.

"I have an idea for a gift for Wes." April saw his eyebrows lift in question, but she hurried on before he could ask her anything. "Can we go inside? I don't want to talk on the sidewalk."

Her mysterious request moved him into action, so he swung the door open and, with a sweep of his hand, motioned her inside. "I'll see what I can do for you."

Fifteen minutes later, April emerged with a smile on her face and a package underneath her arm. She couldn't wait to give it to Wes. It was only a little something, but she hoped he'd be pleased.

When she entered the depot, she was surprised to see Morgan talking with Billy. Lenora was serving coffee while they sat at a small table, and all three looked up as she entered.

"Howdy, Miss April," Billy said warmly with his usual bright smile.

"Hello, everyone. I wanted to stop in and see how you're doing, Morgan." April approached the passengers' waiting area. "From the looks of it, I'd say you're doing well."

"I'm doing great, and grateful to be alive." He stood up, moving a little stiffly from his seat. "I owe you my thanks. Here, please have a seat." He pulled out a wooden chair.

"You don't owe me a thing. I'll think of it as my first Montana adventure! But I'm sorry about Leon. He was very kind to me."

Lenora gave April a big smile. An apron was tied neatly at her back, and she carried a cookie sheet. Placing the cookies on the table, Lenora got another cup and poured coffee for April. "I have some warm oatmeal cookies. Would you care for one?"

"I'd love to sample one," she said, lifting a cookie off the tray and taking a bite. "Delightful, Lenora. Billy, how have you been?"

Billy stood straighter and pushed back his shoulders. "Just fine, Miss April. I've been helping Morgan around here as much as I'm able."

Morgan cocked his head to look at the boy. "You've been a great help. I don't know what I would've done without you around here." Morgan smiled broadly, exposing his mouthful of white teeth.

Billy looked as though his chest might burst, and April was happy he'd found a place to live and work. "He's a quick learner, and soon he'll be driving that stage for you, Morgan."

"I can hardly wait until you're better, Boss, so you can teach me." Billy smiled broadly.

"Don't you worry none, Billy, it'll be sooner than you think," Morgan said, giving him a clap on the back.

"How's Jane and the riding lessons?" Billy asked April with a sheepish look.

"Wes tells me she's doing much better." April tilted her head as a thought formed. "Why don't you come with me? I'm going out there, and I know she'd be glad to have someone close to her age to ride with. You can see for yourself how she's doing. That is, if Morgan can spare you for a couple of hours."

"You go, Billy. You haven't had any free time since all this started."

"I can?"

Morgan nodded, smiling back at the boy. "Finish your cookies and saddle up Star. Will and I can handle things this afternoon."

"I'll be outside waiting for you, Miss April." Billy took off like the room was on fire.

"Don't go off without your jacket," Lenora called after him. "It's colder this morning." The three of them laughed at Billy's excitement and Lenora's motherly advice.

"Is Will around?" April asked. "I need to send a telegram."

"I'm here." Will appeared from the office in his usual white shirt and black suspenders, looking like a true office clerk. "What can I do for you?"

"Oh, I didn't see you back there, Will. I have a telegram to send back home." April turned to Morgan and Lenora. "If you will excuse me." She walked over to where Will stood with his tablet in hand, awaiting her instructions. She gave him the particulars and paid for the telegram, fully aware that Lenora and Morgan could hear their conversation.

"I'll let you know if you get a gram back, or I'll run it over to you," Will said as he closed the cash drawer.

She thanked him, then went back to the waiting area. "Morgan, who's going to drive the stage next week?" she asked while watching Lenora pick up the coffee cups and napkins. "I saw your sign in the window that your route was postponed."

"Oh, are you offering?" He chortled and winked at Lenora.

"Hardly. I was just curious . . . but if you really needed me to, I suppose I could."

"I'm a little sore and stiff, but the doc says I can get back on the road Monday, and I'll take Billy with me. Now that Lenora's here, she can help Will out with tickets or anything else that needs seeing to."

"I'll be cooking dinner for the passengers who'd like to buy a meal. I love meeting new people," Lenora said. "I'm looking forward to it."

"Then I can't wait to taste some of your Southern cooking. I just sent a wire to my maid, Tilly, back in Colorado. I want to see if she'll make a trip out here."

Lenora gave her a strange look, but Morgan teased, "Guess you need a maid to dress you with all those new frocks you bought out here. But I thought you were leaving soon."

"It looks as though I might be here awhile, and you'll get a chance to get to know me even better," she teased back, knowing she'd been a bit of a thorn in his flesh. "I know you're just *dying* to do that."

"Won't matter to me. I can always use a hand with the team," Morgan said.

"You don't mean stay permanently, do you?" Lenora asked. She wiped the crumbs from the table, then paused to wait for April's response, her hands on her hips.

"Could be, Lenora," she answered coyly.

"Then it has to be a man! That'd be the only way you'd ever leave home, I'll declare. I know that from experience—and by the look on your face."

April laughed and tossed her hair back off her shoulders. "That's exactly what Tilly would say. You'll get along well with her, if I can talk her into coming."

"I figure that man to be Wes," Morgan said. "It's no surprise to me. Leon and I knew it would happen because of the way you two quarreled and looked at each other." His faced saddened when he mentioned Leon.

April didn't deny the observation. "I've agreed to stay awhile for now."

"Good thinking. We love having you around," Morgan expressed with a serious face.

April scurried over to give him a quick hug. "You may change your mind about that later. But you've treated me like a daughter, and I want you to know I appreciate yours and Lenora's friendship. Between you and Miss Margaret, I didn't have a chance."

Tears misted Morgan's eyes, and he said, "Here now, you're gonna make Lenora jealous!" But April knew he was pleased.

April turned to leave. "I'd better go find Billy so we can ride out to the Rusty Spur." She hurried out, anxious to see Wes.

Watching April dash out the door, Lenora turned to look at her husband. "I really like that girl. She's all right. At first I didn't know how to take her."

Morgan narrowed his eyes, looked out the window, and watched April and Billy mount their horses then trot down the road. "I know what you mean, honey. I've seen changes in her, and I think besides Wes, Miss Margaret has been a positive influence on her." Morgan said a silent prayer that God would watch over April and guide any decision where Wes was concerned. They would struggle, but the effort would be worth it in the long run.

It pleased him the way April had treated Lenora from the beginning. Not everyone wanted to be friends with black folks, but it didn't seem to matter one bit to her. He was grateful for the friends he had, especially Miss Margaret. *I wonder what Josh will think about Wes courting April? I never dreamed a man like Wes could change so much. Change in the hearts of men comes slowly, so that has be the work of the good Lord.*

Morgan reached for Lenora's hand. "Have I told you lately how much I love you?"

Lenora let herself be pulled close and blinked her eyes. "Let's see . . . this morning before we got out of bed. But I always want to hear it. I've missed you, and I'm so glad the robber was a bad shot."

Morgan gazed into his lovely wife's dark eyes, appreciating the love he saw reflected there. A single tear rolled down his cheek and disappeared into his beard. He was a very happy man. Very happy indeed.

"Morgan! You're crying." Lenora reached up, caressing his wet cheek.

Morgan cleared his throat, embarrassed at his sudden emotional state. "Naw, I'm not . . . I'm just happy that you're home at last. Right where you need to be." He pulled her to his chest and kissed the top of her head. She released a deep, contented sigh. "Want to go back upstairs for a while?" he whispered in her ear.

Will smiled from behind the ticket counter as the couple mounted the stairs, arm in arm.

26

"Billy, I'm glad you rode over today!" Jane was already on the back of Cinnamon when they arrived. Her face was flushed despite the chill in the air, and April figured it was more from the fact that Billy was nearby than from the riding lesson.

"Hey, yourself! Morgan gave me a couple of hours off today." Billy drew his horse up close to the corral where Jane was. "Nice horse you got there."

Wes stood inside the corral with Jane, leaning against the railing. He glanced up as April and Billy came into view. "Looks like this might call for a picnic down by the stream later. How are you two this morning?"

"Good, Wes. How's our star pupil?" April's heart thumped when she saw Wes's friendly smile and his gaze sweep over her. "A picnic might be just the thing today." She smiled back.

"I've packed us some sandwiches and fruit. Let's all ride down to Big Spring Creek. What do you say?"

Billy's eyes gleamed with delight. "Wow, I've never been on a picnic before."

"You haven't?" Jane gave him a dubious look. "It's fun. Follow me and I'll lead the way." Billy fell in next to Jane, and soon they were chatting about the start of school.

Wes reached through the fence and touched April's hand. "I'll go get the lunch and be right out. Don't go away."

"I promise I'll be right here. You'd better hurry, they're leaving us behind. Seems Jane's in very happy spirits. You'll have to tell me what happened." April's tone was hushed so Jane couldn't hear. Her eyes slid over Wes's lean body in approval. He was dressed in worn but clean jeans, a green plaid shirt that set off his hazel eyes, a coffee-colored leather vest, and a matching leather hat. One thing she knew for certain, besides a love of horses, they both loved leather outfittings. She'd have to ask Tilly to bring her another pair of boots and a belt if she came to Montana. After her bargaining for Sassy with her good boots and belt, April hadn't found a way to replace anything as fine as those, but she'd try. She didn't begrudge Jane having them now. Wearing them made Jane seem happy and look like a real horsewoman.

Wes hurried inside, and true to his word, he was back in a flash carrying a basket with a blue-checkered cloth, which he handed to her. It thrilled April that he would be so romantic to think of doing something like that. He got on his horse, then edged Dakota up next to her, close enough to talk.

The earlier winds had died down, and the hawthorn blazed deep red along the thick wooded trail on the way to Big Spring Creek. It was a perfect day in April's mind—peaceful, with only the sound of the horses' hoofbeats clomping on the packed trail, an occasional crow cawing overhead, and the distant sound of the young people's chatter. All was right with the world, and she felt a contentment she'd never had before. Was it because of the man riding next to her?

"Wes, what was the outcome of Jane's walking?' April kept her eyes focused on the trail before her.

"She told the truth to her mother, which was what I was hoping for. But sadly, not walking or standing for months did take its toll on her leg muscles. It'll take awhile before they're strong again, so she's somewhat shaky when she walks." Wes flicked a bug off his arm absentmindedly. "I think it's best we suggest that the riding and passing of time is making her legs stronger, which is partially true. Cynthia agreed to save her from embarrassment. I felt sure she would."

"You must have been very persuasive to be able to convince Jane to be truthful."

Wes shrugged. "I don't know. I did try to help by sharing my own mistakes. Jane's a good kid, she's going through a hard time." When April raised an eyebrow, he added, "She just happened to make a wrong decision based on her feelings. I think it all stems from losing her dad in a mining explosion."

"I think she has a new friend in Billy. They played board games together when he didn't know she could walk. But was Cynthia angry with her?"

"She didn't say too much about it. I think she's just happy that Jane can walk. She loves her daughter, although she admitted Jane is a little spoiled." Wes glanced over at her. "Do you see much of Cynthia with Mark at the boardinghouse?"

"Not really. She comes right after lunch to help in the kitchen and leaves by supper time. I believe she and Mark were brought together in friendship because of Jane. He's beginning to court

Louise now, or didn't you notice the other night at Miss Margaret's?"

Wes nodded. "I wondered about that. It looked to me like they were enjoying their time together in the parlor before we left on our walk. Louise looked different . . . prettier and not as stiff." He wrinkled his nose in thought.

April giggled. "I may have had something to do with that."

Wes's laughter reverberated throughout the wooded glen, causing Jane and Billy to glance back at them. "I have no doubt you did."

The scenery before them was spectacular. The autumn purple ash trees splashed brilliant red to tinges of purple, which would later become deep purple. The trail opened wide as they approached Big Spring Creek. They could hear its rushing water, and the pungent smell of spruce was fragrant in the air. Long willow limbs trailed to the ground, and huge cottonwoods flourished near the creek.

Wes yelled at the kids, "This is a good place to stop for lunch." He slid off Dakota and held Sassy's reins while April dismounted. "Billy, there's a blanket rolled up on the back of Cinnamon. Could you fetch it?"

"Sure thing." Billy hopped down and untied the blanket. Walking over to them, he handed the blanket to April, who unrolled it and placed it on the grassy meadow. "Wes, how do we get Jane down?"

Wes clapped the boy on his back. "Easier than you think." They walked back to where Jane was with Cinnamon. She stared down and chewed her lip.

"Wes, if you'll give me a hand, I'm pretty sure I can do this," Jane said.

April walked up and stood behind them to watch.

"Billy, hold on to Cinnamon's reins to keep her steady." Wes reached up to lift Jane's right leg across the horse's back, and she half slid down the side of the horse. She stood with wobbly legs, then held out her hand to take Billy's while still holding on to Wes with her other hand.

Billy stared in disbelief as she took a small step in the direction of the blanket. "Jane! You're moving your legs!"

Jane took another tentative step, her face beaming pink. "I can walk some, Billy. I'm just shaky."

"You're doing fine, Jane. This is wonderful!" April clapped her hands.

"But why didn't you tell me?" Billy's look was mystified. "How'd this happen?"

Jane took a few more steps, and her walking became steadier. "I wanted to surprise you."

"We think it's a combination of passing time and the horseback riding somehow," Wes added.

"Well, whatever it is, I'm mighty happy for you! Now you'll be able to attend school with the rest of us instead of doing your lessons at home."

After they tied their mounts close enough to the stream for drinking, they settled down on the blanket. April reached inside the basket and found roast beef sandwiches and McIntosh apples. Wes had even remembered to pack napkins. She handed the sandwiches around, and Billy was nearly finished with his before she took her second bite.

"It's a good thing I packed two for us, Billy. I think you have a hollow leg." Wes laughed and the rest joined in.

"Lenora is a good cook, but I can always eat," Billy said, patting his stomach.

They ate the shiny red apples for dessert and enjoyed the pleasant fall weather while chatting. Wes asked April if she'd like to walk along the creek, and when she said yes, he pulled her up from the blanket with both hands. Billy lazed back with his arms under his head while Jane propped up on one arm talking with him.

When they were out of earshot, April said, "Thank you for doing this today. Jane seems a changed girl, and I think she and Billy will become great friends."

"Like us?" Wes asked, his arm firmly planted around April's waist.

"Yes, like us. I have a good feeling about them. This has been good for Jane and no doubt for Cynthia." They continued walking until they got to the water's edge and found a seat on the fallen trunk of a ponderosa pine. April tucked her arms around her legs, and Wes scooted closer to her. He smelled of shaving cream and the outdoors, and his leather vest gave off a pleasant smell that was becoming familiar to her. His spurs gave a light jingle at the slightest movement. She loved the manliness of him all the way down to the tops of his leather boots.

Wes lifted her hair and took a deep breath. "You smell so good. If you were a glass of water, I'd drink you up."

"Wes, you're getting to be a poet, I declare." April felt heat rising in her cheeks.

"I'm not totally uneducated, you know," he said, still playing with her hair.

"You never told me so." It seemed there was another side to him that she didn't know, and she was secretly pleased that he may have had more schooling than she'd first thought.

"It hadn't come up yet. I attended Montana State College of

Agriculture in Bozeman, and I have a degree in agriculture, but I do minimal farming. I'd rather be handling horses. I never know how much money I'll make from month to month with farming." He paused and gave her a level stare. "I may have an order coming up soon for several horses for a rancher in Bozeman, but the deal's not firm yet. Do you think you could be happy with that kind of uncertainty?"

"I think as long as we're doing what we like together, I can be." She reached over and clasped his hand. "I'll have some of my own money from my father. Who knows, perhaps we could open up a business. I think there's a need for a good leather or tack shop here, instead of always ordering from a catalog. Maybe things made by hand and such."

"You *have* done some thinking." He squeezed her hand hard, then gave it a swift kiss. His eyes smoldered with love for her, and April's heart did a somersault.

Was she doing the right thing? She couldn't wait to talk to Josh. She couldn't believe she was already considering moving here. "I wired my maid Tilly to see if she'd come to Montana. That's how serious I am." She leaned over and kissed him on the cheek, but he grabbed her arms.

"Oh no you don't . . . you can't tease me that way and get away with it. I need the real thing."

Wes placed his hand behind her neck beneath her silky hair, pulled her closer, and kissed her pouting mouth. He never knew that a kiss could taste so good. A flash of desire like a fire hit him in his belly, surprising him. He never wanted to let her out of his sight. She returned his kiss with a passionate one of her own that only ignited his craving for her. Wes pulled back, touched his fingertip to the end of her nose, and drew it down to her mouth, where she kissed it tenderly.

"Ever since you rode into town dressed like a man, and when I saw you at the wedding in that crumpled yellow gown, I knew there was something different about you. You're feisty, determined, and sometimes downright exasperating, but you are the woman I want to share my life with."

"I may make you wish you could take that back in a few months," she teased, then batted her eyelids.

"Sweet thing, you will be a pleasure to fight with."

"I don't—"

Wes crushed her mouth with his to silence her protestations and felt her ragged breathing. "No need to say more." His hands were trembling, and he decided that he'd better stop now, or heaven help him, he wouldn't be responsible for what he might do. "It's time to go." He puffed out a breath of air. "The kids will wonder what happened to us."

He searched her dreamy blue irises, and she huffed in exasperation. "You're right, but it's so nice being in your arms. I never want to leave them." She pulled away and stood up, her chest heaving in and out, and Wes thought she couldn't look any more desirable than she did at that moment.

"I feel the same way, but one of us needs to stay in control, or Miss Margaret or Morgan will skin us alive. I don't know about you, but I don't want to have to face either of them . . . or Josh." He took her hand and led her back to the picnic area, his heart full of this incredibly beautiful woman from Colorado. She might drive him crazy sometimes, but that was worth the risk to have her enduring love.

27

Miss Margaret sat with her chair pulled up close to the window so she could see outside. She wanted to be on the front porch in her rocker, but earlier there had been a sharp wind, and though it had died to a gentle breeze, she still found it chilly. Better to be inside with a fire in the grate, she decided. She'd been making notes in the journal she kept with her Bible, and she penciled a big check mark of praise next to Wes's name. *God, You're always faithful to me. All that I have and all that I need has come from You, Lord. Thank You for Your tremendous love and sacrifice.* As soon as her quick prayer was offered, Margaret felt a warmth flood her heart.

She closed the leather journal, recalling her conversation with April, whom she'd grown to love. She hoped that she'd been able to instill more confidence in April. She should be returning any moment from her trip out to the Rusty Spur, and Margaret wanted to know how things went. Cynthia had confided Jane's lie to her when she had come to work yesterday. Over the last few months, Cynthia and Margaret had prayed about Jane's healing together. And indeed, that prayer had been answered. As Margaret had pointed out to Cynthia, Jane's truth was a type of healing. Now, the two of them knew the truth, and the truth would set them free. Already she noticed that Cynthia stepped lighter, and her shoulders weren't hunched over from the burden of caring for a crippled child alone. Margaret hadn't said anything to a soul about Jane being able to walk, but she was sure that Jane would say something today.

She saw April and Sassy appear next to the side of the house, heading to the barn. She'd go make a pot of hot tea and slice some pound cake for a little snack before supper. Louise and Natalie should be through with their chores by now. She rapped on the Wingates' door with her cane to invite them to join her as well, but there was no answer. May and Willard had spent the day with their daughter, but she guessed they hadn't come back yet. So she moved on to the kitchen to make the tea.

Delicious smells of beef stew tickled her nostrils. Margaret loved the smell of supper cooking in the afternoon, permeating her household with its homey aroma when guests arrived. Natalie, in her apron, her hair tied back with a kerchief, turned from the sink with soap suds on her hands as her mother entered the kitchen. "I thought you were resting."

"I was, but I have a chill and I thought a cup of hot tea would chase it away. I saw April ride up and head to the barn, so maybe she can join us," she answered, taking a knife out of the drawer to slice the cake. "Where's Louise?"

"Here I am, Mother," Louise answered as she pushed through the swinging doors to the kitchen. "I'm ready for a break. I've just set the table for supper. Oh, and I invited Mark too, if that's okay?"

Margaret paused with the knife and looked up with a smile at her oldest daughter. "Louise, you know that's fine with me. Dr. Mark would make a wonderful husband."

"Not so fast, Mother, we just started seeing each other." Louise's face mirrored her excitement, and she stepped up to kiss her mother on the cheek. "But he is wonderful, isn't he?" She twirled around, her skirts swishing like a schoolgirl's.

Natalie leaned her head back and laughed at her sister. "You care for the nice doctor a lot, don't you?"

Louise popped her with her dish towel. "Oh, shush, it'll be you soon enough, my dear sister."

"Could one of you carry this tray to the parlor for me?" Margaret asked. The happy banter between her daughters filled her with joy, especially where Louise was concerned. April had burst in like a tornado and stirred things up a bit, and even though Natalie had lost out on Wes, Margaret knew there was someone, somewhere, for her daughter.

She followed Louise out to the parlor as her daughter balanced the tray of tea and cake.

Natalie called out, "I'll be right there as soon I dry my hands."

April was just entering the hallway, looking flushed and happy from her afternoon outing. Margaret caught her breath. *She has no idea how really beautiful she is with the first blush of love on her face.* "April, as you can see, we are about to have afternoon tea. Would you care to join us?" She waited for April's response and leaned heavily on her cane.

"Let me freshen up a bit and change out of these jeans, and I'll be right down." April stopped with one foot on the bottom stair.

"I'm sure I smell like horses and the barnyard, and I don't want people talking about me behind my back again," she teased. She posed in a hoity-toity fashion and held her nose between her thumb and forefinger, her pinky finger sticking out to the side.

Louise giggled at her. "I don't think you'll have to worry about that anymore. People are getting used to you wearing britches and riding your horse."

"Mmm . . . Wes likes the jeans, but he seems to love me in a dress, so you may be seeing more of me like that."

"You mean you're willing to compromise? I'm shocked!" Louise dramatically clasped her hand over her forehead.

April poked her tongue out at her friend. "I'll be down in five minutes."

Margaret just shook her head at the two of them and nudged Louise to move ahead. "Best hurry. The tea won't be hot or fit to drink if we stand here jawin' all day!"

❧

It was a delicious feeling, sinking down beneath her quilt after such a long, sweet day. April's thoughts tumbled around in her head. So many things had happened since she'd left Steamboat Springs. Some good, some not so good, but overall, she was very happy she had come for Josh's wedding. April had filled in Miss Margaret and her daughters on Jane's slow but definite recovery, while omitting the truth about Jane's lying.

Sunday they would attend the mayor's meeting at noon in the square. *Maybe Josh will return next week. He might be surprised to see Wes and me together.* April laughed to herself. *It will be delicious to see the look on his face.* Knowing that he never knew what to expect from his little sister made life so much more fun for April.

When fuzziness crept over her eyes into that place of neither awake nor asleep, all April could see was the strong, chiseled jaw of Wes's profile as they rode side by side today, and then she could feel the taste of his lips on hers . . .

Over the next few days, April could sense distinct anticipation around Lewistown, with people standing on street corners and in the general store wondering what the mayor's special meeting in the town's square was all about. Miss Margaret and her daughters stayed busy baking pies and cakes to add to the refreshments that Helen was preparing. Billy and Mark got involved in setting up sawhorses with wood planks that would serve as tables. April pitched in to help Lenora hang the red, white, and blue bunting across the railing of the gazebo.

It seemed almost like a holiday celebration, and April felt like she was one of the townsfolk by doing her part in the preparations. She never thought she'd do something like this and gain so much satisfaction. She just wished that Wes could've been there to work alongside her, but he'd had work to do before Sunday. Still, she found herself daydreaming about going to church with him.

Finally Sunday came. Sunlight streamed through the sheers, waking April, and she stared at the clock. It was nearly eight. Since living at the boardinghouse, April's body clock had been timed to wake up by seven, so she jumped out of bed, hoping not to miss breakfast before church.

She wanted to look nice today. After pulling out several items and tossing them aside on her bed, she chose a pale blue lacy blouse fitted at the waist. The robin's-egg blue moiré skirt, gored and widened at the bottom, balanced the wider long sleeves of the tight-fitting bolero with its notched, edged collar and black braiding. The skirt looked passable enough without having to iron it, one of her least favorite chores. Tilly would have scoffed at it, though, and April was sure she wouldn't have let her out the front door until it was steamed and pressed perfectly. On her feet April wore high, curved Louis heels, but only because she decided her low-heeled cowboy boots would have looked ridiculous. *Ahh . . . it won't be all day. I can always change into something more comfortable later. But today I want to turn Wes's head so he has eyes only for me!*

She brushed her hair and deftly braided it, securing the plaits daintily around her head with silver hair combs. Taking a step back, April admired her toilette in the long cheval mirror. Satisfied with the outcome, she snatched up her handbag and stuffed Wes's present inside, then practically ran down the stairs.

After church, townsfolk began to amble toward the direction of the town square in anticipation of the afternoon activities. Already the town band members had arrived and were tuning their instruments.

Mayor Brown clapped Wes on the back, then after a firm hand-shake, he made his way to a group of dignitaries who represented the superiors in Washington. They were clustered near the gazebo in the town square, which was decorated with red, white, and blue bunting. Wes had been in luck to be able to have a word with him before the mayor made his speech. He craned his neck above the burgeoning crowd to see whether or not April had come.

This was the largest number of people he'd seen in one spot since Josh's wedding. Carriages with ladies dressed in their finery filled the streets. The band was now playing as anticipation grew. He saw Cynthia talking to Marion Stockton, with Billy standing close to Jane's side, lending his arm for support. He waved to Andy and Nellie standing next to Reverend Carlson just as Lenora and Morgan joined them. Morgan looked to be in great shape, and Wes was glad that Lenora was by his side now, for good.

When Wes had arrived earlier today, he'd sprinted over to Power Mercantile to pick up his order, and now it was tucked safely on Dakota's back. Wes felt all knotted up inside and hadn't been able to think of anything except April since they'd parted at the picnic yesterday. He couldn't even eat today. How could a woman do that to a man's head? He didn't know and he didn't care. He just wanted to build a life with April as his partner, but he was afraid she'd go back to Colorado and that would be the end of it. He couldn't let that happen, and as he lived and breathed today, it wouldn't, not if he got his way.

His eyes caught hers and held across the meticulous lawn of the square. She moved toward him, never taking her eyes off his, dressed like a fashion plate that must have cost a fortune. He gulped for air. Her hair, normally worn hanging down her back, was wound up in braids held by silver combs, and she wore a tight-fitting jacket across her slim shoulders. She was a vision of loveliness, and he couldn't take his eyes off her sweet face.

She gave him a brief brush on the lips in greeting, right in front of Miss Margaret, Natalie, and Louise. He couldn't believe it. It was daring to say the least, but he knew he'd better get used to April's ways. "You are beautiful, April, and maybe a little overdressed for the mayor's speech," Wes said, taking her hand and tucking it inside his elbow. Her scent drove him crazy and lingered in his thoughts.

April giggled. "Oh? What about yourself? I don't recall seeing you in a starched white shirt and tie before. The black leather vest is a very nice touch, Wes." Her eyes focused on his.

"Just wanted to clean up a bit today—you never know who you'll meet or what will happen."

"What do you mean?" she asked. He smelled like musk soap and had shaved his usual stubble from his face. *He must have had the same idea about looking nice for me.* At least she wanted to think so, and her heart was full of love for him.

"Aw, nothing, really." He patted her hand, then said hello to the other ladies. Natalie was cordial to him but looked away, seeming interested in the band.

Wes handed April a package. "Here, I want you to open this now."

"I love surprises," April said, tearing into the wrapping. "Oh, Wes! My goodness. Where did you get these?" April ran her hand over the brown hand-tooled boots in awe. A matching belt was rolled and tucked into one of the boots. "How did you ever find something so close to mine?"

"Let's just say I have several connections down in Texas." A broad grin split his face. "I take it you like them?"

"Like them? I love them! Thank you so much!" She asked Louise to hold the gift for her, then untied the string of her handbag. "I have something for you as well," she said with excitement, and handed him a package.

"What? You have one for me? I'd say our minds think alike." Wes pushed back his hat to see better.

"Just open it, Wes," Louise said, now that everyone was looking on.

He ripped back the paper to reveal a book. "Well, boy howdy. This is just great, April." He opened the book and peeked inside.

"Well, what kind of book is it? A mystery?" Willard asked as he and May walked over.

"No, even better. It's *The Fannie Farmer Cookbook*. Now I can figure out some of those dishes I've been wanting to try. I'll be able to give Andy a run for his money!"

Everyone laughed and then sighed when Wes leaned down to kiss April softly on her check. "Thank you. I really love it."

"I thought you might." She smiled back at him, a funny, tight feeling squeezing her chest.

The crowd suddenly quieted down, and April looked up to the platform where the mayor was about to speak. The band stopped playing, and everyone clapped as Harry Brown stepped up to the podium.

"My wonderful citizens, I'm so happy that you're here on this spectacular fall day with a bit of chill in the air. We all know that winter will be here soon enough. So let's enjoy today." He cleared his throat. "Some of you may not be aware that a few months ago, the United States government began to negotiate with the Blackfeet to purchase 800,000 acres of land for the preservation of the beautiful forest and mountains that Montana is privy to. That treaty was framed and signed by members of the Blackfeet tribe for the sum of 1.5 million dollars for a period of ten years, with

4 percent interest. This land I'm speaking about is the western boundary of our wonderful state that runs as far up as Canada."

The mayor paused and turned to introduce his guests. "President Cleveland chose representatives to help with this purchase and bring awareness of that fact to our great United States and to the citizens of Montana. We are happy that we are one of the cities on their statewide tour. Please give a Montana welcome to Dr. George Bird Grinnell, the editor of *Forest and Stream* magazine and a naturalist who was very instrumental in convincing his dear friends the Blackfeet to sell the land for preservation."

Applause erupted all around. Dr. Grinnell smiled at the crowd and waved. The mayor smiled. "I'd also like to introduce to you US Indian agent George Steele, who was instrumental in persuading the Blackfeet that this was in their people's best interests. Also, please welcome Chief White Calf, who was one of the original signers of the documents for the Blackfeet tribe. Let's give them all a warm welcome." The mayor started clapping, and others, even if they were doubtful, did likewise.

The two men and the chief stood before the crowd. Wearing soft buckskin pants and a beaded tunic trimmed in long fringe the color of churned butter, the chief had a regal air of dignity in his stance with his arms folded across his chest. He neither smiled nor moved but looked straight ahead.

Wes leaned down and whispered in April's ear. "I'm not sure Chief White Calf is all too happy with this purchase."

April asked quietly, "Then why would he sign it?" She watched the chief without turning her head to look at Wes. She'd never been this close to a real Indian in her life, and she was fascinated.

"There was some talk that miners were breathing down the

officials' necks to secure the land for mining gold and copper. The Blackfeet lost two-thirds of their tribe to smallpox back in 1837. Then many died from starvation when the buffalo herds declined about fifteen years ago. I figured the tribe was nearly destitute. I think they had little choice if they were going to save their people."

"Well, you might be right, by the look on Chief White Calf's face." April saw sadness transparent in the chief's eyes. "I understand why the government might want to own it, but how much of this was forced upon them, do you think?"

"I honestly don't know the answer to your question, but I have one for you," Wes said.

She spun her head around. "Is that right? And what might that be?"

Before Wes could say anything further, the mayor invited everyone to join them for refreshments set up on the side of the gazebo. The band struck up a loud marching tune, and Miss Margaret suggested they join the others. Instead, Wes took April by her elbow, and she traipsed behind him until they reached the edge of the square. She saw the curious looks of her friends but tried not to make eye contact.

"What is it, Wes? I thought we could have some lemonade—"

"Shh." Wes pressed his fingers to her lips. "There's no time to lose."

"What are you talking about? There's nothing we can do about the sale of the land."

"I'm not talking about that. I'm talking about us." Wes took a deep breath, then continued. "Did you decide to stay in Montana?" He stared down at her with a peculiar look on his face that April couldn't read.

"I told you I would stay awhile longer. Why?"

Wes took his hat off and held it with trembling hands. "I have to know—do you love me?" he choked out in a whisper.

"Wes, I . . ." *What is the matter with him?*

"Do you love me? It's not a hard question, April." He shifted on one foot, impatience in his face.

"Yes, I do, Wes. I thought you knew." Suddenly her throat went dry, and she licked her lips.

"Will you marry me then?" His eyes held hers, and April watched his Adam's apple move when he swallowed hard.

April's jaw dropped. "I thought we were going to think about this for a while."

"I mean now, April. Right here—right now." His voice was pleading, and his eyes were filled with passion.

"Have you lost your mind, Wes Owen?" April thought surely he must be joking, but another look at his face told her he was serious. His eyes penetrated hers and mirrored deep longing and love. Her lips parted to speak, but the words caught in her throat. What about the big wedding she'd always planned? And what about her parents? They would be furious!

After a long minute she found her voice. "How do you intend to do that right now?"

Wes dropped to one knee, laid his hat aside, and reached for her hands. "Will you marry me? I love you with all my heart. I'd be the luckiest man alive if you'd want to spend the rest of your life with me."

April's heart was pounding. "But how, Wes? We have to make plans . . . I wanted a big wedding."

"We don't need all that, do we? All of that is just trimming. We don't have to wait. You're a lot like me—I've waited too long and you've waited long enough. I don't want to lose you."

"But I wanted a beautiful wedding dress. I wanted to look pretty."

"You look beautiful to me in the dress you're wearing." His eyes traveled over her body, then he lifted her hand and kissed her fingertips.

April's stomach lurched. Her bolero jacket was suddenly beginning to feel hot. "I don't know . . ."

"Just say yes and we can exchange our vows today."

Excitement shot through her at the possibility. She felt nearly breathless.

"I've talked to the reverend, and it's all set if you'll agree. The mayor said we can use the gazebo with the decorations and the band. There's plenty of food, and all of our friends are present. You can't beat that. I even made reservations tonight at the Day House Hotel in town!" Wes's face blotched red. "I hate wasting time when I love you and you love me. What do you say?" He squirmed on his bent knee. "Hurry, my leg is going numb," he said with a half smile.

She hesitated, remembering the big wedding she and her mother had planned four years ago, and the shadow it had left over her when Luke called it off. Did she really want to go through that again? She knew she didn't. What was the point of waiting? Wes was right. But she wished Josh and Juliana were back from their honeymoon. She chewed her bottom lip. "I just might consider it, if Josh were here . . ."

A movement from behind caused her to turn, and she gasped when she saw her beloved brother walking toward her with Juliana a few steps behind him. "Josh! You're back!"

"I am, little sister," he answered as he reached and gave her a bear hug. "And I'm here to give your hand in marriage to Wes with my most hearty approval!"

April felt tears well up in her eyes, and she pulled away from Josh's embrace, looking him straight in the eye. "But . . . you've been away! How did you know he was even going to ask me?" April swung a look from Josh to Wes with an arched brow, thoroughly confused now. First an offer of marriage, then Josh back from his honeymoon and she didn't know it? How could that be?

Josh clapped Wes on his back. "We got back on Friday but went straight to the ranch and found Wes waiting there for us on the porch." Wes, still kneeling in the thick grass, smiled sheepishly at April. Josh continued. "Wes told me about his plan to ask you to marry him today and said he needed my help."

April took a teasing swipe at her brother with her reticule, and he feigned hurt. "You've been home and I didn't know?" she asked. It was hard to be mad at Josh when he was grinning broadly at her, giving her his sweetest brotherly look that had always caused her to give in when they were children.

Juliana timidly approached April, then stood next to Josh, who clasped her hand. Her beautiful blue eyes shone in her lovely face, and April thought they made a handsome couple. "April, it was the only way we could keep it from you. We decided not to come to town until today or Josh would've spoiled all the fun. It was hard for him to keep a secret," she said with a cheerful giggle.

"Wes is a good man, April, and I believe you've finally met your match." Josh laughed. "Why don't you say yes so he can get up before he falls over?"

April turned to Wes, love bursting inside her chest. "Yes, let's get married today!" April flung herself into his arms, and they both tumbled to the ground in a heap, laughing. She lay with her skirts tangled across him and leaned over his chest to give him a long, satisfying kiss. Wes tightened his grip around her waist and hugged her tight, kissing her eyelids and brow.

"I love you, Wes. God help me—I do." She stifled his words of love with another kiss.

Applause burst out all around them, and when April looked up, their friends and the reverend were standing in a semicircle, smiling and cheering. Miss Margaret was wiping tears from her eyes with her handkerchief. April untangled herself, then Wes pulled her to her feet. Juliana reached out and smoothed down April's rumpled skirts, then repinned April's escaping hair as if she were her own sister. The act of kindness was not lost on April, and she briefly embraced Juliana. April was fully aware that her cheeks were burning after Wes's public proposal and their tumble in front of the crowd, but her heart was soaring. Wes brushed off his sleeves and crooked his arm out for her. Everyone crowded around to congratulate them with a slap on the back for Wes and a kiss on the cheek for April.

Wes turned to his future brother-in-law and said, "Josh, I owe you one."

"Friends don't keep score, Wes. Just take good care of her, because I know the trail to the Rusty Spur," Josh said, his eyes dancing with mischief.

April couldn't be happier than she was right now. The man she loved and her dear brother were good friends.

"Thanks just the same, Josh," Wes choked out, then shook Josh's hand.

"Well, we'd better hurry. We have a wedding to perform," Reverend Carlson said to everyone, gesturing toward the gazebo.

April walked with Wes to the gazebo, and the others followed behind. Leaves of orange, gold, and red from the ash trees swirled in a circle and were swept across the lawn with the stiff autumn breeze. A showy yellow tanager, his head cocked to the side, warbled a sweet melody from his perch on the gazebo's railing. Lenora handed April a handful of sunflowers that she'd picked, and April clutched them tightly, hardly believing that her wedding was taking place. *Am I dreaming?* She blinked and saw Wes gazing at her with that beguiling smile. She tensed for a moment.

But what was it Miss Margaret had said to her one night? *What is it you want for your life—your daddy's approval or to live life your own way?* Wasn't that what Josh had done? Well, April knew what she wanted, and it was Wes. To raise horses, have his children, and grow old with him, holding hands as they watched the sun set over the Judith Mountains from their front porch. Their new and improved front porch. April giggled under her breath. Wes winked at her and took her hand.

April and Wes stood side by side, repeating their vows. Though there was no ring, it didn't seem to matter. That would come later. All that mattered was God had kept His promise to heal her heart, and April was glad that she'd waited on Him. Oh, she and Wes would probably have a few tiffs now and then, but that would make life all the more fun and interesting.

A tingle went down her spine. Wes loved her, and he was definitely worth the wait, however long it had taken.

When their kiss had sealed their vows, April's heart swelled, and she thought it couldn't hold all the love she felt at this moment.

The couple turned, still holding hands, and looked down over the railing at their friends who'd gathered along with the townsfolk to celebrate their vows. Through April's tears, she said a prayer for her new husband and all the wonderful people she had grown to love under this vast, cloudless Montana sky.

Author's Note

My love of history dictates that I research and try to stay as factual as I possibly can in my story. Many of the buildings mentioned throughout the book are historical to Lewistown. Power Mercantile really existed and was built in 1884 on the corner of Main Street and 3rd Avenue South. It boasted supplies such as groceries, clothing, dry goods, furniture, shoes, and men's goods. The Bank of Fergus County was directly across the street on the opposite corner. Phillips Drug Company, where Wes and Natalie have their soda water, was also on Main Street. The Day House Hotel, where Wes makes reservations, was built in 1880 and was located on the corner of 4th Avenue North and Main Street. Beaver Creek Church was situated on Lower Spring Creek Street. The Stockton Hotel is purely fictitious.

The Big Spring Creek runs northwest for thirty miles near Wes's ranch, the Rusty Spur, and is one of the largest spring-fed streams in Montana.

Morgan Kincaid is a fictitious character who ran a franchise of the Wells Fargo stagecoach depot. Mary Fields, or "Stagecoach Mary," was a colorful, gun-toting historical character who delivered the US mail by stagecoach in Montana. Raised as a slave, she lived a rugged life out West. She eventually retired from delivering mail in her seventies to open a laundry and lived out her last years in Cascade, Montana. Montana State College of Agriculture in Bozeman was a land-grant college founded in 1893, and later its name was changed to Montana State University. *The Fannie Farmer Cookbook* that April gives to Wes made its debut in January 1896. It's been my favorite cooking companion since I received a copy in 1967.

Much of my fascination with Glacier National Park comes from its phenomenal beauty and rich culture and history. I have no proof that any mayor ever spoke in Lewistown about a glacier reserve, but I do know that President Grover Cleveland appointed a committee to make a treaty with the Blackfeet Indians for the purchase of the western land of Montana. George Bird Grinnell, naturalist and editor of *Forest and Streams* magazine, was personally requested by the Blackfeet for the negotiations. Indian agent and local trader George Steele played a significant role to persuade the Indians of the benefit to sell their reserve. White Calf, the Piegan chief of the Blackfeet tribe, was an original signer of the commission and authorized the sale of 800,000 acres to the US government for $1.5 million. (Note: The different tribes of the Algonquian, Bloods, Blackfeet, and Piegan are designated collectively as the Blackfeet.) White Calf later died from pneumonia as he was visiting Washington in 1903.

The commission was confirmed later by Congress in June 1896. It wasn't until 1910 that Glacier National Park was officially designated by President William Howard Taft as a national park.

If you've never visited Glacier National Park, I urge you to make it one of your dream trips. Be sure to travel on Going-to-the-Sun Road. Your life will be richer for it. You can find more information at http://www.nps.gov/glac.

Acknowledgments

To my daughter, Sheri Christine, for being my personal editor. She kept me laughing throughout the late-night edits by email and accommodated me in spite of her own busy schedule. I also appreciate Gaye Orsini's last-minute edits and tweaks.

To my best friend and critique partner, Kelly Long, for her insightful suggestions. She also carried me during the hard times that life dropped in my lap while I wrote this book, especially the loss of a third brother, Sam. Thank you, my friend!

To Charles Riggs of Wells Fargo Historical Services, who kindly supplied me with the cost of a typical stagecoach fare.

To all of my family, who loves me and supports my writing. I love you more than words can say. Forgive me if my writing isolated you for long stretches of time.

To the sweetest gifts in my life—my grandchildren Maggie, Angelina, Peter, and Sarah, who keep me centered. Mimi loves you all so much!

To Dottie and my personal cheering section of The Bookmark, Barbara and Sara Sue.

To my wonderful choir buddies.

To Jan Tilton and Debbie Kotyuk of the prayer room at Johnson Ferry Baptist Church in Marietta, Georgia. Your constant prayers for my family made all the difference.

To my encouraging friend and agent, Tamela Hancock Murray, and the superb team at Revell. I couldn't have done this without you. Many thanks for keeping my dream going.

To my readers who have taken the time to write me personal notes. Your kind words are like sunshine on a cloudy day!

To my dearest mother, who shaped me into the person I've become today with her love of God's Word. It's because of her that Scripture pops into my head just when I need it most. She had the tenacity needed to hold our family together during the worst of times because of her unconditional love, much like Jesus's love for us. What a sweet reunion we'll have someday.

Most importantly, to my Lord, who whispered the desire for me to write at the early age of nine and who leads me all the way.

Maggie Brendan is a member of the American Christian Writers (ACW) and the American Christian Fiction Writers (ACFW). She was also a recipient of the 2004 ACW Persistence Award.

Maggie led a writers' critique group in her home for six years and was quoted in *Word Weavers: The Story of a Successful Writers' Critique Group*. She was a guest speaker at a recent Regional Church Bookstores and Libraries conference in Marietta, Georgia, on the value of Christian fiction.

A TV film version is currently in development of her first novel, *No Place for a Lady*, book 1 of the Heart of the West series. *Romantic Times* awarded *No Place for a Lady* a 4.5-star review and also gave *The Jewel of His Heart* a 4-star review.

Maggie is married and lives in Marietta, Georgia. She has two grown children and four grandchildren. When she's not writing, she enjoys reading, singing, painting, scrapbooking, and being with her family. You can find Maggie on her blog, http://southernbellewriter.blogspot.com. She is also a resident blogger on www.bustlesandspurs.com.

Journey into the
Heart of the West

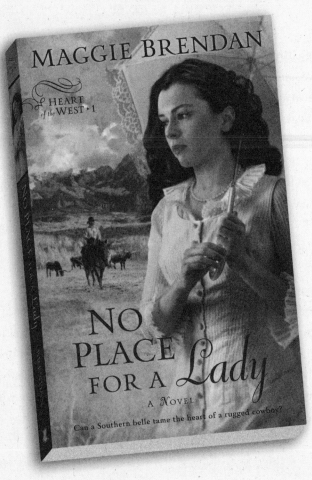

Can a Southern belle tame the heart of a rugged cowboy?

Revell
a division of Baker Publishing Group
www.RevellBooks.com

Sweet Romances
That Capture the Heart

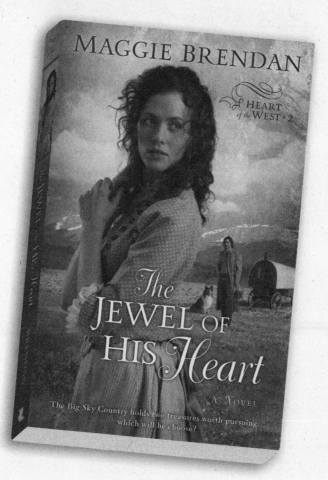

The Big Sky Country holds two treasures worth pursuing . . .
which will he choose?

If You Loved This Book,

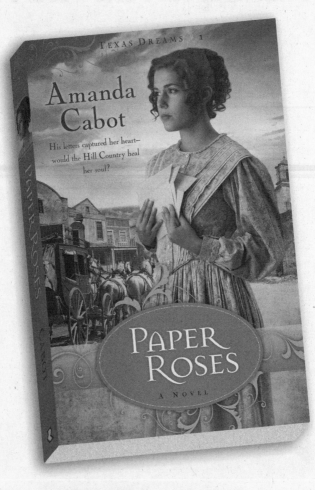

His letters captured her heart—
would the Hill Country heal her soul?

You Will Love the
Texas Dreams Series!

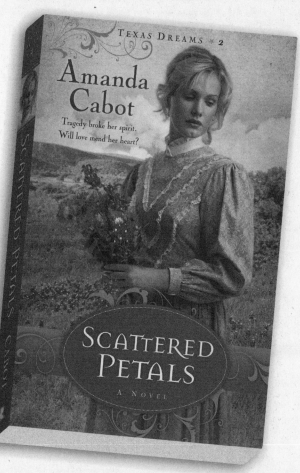

Tragedy broke her spirit.
Will love mend her heart?

When tragedy strikes, how will Molly McGarvie survive?

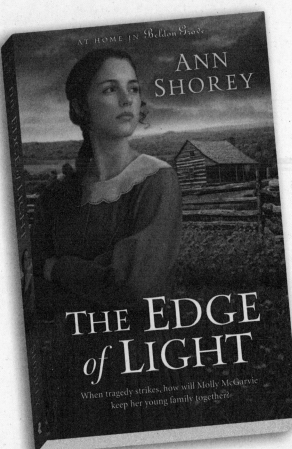

Experience the wonder and hardship of life on the prairie with Molly McGarvie as she fights to survive loss and keep her young family together.

When loss drives them apart,
can their faith bring them
back together?

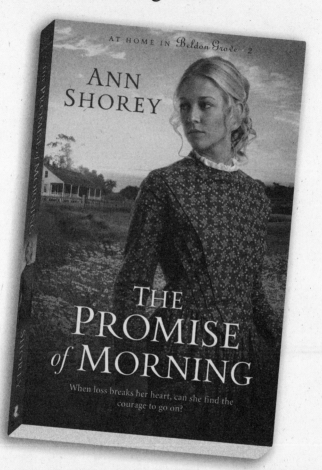